THE UNSPOKEN

Book One in the Keres Trilogy

BY

A. E. Waller

ISBN: 978-1-329-13222-1

"We are the keepers of the ancient secrets; for we walked the world when it was new."

- Eileen Lynch

Chapter One

     The Mothers arrive at 05:00 to dress me. They arrange my hair carefully in tiny braids and curls, some pinned up with delicate ornaments representing the nine different lines of Service. They drape multiple layers of white satin robes with terra-cotta orange bands around the hems and sleeves. A pattern of life in Chelon is woven into the fabric of the outermost robe- Play Groups as children, people working together in the different Services, a Banding Ceremony, and featured prominently on the front are the five Absolute Mothers, the omnipotent rulers of Chelon.

     It takes over two hours to clean and dress me. I wonder if everyone else's preparation takes so long or if it's just the two years of neglect that causes mine to be so lengthy. Once dressed, I am told to kneel in the center of the room until I am collected for the Oath. There isn't much else I can do in this getup. I cannot lean on anything because of the elaborate hair arrangement and I cannot sit on a chair because the robes are too stiff. So I kneel with the thirty pounds of dense fabric billowing around me.

     I am dressed up like a goddess to be told how I will serve Chelon for the rest of my life. I turn my head to look at myself in the long glass on the wall. My breath catches in my chest. The makeup The Mothers have applied hides my sunken eyes and hollow cheeks. I have been given the Chelon red lips and blue star under my right eye. The robes are heart breaking; they are so exquisite and made specifically for me. The Service ornaments fixed in the mass of black hair on my head draw attention like a mystical crown.

I am beautiful.

The door tone rings and a Mother comes in, helps me to my feet and leads me to the line of Play Groups from my year. We are all dressed with care, the girls much like me with hair ornaments of the Services and robes with elaborate patterns woven especially for them. The only thing alike on us is the black diamond pin over our left ears. The boys, dressed in leggings with scenes embroidered in silk threads and patterned with jewels creeping up the legs are topped with shirts of almost transparent white gauze. A masculine version of Service ornaments hang from their belts.

Our biological parents make our ceremonial clothes and ornaments. They begin the day we are born, as the activity is supposed to distract them from the removal of their children. It takes most parents over ten years to gather materials to create these outward signs of ceremony. Some of these robes were only completed last night. The goal is to make them more beautiful than any that have been seen before, to make them especially unique and easy to spot from a distance. This will be the first time they will be able to identify us as their own blood line. The day we are no longer children, the day we become full citizens, serving the city.

The line of Play Groups travels silently to the center of the Quad, four large residence compounds shaped like pie wedges meeting at their points in a vast courtyard. It is already strung with lights for the celebration later tonight. Our line slowly arranges itself around the center stage while the rest of Chelon gathers in close. People eager to spot the robes and leggings they have made, eager to see their children for the first time. Not that they will be allowed to make themselves known to us.

The five Absolute Mothers appear at the balcony on the north residence compound, their elaborate headdresses of hammered copper reflecting in the morning sun, their deep purple robes standing out against the stark white of the building. They survey the stillness that has spread through the crowd. The appearance of the Chelon flag signals the start of the Pledge.

We, the children of Chelon,
Pledge our lives to our lines of Service.
We, the children of Chelon,
Pledge our lives to our city.
We, the children of Chelon,
Pledge our lives to The Mothers.

After a single long note plays on a brass horn, everyone turns their attention to The Mother on stage with us. Her image appears on the two large television screens on either side of the stage. In a sugar sweet voice, dripping with honey and caramel, she recites the Play Group numbers who are being assigned to

3

Service this year. It's when she is talking about the importance of each line of Service that I see him. Wex. Tall, so much taller than I remember him that I have to tilt my head up to see all of him at once. His eyes meet mine and I can see his chest rising and falling, slowly. Two years is a long time, especially between the ages of 13 and 15. And then to see each other bejeweled like celestial beings for the Oath instead of how we are naturally. How he even recognizes me under all the makeup and finery is beyond reason. Everything around me melts away, and I see nothing but Wex. I hear nothing but his breath.

The Mother suddenly changes her tone, "PG3446!" This rattles me, reminds me we shouldn't have shown any sign of remembering each other. I rip my eyes away from him to look at PG3446, dazzling in blues and oranges. The Mother calls for one of the girls to step forward, center stage. A young woman, a novice Mother by her white tunic and lavender apron, steps with her and slowly pulls out different hair ornaments while The Mother speaks of this girl's individual traits and talents. Soon, only one ornament is left, the tiny leather bound book with gold lettering of Pedagogics. She will be trained as a teacher. The crowd applauds and the girl steps back to her place with her Play Group, glancing with relief at another girl from PG3446.

The assignments continue, future miners, factory workers, and Keepers being the most frequent. There are several farmers, healers, and educators which all receive a tangible feeling of relief from the crowd. These kids won't be in direct danger of a cave in or a mangling by the machines. Exactly fifty-four of us are assigned before The Mother calls out "PG3456!" I'm surprised we are called as a group considering we have just completed the longest Solace in the history of Chelon. We aren't even standing together on the stage. Shuffling motions are all around me as girls try to move sideways in their weighty robes, making room for the six of us to gather for the first time in two years.

There they all are to my left and right. Doe, a full head shorter than me with her honey-blond hair piled on top of her head, Harc's gray eyes gazing resolutely before her, Frehn whose muscle mass has doubled since I last saw him, his eyes darting through the crowd. Merit, long and lean as ever, and Wex, who towers over all of us. We stand in a line, not a group as the others have done, staring straight before us.

"PG3456, just this morning returned to us from Solace," says The Mother in her sticky sweet tone. "It is so good to have you among us again, darlings." My stomach turns over. "Merit."

Merit moves forward to the center of the stage. Is this it? Is that all the public humiliation we are to endure? No additional punishments? Are we allowed to remain a Play Group? There will be something else, surely. The Mother is talking about Merit's virtues. Quiet and loving, obedient and purposeful in his studies. The novice removes ornaments with long fingers, and my head swims. There is a dramatic pause over the last two ornaments, an elaborately carved jade horse and a long silk tassel strung with jewels. As the novice reaches for the last ornament, her fingers graze his leg and Merit jerks away from the touch.

Suddenly I wonder what they did to him during Solace. For the first thirteen years of our lives, he was always reaching

5

for the comfort of others. While the overwhelming Heavy Weight of guilt and despair was enough to immobilize me with its darkness, did Merit not give into it as I did? Was something else necessary to press him into submission? He recovers quickly and I can see the muscles twitch on the side of his face. The novice removes the tassel- Merit will work with the animals. I breathe for the first time since his name was called. Animals will not hurt him like people can. He is safe.

Doe is called forward, her large soft brown eyes looking down at the stage floor. She's the youngest member of PG3456, born two hours before we were grouped. "Strength of mind coupled with the elevation of spirit," oozes the Mother, "Poised for action with a steady hand." Doe's shoulders droop slightly when she looks at all the removed ornaments and deduces she is left with the Healers' bandages, bronzed and gathered in rosettes. Then she quickly straightens and returns to her spot to my right, avoiding my sideways glance. Healers are one of the coveted Services, as they are considered safe from pain and physical catastrophe. They have access to medicine and soothing drugs. Maybe too much access in some cases.

"Harc," the Mother says it as though it's a call and not a name. It sends a shot of loathing through me that I can't explain. "Harc, our own little gray dove," The Mother purrs. She is using PG3456's pet name for Harc and it transmits a stab of palpable pain down our line. Harc's velvet gray hair is always in perfect order like the feathers of a bird. Hers isn't the coarse white-gray hair of the aged, Harc's is the soft gray of a heavy thundercloud. Smooth and cool to the touch. I know we will never call her Dove again. "Refreshing as a summer rain, powerful as the thunder that follows. And with the ability to electrify all of Chelon with fragile hands." Harc twists her long fingers and I see the white and red scars. Then it's true. PG3456 has been tortured, their strengths turned to liabilities. Why then was I left virtually untouched? Why wasn't I tortured? I could have handled pain with more fortitude than I could the emptiness of the Heavy.

Harc steps back in line with only the tiny crown of circuits and silk in her hair. Factories. I see a vision of her losing one of her beautiful long fingers in the machines and I almost choke on a sob.

"Wex." My heart is in my stomach again, as it was for Merit. Only there is a burning sensation in my throat now, and my eyes begin to prick. I feel the stage move under me as he walks to the center. There's a buzzing in my ears as I strain all my senses to discover what they have done to him during our Solace. "Powerful as the river water coming down from the distant mountains, Wex can serve Chelon with the strength of ten boys his age, though he is wise enough to realize his own limitations. Never crossing boundaries and always responsive to a request."

The crowd presses forward as Wex is left with two ornaments, a string of golden corn with ruby tomatoes studded in-between and a sparkly circular wreath of coal. The novice moves in front of him so the crowd can't see which is removed and placed on the table in front of him. Wex runs his eyes over the table and narrows them for an instant. The string of corn. Nutriment Cultivation. Wex is in the fields. It seems unreal. Wex has achieved the ultimate goal of working outside of the

7

inner wall, out from under constant observation. Something reserved for the most obedient, not for someone just this morning released from Solace.

Before I can fully comprehend Wex's assigned line of Service, Frehn is already in the center with ornaments being removed. "Power needs structure, patience needs guidance. He excels in Physical Assessment, as you can all imagine," there is a demure giggle from all the girls, "Frehn is a young man on the verge of being someone on whom all of Chelon can depend, if he chooses." They say things like this so we all feel dependent on each other's cooperation. So we feel that we must comply in order to keep the rest of Chelon from punishment.

Charming and mischievous, Frehn had stolen kisses from all three of us girls by the time we were nine. And we all had been in love with him for it. Unafraid and steadfast, remarkable. He had the misfortune to be born a twin just minutes after the Spring Grouping. He was raised with his twin for a year before the next Grouping took place, and because we cannot have blood families, his twin was removed from him and placed with another Play Group. But he remembers, and whenever we passed others from our year in the halls, his eyes were always searching their faces, looking for a face that matched his own.

And his eyes dart now, not at the crowd before us, but at the people on stage. He has not looked forward once since called. His movement is not unnoticed, but as he is not looking at PG3456, he is not likely to be punished harshly. The novice places her hands on his hips in an effort to remind him of where he is. He looks down at her as if it's the first time he has seen her and smiles wearily. She has removed the last ornament, leaving a looping chain of diamonds and coal laced with emeralds that match his eyes. My head reels. Frehn is in the mines. Uncontainable Frehn underground.

I lock my eyes on him as he walks back to the line, back tall and strong as ever, resolute. He glances at me and winks.

So they haven't broken you after all. I feel his strength in that wink, defiant and patiently waiting for his moment.

"Keres!" It's almost said harshly and I suspect the Mother needed to repeat herself. I'm filled with a desire to present a good show for Chelon, for the Absolute Mothers watching from their balcony, and for PG3456. I am not broken. At least for the next three minutes. I am whole, unchanged. Assign me in the textile factories, let me frantically work to keep my hair and limbs out of the weaving machines, leaving me no spare minute to let my mind wander and plot.

I force my back straight and attempt to glide to the center of the stage, tying to emulate a dancer's smooth movements. I purposefully avoid looking at anyone, pinning my eyes to the corner of the opposite residence compound. With a slight smile that I hope is steady, I try to raise my hollow cheeks so the blue star under my eye catches the sunlight. There is a rustle in the crowd as a woman moves forward slightly.

"Keres, born on a summer's morning in the height of growing season. Her hands are nimble, top of her class in all the Pedagogics. Physical Assessment marks higher than most of the boys." She glances around the Play Groups at this, waiting for the boys to make noises of disbelief. They don't. "She is quick of mind and resistant to bodily harm." Yes, and won't that help me when I am fighting against the machines. She's not talking anymore. The crowd is not moving, PG3456 are statues. I glance down at the table in front of me to count the removed ornaments. Nutriment Cultivation, Mineral Recovery, Architects, Healers, Pedagogics, Fauna Management, Keeping... and Component Fabrication. What's left? I instinctively reach up to my hair and pat, and I feel it. The cold black diamond of the Unspoken.

Chapter Two

I try to remember the last time I saw someone left with
the black diamond. Like water swirling down a drain, my mind
pulls me down into the past. All the years blur together in an
eddy of colors and sounds. I remember an Oath of Service
exactly like this one, only I was looking up at the stage rather
than down from it. There was a boy, left with just the sparkling
black diamond hanging from his belt. He looked perplexed. I
suppose the same way I do now. His brow creased as if he was
trying to remember a time before him when the black diamond
remained. No one in the audience clapped for him either.

I feel like an empty shell standing on the stage, my
hand on the black diamond, my soul hovering somewhere
above my body. Everything goes in and out of focus around
me, and the soundless crowd before me melts into a myriad of
visions.

Over the past two years of my life there were days
when the Heavy Feeling threatened to overcome me. It pressed
me back down when I tried to get out of bed. I could visualize
its long black smoke fingers sinking into my chest, pushing me
further away from what I knew I needed to do. I needed to get
up. I needed to move. The Heavy wouldn't allow it.

Late yesterday afternoon there was a sound at the door followed by a light clicking on in my room. The Mothers had come in to take the lunch tray and replace it with the dinner version. I couldn't open my eyes to see which Mother brushed the crumbs away from my sheets. It was as if she's brushed my mind clean and I couldn't remember anything. I had to wait until they were gone and the light was off to sink back and hide in my memories. It wasn't difficult to remain perfectly still while they wiped my face and hands with a wet cloth. They spoke to me in low soothing tones while they bustled around me. Reminding me that tomorrow was a big day and I would have to get up.

I wondered then what they would do if I just stayed like this, immobile and void of emotion. Prop me up on a dolly and wheel me down to the center courtyard to be assigned to Service? The thought of The Mothers having to cover up my current state at a public ceremony cheered me a little. I could picture them gathered in groups, their large white headdresses rubbing against each other, franticly trying to piece a plan together that would appease the crowd. No one wants to see a fifteen year old girl who has been devoured by the Heavy. People may become upset if they see the Solace has not reformed but broken me. That would be a waste of resources.

The light switched off and The Mothers left at last. In reality they were probably only in the room for a few minutes. But since my Solace had begun, minutes had felt like days. Alone again, I inhaled deeply trying to smell what they had left for dinner. Soup. Knowing I would have to eat to get through the ceremony, they would leave something I'd have to sit up to eat. Just an extra reminder of their control, even if they let me wallow, despondent under the Heavy.

Slowly, I pushed myself up the headboard into a sitting position and swung the tray forward over me. The spoon felt like it was made of lead and the soup was thick. The clock's face showed it took me more than an hour to finish and slide back down in the sheets. Now that the business of surviving to the next meal was over, my mind was free to wander again.

I had shut my eyes and tried to think about what brought us to this place. In my mind I could hear the sharp intake of breath at the door and a great deal of tisk-ing noises. I remembered being jolted awake; we were in the common room and it was long after power down. PG3456 in a mass on the floor. We had fallen asleep in each other's arms. The Mothers' faces were white with horror. We were picked up, taken to our rooms, and told punishments would come in the morning. And they did of course, but perhaps because we were only ten or maybe because we were all together rather than in pairs that night, the punishment was light. We hauled water barrels for Fauna Management. But after that night, someone came to be sure our solitary doors were locked every night after power down.

When I was thirteen, PG3456 finally found the limit to The Mothers' tolerance. It started in a Traditions lecture. The instructor was reviewing the details of Play Groupings and how they are essential to Chelon's success as a city. He paused to ask if there were any questions. Doe raised her hand to ask what made a baby a boy or a girl. When the anatomy chart was pulled down and explained again, Doe shook her head, "No, I

13

mean what decides if a baby will become a boy or a girl? Is it The Mothers?" A pained expression flashed across the Pedagogic's face, and he ignored the question, continuing on with the lecture. Doe slipped down low in her seat so as not to catch his eye again, silently thankful he did not press his button, summoning The Mothers.

The rest of the morning lectures passed without anything out of the ordinary and we let the tension go with a sigh of relief.

After lunch, we opted to walk near the outer wall, which afforded us a marginal level of privacy instead of attending one of the voluntary activities taking place around the Quad.

"Why wouldn't the Pedagogic answer Doe? She gave credit to The Mothers after all," Wex began immediately.

"Maybe it's because The Mothers don't pick. It's probably biology just like the animals. It's just chance who ends up a boy, and that riles them up," Frehn said.

The question that biology and animals related to us somehow sent us all into pensive silence for the rest of our walk. That night at dinner, a Mother approached and asked us to follow her. We left our trays where they sat and complied. She led us to her sitting room and began to ask us questions about what we learned in lectures that day. We knew what was coming. Without an outward signal of any kind, we unilaterally agreed not to speak about the Traditions lecture. We would force the Mother to ask us about it directly.

"We were only confirming that The Mothers choose who is a boy and who is a girl," snapped Harc from my left.

14

Without warning, The Mother reached out and slapped Harc hard across the cheek. I felt the air push by my face as if she were slapping me too.

The Mother gasped and put her hands to her cheeks with a sickening mock face of regret, "Oh! See now what your words have made me do? You've made me hurt someone I love!"

Merit was on his feet immediately, hands clenched into fists. Wex and Frehn were standing an instant later, I think more to remind Merit of where he was than to aid in his fury against The Mother. Doe started applying her handkerchief to the deep cut on Harc's cheek made by one of The Mother's spiked rings. No one was watching me. No one saw the rage that boiled over inside me, spilling out of my eyes in hot tears. No one noticed that I lurched to hurl myself forward at The Mother. Just before my fingernails could dig into The Mother's eyes, Wex dove in front of me, his mouth on mine.

Wex and I were pried apart, all six of us locked into our separate rooms. Which was a blessing really. If The Mother had known I was going to attack her, I would have been killed on the spot. And probably my entire Play Group with me.

My first kiss saved my, our, lives.

I'm sure there was great debate on our punishment among The Mothers. I was left alone in my room for ten days, the only sign of life the oat mash and water which appeared twice daily in the little passthrough by the door. On the tenth day, our televisions lit up and our punishment announced to the entire city. Solace for 720 days. One day for each second of our rebellion, our two minutes with The Mother in her sitting room,

15

times six. I would not see Wex or the others again until we were fifteen. To me it seemed like a lifetime.

Today is the 721st day of our Solace and 731 days from the last moment I saw PG3456. We celebrated our return by attending the Oath of Service festival where everyone in our year was assigned to a line of industry. I spent the last two years thinking, believing, our Play Group would be publicly dissolved during the Oath, leaving us to live out the rest of our lives in work and solitude.

From the moment we attended our first lecture in Traditions, PG3456 set our sights on serving side by side in Nutriment Cultivation. Being out of doors and free to walk among the crops or through the enormous open air kitchens was our primary goal, breathing in the clean air outside of the inner wall. We worked towards that goal in lectures and physical instructions. We bent our minds to show our teachers any traits that might be thought suited to the fields. No complaints from hard labor, building up a tolerance to sun and windburn by spending all of our free time outside with no regard for the weather. We volunteered to care for the flowers in the container gardens around the residence blocks and showed as much interest as we dared in the people who were already assigned to work the crops.

Now that we had been in Solace for two years, it seemed unlikely we would be assigned to anything but the mines and factories. My limited contact with other living things had been under observation and strict control. I continued hearing the Pedagogics lectures over the television in my room, and I assume the rest of PG3456 had as well. We would have to be reintroduced to life outside our rooms when this was over and education was essential to our usefulness to Chelon. But I had not been able to interact with the instructors.

The Mothers would certainly not have risked giving us so much freedom in the fields, not after our 720 second display of unified defiance. The fields are so widespread, we could have been off on our own for hours at a time with no supervision. I was certain I would be put in the factories because I am dextrous and have a quick mind. Those two traits would have kept my fingers out of the machines while I manufactured goods Chelon needs for trade with the other cities.

The night before the Oath, I dreamt of my seven year old self, of the day I tried to walk down a set of stairs backwards. My friends screamed as I tripped and rolled down two flights. Scooped up by the Healers and taken to their building, I felt no pain. Just a sense of foggy amazement that I was not dead.

While I was being looked over for broken bones, I heard the pains of birth from a room across the hall, then a joyous cry from a woman that quickly turned to an anguished sob as the baby was taken from her. There was a quick hurried sound to hush the woman as one of The Mothers came gliding down the hall in her lavender and white tunic to collect the newborn infant. She cooed and stroked the baby's tiny fingers as she bustled off with it in her arms. We were all once that baby. And all the girls in Chelon would be that woman. Pain, brief joy, and then never ending agony. They will not permit us to have families.

Instead we are grouped in sets of six, three boys and three girls. When my Play Group was formed, people looked at us as the left overs. We had a wide swing in ages for a Play Group, ranging from just shy of 12 months to a matter of hours old. Even our assigned number was strange. The last group formed that day, we were PG3456. We were the first consecutive number set for 111 years, 1,111 Play Groups ago. Healer Fednum told me once that PG3456 was like a pack of wild dogs from the other side of the outer wall. Coarse and untamed from the beginning. Even our appearance was ragged compared to the Chelon standard. None of us wore the issued clothes as they were intended. But because we didn't physically alter them, we weren't breaking any rules. So we were left alone and allowed to ignore the opinions of others.

"Keres?"

My dreams, projected memories on the backs of my eyes, were coming in with sound. I must be deep into the Heavy tonight.

"Keres?"

No. That wasn't in my memory. That wasn't in my dream. That was on the other side of the room. I raised my head slightly to peer over the edge of my round bed. Eyes sweeping the room. No one. Exhausted from the effort, I fell back into the sheets.

"Keres, it's me. Wex."

Wex. Where are you now, Wex? Pain swept through me like poison, eating away at what little strength the soup had given me. I sank back down into my bed and gave into it.

On the backs of my eyes I saw us, all of us, in the fields running toward the horse barn. Jumping over crop rows and laughing when Frehn scoops up a handful of fresh greens to carry like a Banding Bouquet. We collapse by the stream at the back of the barn and dunk our heads in the cool water. The boys whip their heads back, causing arcs of water to fly through the air.

I catch Wex's brown eyes on me while I wring the water from my own hair onto my bare feet. Already tall for thirteen, I take in Wex's shoulders. They completely eclipse Merit's entire body behind him. Frehn nudges me with his elbow and motions towards Doe, perched on the edge of the bank trying to pick a flower from the patch of grass in the center of the creek. Frehn jumps into the water, sending a huge wave over her. Before she has time to react, the flower is in her hand and Frehn is laughing as he kicks up the water, soaking us all.

I turned my head into the pillow and choked out my grief; the memory stabbed me deep. I wanted the Heavy to press me into the pillow, smothering out everything. I wanted to die there, that instant. Darkness crept over me and I heard his voice again. Deeper, stronger than I last heard it two years ago. But it was Wex's voice.

"In the vent. Keres!"

Instantly, I was at the ventilation entry point in the back of my room without knowing how I got there.

"Wex?!" my voice caught in my throat.

"Yes, keep your voice down. We can talk while the air is blowing without anyone overhearing but you must keep your voice low. We only have a few seconds left."

19

"Wex." Wex. Hexes on the Absolute Mothers, it was Wex.

"Listen to me, tomorrow when we are assigned to Services, we must pay attention to where everyone goes, even those outside of PG3456. We have a plan, Keres. To leave Chelon."

Chapter Three

Like pulling my head out of water, I am brought back to the here and now. My memories are yanked away from me and I am left standing in the silk and satin robes of ceremony, disoriented and unnerved. The novice has guided us off stage to a room just inside the north residence compound. She is trying to group us by service so we can receive the appropriate uniform tickets. I stand alone, willing myself to stay upright. The weight of the robes seems to have doubled since they were put on me before dawn. I want to scream and frantically knock the black diamond out of my hair, as if it's a spider.

Someone places two thin metal squares in my hands and moves on quickly. I don't look down. I know one is the ticket I will present at the clothier counter and the other is my new schedule. I can feel myself swaying, pushed by the black smoke fingers. Not yet, I repeat over and over. Not. Yet. I cannot give into the despondency of the Heavy until I am safe in my room. I have to get out of these robes and take this makeup off my face. I am unbearably hot.

The Mother who led the Oath finally dismisses us with cheery instructions to use this rare free afternoon to gather our uniforms and check in with our Service Leaders before the feast tonight. We begin training at 08:00 tomorrow. Doe and

Harc are at my elbows, guiding me out of the room. Merit whispers through slightly parted lips and clenched teeth directly behind me, instructing me to walk quietly until we are changed and can meet together in our common room. I blink at the idea. Meet in our common room. Together and alone. Impossible.

Somehow I make it to my room where a novice waits to help me undress and wash off the makeup. Apparently it takes four Mothers to dress me up but only one in training to get me back to normal. She packs the robes neatly away in a crate and slips out of the room, closing the door behind her.

I walk to the door, place my hand on the knob and hold my breath. The latch clicks open. I close it and open it again, looking out into the common room as I used to a thousand times, a lifetime ago. My door is unlocked. With no announcement, no instructions, no new rules, Solace is over. I want an explanation, I want someone to tell me what my new normal is. An unlocked door, finding myself still in the same block with PG3456 seems anticlimactic. It feels like a trap.

Realizing I'm standing in my doorway with nothing on but the thin dressing robe the novice draped over me, I close the door again and move across the room slowly. It feels foreign to move this much. In the closet I find the assigned allotment of clothes for my fifteenth year. I vaguely remember the day they were brought in by The Mothers, as I was unable to join the others in the annual trade out. How I ached for these clothes three years ago. They seemed so grownup to me then. Careful to choose items that were intended to go together rather than an outfit I would have created two years ago, I get dressed. When I look in the long mirror I don't recognize myself. The goddess who was reflected back this morning has been replaced by a young woman, neat and presentable if a little too thin, dressed in dark brown pants, white shirt and flat leather shoes. A young woman who looks a little like me about the eyes with a black diamond pin over her left ear. "Who are you?" I can't help asking the reflection. The girl in the mirror has a massive amount of black hair I don't remember having and her chin is razor sharp. The only thing recognizable in the reflection are my blue eyes.

There's a quiet knock on my door. I jump at the now unfamiliar noise. The Mothers never knock, they always ring the bell tone. Doe gently opens the door and sticks her head around the edge.

"Will you come out?"

Suddenly shy, I hesitate, reminded of the day Doe tripped in the canteen, her tray flying across the floor, spreading her lunch ration as it went. We couldn't have been more than six years old. In unison, the rest of us went to her before the laughter in the room could make her feel alone enough to cry. Picking her and the tray up, we all kissed and hugged and cuddled her. All of us. The Mothers watched us from their positions on the edges of the room with grave faces.

If some other girl had tripped, The Mothers would have come forward to clean her up and set her right. Perhaps the girls, or at least one girl, in her Play Group would have gone to help as well. Never the boys. It is unheard of for boys to caress and soothe a girl outside the privacy of their own residence block. And especially not one they weren't Banded to. I

23

remember feeling the hard floor on my knees as we cleaned the mess of food. When I glanced up, I saw a Mother watching me, the corner of her eye twitching with concentration. The Heavy's fingers slinking around the back of my neck were as cold and hard as the slate floor of the canteen.

What's wrong with me? PG3456 is feet away from me, I am free to speak to them, touch them, look at them and I am suddenly afraid? Doe seems unfazed by my lack of movement and just leaves the door ajar. Shaking myself for being so stupid, I lunge for it and swing it open.

Standing around our common room are my five friends. They are not dressed like gods now but like all the other teenagers in Chelon. We take each other in for a second and, slowly as if introducing myself for the first time, I reach out to shake hands. The Heavy is shoved aside and the shyness falls away, and we collapse into each other with tears welling up in our eyes.

"This is idiotic," Frehn says as he rubs the back of his hand across his cheek. He doesn't pull away though. Some of us give an anxious laugh out of relief. It must make an odd picture. Six people, just pushed into adulthood, grouped in a circle, arms on each others' shoulders, laughing and sniffing and crying.

No one says anything else, sure that The Mothers are monitoring us in some way. I try to absorb everyone, all the changes time has made. I want to be familiar with their faces again. There are hard adult angles replacing the soft roundness on noses and cheeks I remember. The boys are unable to sit still after being caged in their rooms and smelling fresh air at the Oath this morning. At least the restlessness is familiar. Wex is the first to suggest we walk outside before we join the line for uniforms.

Now alone and not in the Oath line, I am free to look about as we leave our block and walk to the elevators. When I notice something out of place, a different type of flower in one of the numerous container gardens or a new pattern in the hall tiles it jars me. It's as if Chelon shoves me backward with each step.

My body isn't used to moving this much and it begins to protest loudly by the time we reach the Quad. Merit doesn't seem to be faring much better so we rest in the grass. My senses on the verge of overload, I close my eyes and just smell the world. It smells a lot better than my terra-cotta pot bed. An old feeling of relative freedom surges up within me and I smile to myself.

PG3456 has spent hours just like this, sprawled out in the grass, not talking. Merit would reach out now and again to be sure we were all still there. I would weave grasses together to make animals for Doe to play with. She was so much smaller than us, she became something of a pet. Wex would stroke her back like she was a calf or a colt.

The black diamond pin scratches my scalp when I shift in the grass to look at Doe now. She is still small for our age, but the Solace doesn't seem to have stunted her. She actually looks more toned than she ever did before. Her hair is swept back into a braid, no longer in the elaborate style from this morning. She moves her head to look slowly around the Quad. I imagine she is searching for things that have changed, things

25

that have stayed the same. A sad mien on her face, as if she regrets our returned freedom to roam.

"We should get in line," I say. Avoiding the rest of today's tasks is only letting the Heavy press into me again. Everyone else knows what they will be doing tomorrow and has a general idea what they will be wearing during Service hours. Each one has landed in a Service that will be a clear benefit to us if there really is a plan to escape Chelon. My Service, my contribution is unknown, unspoken.

We know who is an Unspoken by their distinctive hairstyles and tattoos, or their black diamonds if they are still in the early apprentice stages. The Unspoken is not what they are officially called. They don't have a Service title, at least not one that's known. They are still members of their Play Groups, of course, but beyond reporting to a room in the basement of the Gratis Building, their Service to Chelon is a complete mystery.

Most people don't think about them much because there are so few of them and so little is known about their activities it makes for poor conversation around the common rooms. I always thought of the black diamond ornaments on Oath day as more symbolic of dread. Dread that one day it would be my turn to be assigned a Service and PG3456 would no longer spend entire days together. We couldn't all land in Nutriment Cultivation, even before the Solace.

Once we reach the Necessities Center, an enormous marble building covered in scroll work and statues, there are only a handful of people left in line for uniforms. I reach the counter first and hand the Keeper my ticket; he doesn't even look at it. He was probably at the Oath and knows who I am.

All of Chelon will know who I am now. He hands me a matte black box with a mother of pearl clasp. "Instructions on the card," he wheezes as he looks me up and down. I manage to whisper a thank you and move over so Doe can present her ticket.

When Merit has received his box, a straw hamper held closed with a leather loop, it's noon. No one is hungry, as the boxes are consuming our whole attention. Our new schedules aren't active until tomorrow so we go back to our block, uncertain if there would even be a meal for us in the canteen. We walk slowly down the streets and through the Quad in a very traditional and submissive two rows, girls in front, boys in back. Not many Play Groups walk in two lines anymore, but they are not being watched by The Mothers for signs of an emotional relapse either. We talk about all the robes from the morning, the potential for a good harvest, the feast planned for that night. We reminisce over past years' performance displays each Service line provides for entertainment while everyone gorges themselves on food- there will be no rationed amounts tonight. Our chatter is so polite we could be any Play Group. No one would guess what lies beneath our friendly, arm's length banter.

The door shut firmly in our common room, we place our boxes on the table. Harc asks, "Who wants to go first?" in an over-bright voice. No one makes a move. She reaches out and pulls the knotted rubber band off her shiny plastic box. Inside lays a neatly folded blue jumpsuit, slippery white underclothes, shoes and head wrap. The included card illustrates how to wear each piece. "Well. It's not the color of

27

my dreams but it compliments my hair rather well, doesn't it?"
She holds the jumpsuit up to her chin and looks at us with a
raised eyebrow.

How is she able make jokes? And how am I able to
laugh at them? How can we just chat lightly like we were never
in Solace, like we never watched The Mother hit her? Like I
never tried to gouge out a pair of cold eyes in retaliation? How
am I doing this? I'm back to going through the motions.
Opening Service boxes one by one, looking at all the contents,
and laughing. It feels forced and vulgar.

My box is the only one still left to open. Everyone has
been looking at it since we sat down, no one really wanting to
know. I can't remember seeing an Unspoken in anything but
the standard issue clothing everyone in Chelon wears. I look
around the room. I want to see it one more time before
everything is changed by what's in this black box. Taking a
deep breath, I press the clasp and the lid swings open. Resting
on top, there is the instruction card with a woman dressed in a
formfitting black suit with terra-cotta orange patches on the
arms, legs and torso, high black boots and a black leather belt
resting at an angle on the painted model's hips. When I pick up
the card, it unfolds showing more instructions for different
versions of the uniform, a short skirt and jacket, a long loose
skirt with leather pouches dangling from the belt, one with a
shirt and not much else, one thick and lined with fur with
zippers up the arms and legs. I reach into the box and pull out
the first suit pictured on the card followed by the boots and
belt. There's nothing else in the box.

"I guess the other ones are seasonal," is all I can think of to say. How can I possibly serve Chelon in a skintight suit like this? It's so small, it doesn't even look like I could pull it past my thighs. The material feels dense and unbreathable. A claustrophobic feeling starts to close me in.

Wex reaches out for the belt, gently pulling my fingers open so he can take it from me. He looks at it with interest. Loaded with pockets, loops and pouches, none of which have anything in them. "A belt like that would be dead useful in the fields. Better than the issued sling bag anyway. A bag, or even our everyday packs, could really get in the way when you're plowing or harvesting the grains. If that strap gets caught on anything, you could lose an arm in the combine." I can feel Doe's hand on mine, she seems so far away, why won't she stand still...

"Catch her, Wex. She's going to faint."

Chapter Four

I do not faint. I vomit. Stomach acid and bile mostly,
but there's also something resembling the soup I had last night.
"Sorry," I choke as I spit the last of it on the floor.

"You just aren't used to all this activity," Doe says
soothingly.

"Neither are the rest of you and you aren't tossing up
last night's dinner," I rasp, looking up from under the curtain of
hair that's fallen across my face to see all of them exchange
glances. "What?" I demand, aware of a change in the mood. It's
gone from sympathetic to concerned.

"Well, most of us have been keeping active," confesses
Harc, "We tried to move about our rooms and do some of the
exercises from Physical Assessment. We thought it would be a
good idea to try to stay alert."

I can't seem to take in what they are saying. Harc
sounds like they developed this alertness plan after we were
separated. I stare at her blankly. I manage to croak out, "We?"

"Wex-" Merit starts.

Wex cuts him off, "Merit, remember." He glances at the
common room door.

"If they were listening, they would have been in here to
clean up Keres already. You know they gravitate towards mess

and sickness are like moths to flames. They can't help themselves," Frehn says with a wave of his hand indicating there are no moths around my flame of sick.

I consider this. Yes, it's true. In the canteen when Doe fell with her lunch tray, The Mothers hovered around us, itching to dive in with the cleaning cloths they keep under their white aprons. But PG3456 got to Harc first and The Mothers couldn't stand it. When we were small, every scrape or sneeze brought a flock of them to us, dripping with coos and simple remedies. The way they lingered over me in my dark days under the Heavy, their white cornets fairly vibrating with their desire to drink in my pain.

We all turn to the common room door leading onto the hall and wait. It remains closed and still. The bell silent, no one comes. Merit begins to move around the room, quietly feeling under the furniture and lamp shades. Harc, Wex and Frehn join him while Doe cleans me up. I protest, saying I'm perfectly capable of cleaning up my own face and vomit, but she resolutely continues. When she is finished she joins the others in their search for monitoring devices.

When they have gone over the room three times, I can't stand it anymore. "What do you mean we decided to stay alert?" I ask again.

Wex comes over and takes the chair in front of me. "A few weeks after the announcement of our Solace, I heard Frehn scream. His yells were saturated with so much pain, I could feel them crash through me. The next day I heard Harc, the same shuddering screams. I knew then that we all must be in our rooms, still together and only separated by walls. I also

31

knew that the Solace wasn't the only punishment handed down by the Absolute Mothers."

"I didn't hear anyone! I would have known you were near and been alright if I had heard you, any of you," I cry in disbelief.

Wex glances at Harc who says quietly, "We think that something different was done in your room. Something that cut you off from the rest of us even more than just walls and a locked door."

I feel stupid and purposefully excluded. They are exchanging knowing looks as if I am a toddler from another Play Group who stumbled into the wrong common room. Putting my hands to the sides of my head, I feel the black diamond. My fingers rip it out and slam it on the table. It leaves a mark in the wood. "Go on," I say quietly to Wex.

He swallows and continues, "The night after they- after they hurt Harc they came for me. Five of them, all in black and masked. They strapped me to a chair and… " his face is white now, he has trouble even saying the words in a barely audible whisper, "and they used needles, hundreds of needles shoved under my nails." He trails off, stands and begins moving around the room, "They injected me with fire, poison, something that burned through my entire body like white hot metal. Blisters erupted all over me and when they burst the pus burned like fire on my skin."

I can see him arching his back in remembrance of the pain. Wincing for him, Doe slides her tiny hand in his. He looks down and smiles, calmed by her touch. He looks back at me and continues, "They tortured each of us in turn for weeks, night after night always in the same succession. Frehn, Harc, me, Merit, Doe. Everyone, expect you. I never heard you scream or cry out."

"No," I breathe, "No, they never came for me."

Wex sits back down. "Exactly. I thought at first that you must have been moved, you couldn't still be on our block. I had to find out. So I began to respond to The Mothers sycophantic simpering when they came in to switch out food trays or change my sheets. I allowed them to feel like they were soothing me, calming me. I let them clean the layers of sweat and pus off me. I started paying close attention to the Pedagogic lectures piped in over the television and asked for materials for study. Because of that the torturing stopped. Gradually, I stopped hearing the others being tortured as well."

"They cut my fingers to the bone with a slaughter knife. A finger a night," Harc spits out. "They poured some kind of liquid on them, until I couldn't keep the screams down any longer. When that wasn't enough, they broke the bones with heavy irons. They moved on to my hands when there wasn't anything left of my fingers. I wasn't as smart as Wex, I should have just pretended to respond to The Mothers' kindness in order to avoid the torture. Instead, I gave in to the pain. When I started crying instead of screaming The Mothers swooped in gushing and kissing and cleaning my hands." Harc swallows hard, looking sick, "I let them wash and bandage me, and I thanked them. After that the five in black didn't come back."

I look at Harc's delicate fingers. There were so beautiful once. Now rows upon rows of ugly scars fill each one. A mutilated finger a night. And where was I when she was being sliced to pieces? In bed. Crying because I was alone. I almost vomit again but put my head between my knees instead.

"We all went through... something," Wex says quietly, "But we found a way to appease The Mothers. After that, things became surprisingly easy. I began searching my room for ways to communicate, to discover where you were, Keres. I figured out I could talk through the vents as long as the air was moving. I made contact with Frehn first, who was still receiving visits from the five. The stubborn mule wouldn't let The Mothers touch him."

"No, and it took a massive amount of convincing from you and Doe to make me," Frehn says almost proudly. "But I saw reason. If we were going to come up on top, find out where you were, I had to give in."

"I tracked the air currents and we worked out a relay system to communicate with each other through the vents and not be overheard," Wex continues after giving Frehn a look.

"And that's when I pulled the television off the wall," Harc says.

"You- what?" Somehow this is what makes me raise my head. She pulled the television out of its encasement in the bookshelf with her broken fingers and hands. "What did The Mothers say to that?"

"Oh, they never knew," Harc says with a shrug, "I had it all back in place once I got what I needed from the back. It's remarkable how much waste there was back there. Lots of wide plastic tubing covering the wires to keep them neat, I guess. Once we got all of it off our TVs, I was able to connect everything into kind of a network. That tube was just enough to connect all our rooms to each other and to reach from Wex's vent straight to yours. If we could figure out how to get it there."

"It took a while but we managed to hear what was happening in the common room. We heard The Mothers going in and out of your room but couldn't hear anything inside it. Finally, Merit was able to get his vent cover off and squeeze through the ducts to look into your room. He saw you, on the bed, and looking in relatively good physical condition. We were all relieved at first, that you had either overcome any physical torture or that you were spared all together."

"Then we began to really worry," interrupts Frehn. "There's no way you would have been spared when you were the one who flew at The Mother. She must have known you were going to attack her, that's not the kind of thing you just miss. We had to make contact with you. Merit laid the network of tube through the ducts so Wex would have a direct connection to you."

"So I did hear you last night." Was it only just last night? "Yes, but you should have heard me months ago. I talked to you every night," Wex says with a sigh. "That's why we think something else, a different kind of torture was happening to you. Something prevented our voices from getting to you or what was happening in your room to get out. Until last night. When you heard me."

Until I heard him. Until I heard him I hadn't been able to move out of bed. When his voice came from the vent, I sprang out of bed and across the room without knowing how it happened. Is the Heavy something manufactured by the five torturers to keep me subdued? I try to remember the early days of the Solace. I search my mind for the days before I didn't leave my bed and I can't remember them. I only remember the Heavy and living in the memories that replayed on the backs of my eyes. Where is my quick mind when I actually need it? I shake my head to clear the confusion.

"The five in black. Black. No one wears black here. The dye is too valuable to the other cities," I say. My eyes turn to my black box with the black suit spilling out of it. It's the only piece of clothing I've ever held in my hands that was black.

"No, oh, no," I whisper. The Unspoken service, the five in black, my black suit. "No."

"You don't know that yet," Frehn is behind my chair, arms around my shoulders, his breath in my ears, "You don't know that. It could be anything, any number of reasons why your uniform is black. It's not the same as the ones the five were wearing. It's not, Keres."

Doe is at my feet, "He's right, Keres. It's not the same, their black was loose and cotton and they had masks. None of the uniforms on your card have masks."

I look at Wex, his eyes are narrow and his jaw tight with pressure. There is a muscle twitching in his neck. "Black," I mouth to him.

"It doesn't matter," he says. "We will not be here long enough for it to matter. They can hardly turn you into a torturer in a couple of years. You'll still be young when we leave and the five were very old. I would have guessed they were long past Disengagement by the wrinkles around their eyes."

Reassurance flows through me like a warm drink. This is the first time he has mentioned leaving Chelon since last night. Hearing him say it with PG3456 around me makes it real again. We are leaving Chelon in... wait. Years?

"Why years, Wex? Why not tomorrow? Or tonight?" I plead. "Everyone in Chelon will be at the feast tonight, it's the perfect night to go over the outer wall."

Wex only smiles and shakes his head. "We don't know anything about living without the canteen, the Necessities Center, and unfortunately, we don't know how to live without The Mothers. We have to gain some skill, we have to find a way for all of us to get out at the same time. That will take some doing. One or two might easily get over the outer wall but certainly not all six of us. We must keep our heads down and learn everything we can in our Services. Even yours, Keres. Whatever it is, it will be valuable on the outside. Besides, you and Merit are in no shape to climb mountains."

He has a point there. I look at Merit, almost emaciated with malnutrition. His eyes are dull and his shoulders hunched. Being out of doors with the animals will strengthen him up; it's exactly what he needs. He seems to think the same thing about me, a sad smile hanging on his lips. As we stand now, we are liabilities to PG3456. We would get them killed, or worse captured, for sure.

The all too quick mind that got me in trouble with The Mothers so many times has abandoned me. Everyone is outthinking me, which rattles me into anger. It's not their fault I had some sort of silencer around my room and they couldn't share their ideas with me, but it still gnaws at my stomach when I think of them in contact with each other and plotting for months without me. They had each other, if only in voice, for months while I had nothing but my round terra-cotta bed and blurs of The Mothers' lavender tunics.

"It must be late," I say. "We still have to check in with the Service Leaders before the feast."

No one moves, so I tap on Frehn's arms and he lets me go. I pack the black suit back in the box, place it in my room and walk out of our block. I don't wait to see if they follow me. I'm as angry as I was two years ago at the sound of The Mother's hand connecting with Harc's check, at the sight of her blood. I get to the Gratis Building before I can clear my thoughts. The building is almost blood red in the late afternoon sun. "Fitting," I snort.

The Keeper at the front desk glances up at me when I enter the vestibule. Without a word, she points to an area in the corner of the hall and buzzes me through to an elevator that will take me to the location where I am to meet my Service Leader. The elevator car drops so fast my stomach lurches again. Inwardly thankful there is nothing left for my stomach to expel, I can't stop a smile from forming when I think of the doors of the elevator opening to an Unspoken with an elaborate hairstyle and a labyrinth of patterns tattooed all over her body gazing down at me in a pool of sick. That would certainly make an impression.

When the car finally stops and the doors slide open, I step out into a hall of doors, each one with a lantern and a number. I stand awkwardly in front of the elevator, not sure where to go. The door in front of me opens and a man with a twisted swirl pattern tattoo that sweeps up from his neck and across his forehead appears. He is wearing a black suit like the one in my box, only his is just form fitting and not skintight like mine will be. "I've been waiting for a while, Keres," he says, not totally void of kindness.

"I'm sorry, I haven't been used to so much, uh, activity," I apologize while trying to avoid looking at his tattoo. It seems to be moving, pulsating.

"Yes. I can imagine. Well, come inside and have a seat."

I follow his lazy gesture and sit in the chair he indicates. He takes a seat at the desk and looks at me, hands behind his head. He looks like he hasn't shaved in days and there is an unsettling scar running the length of his right forearm, cutting through a massive tattoo. Having appraised me for a minute, he introduces himself as Abbot.

"What do you know about us?" he asks abruptly.

"Nothing. I mean just what everyone else knows."

"What do you think you know about us?"

This question startles me. I hesitate, mouth agape.

"That's what I thought. Quick minds make too many assumptions. Assumptions which display gross ignorance. Well, forget everything you think you know. It won't help you to have preconceived ideas of what your training will involve. Tomorrow morning, don't put on your uniform. Just wear your black diamond ornament and everyday clothes. You can carry your uniform in this pack." He hands a brown pack to me, larger than my everyday pack and much sturdier. "We don't wear our uniforms when we are off the hall. Black is not a common color and it would cause a certain level of unease among the others. Come on, I'll show you your den."

I'll bet it would cause unease, I think. If anyone else in Chelon has had a visit from the five, chaos would explode were the Unspoken to prance around the city in black.

We get up and walk down the hall to a door numbered 29. He unlocks it and hands me the key. "You will keep everything for Service in here, you'll change in here and you'll study in here. When you arrive every morning, come to this room and dress. I'll turn up with instructions at some point." We walk into the room.

It's larger than I anticipated from the closeness of the doors in the hall. There is a desk, sitting area with overstuffed chairs and a love seat gathered around a low table. Bookcases cover one of the walls and a large cushioned mat covering the floor in the back of the room. Everything is surprisingly comfortable, even cozy, in appearance. Abbot shows me the light, atmosphere and other control boxes.

"If I don't turn up before lunch tomorrow, you can start with this book." He thumps a volume on the desk. There's no title on the spine and his hand rests on the cover so I can't pick it up. So I just nod assent.

"Any questions?"

"Yes."

"Well?"

"What is our Service to Chelon?"

Abbot only grins and shakes his head. "That is something for which you are not yet ready to know."

He leads me back to his own den and stands me in the center of the room. "This will hurt a lot less if you hold still." He reaches out to grab the collar of my shirt and I instinctively jerk back, knocking his hand to one side. He just smiles wryly and holds up a large metal stamp, then pulls my shirt down so the top of my sternum is visible. He places the stamp flush to my skin.

"Ready?" he asks. I can only blink, but he takes this for a yes. He clicks the stamp down and searing pain surges through me, buckling my knees. Abbot inspects the place where he stamped me, prodding it with one finger. "Not bad," he nods with self satisfaction. "That's your first tattoo and a very remarkable one at that. It will keep you quiet when you are not on the hall. Just try talking about what you see and learn down here and see what happens. You won't like it," he says. The tone he uses is a strange mix of harshness and sympathy. I can't make him out, I can't make anything out but the throbbing pain on my chest. I reach up to feel the place where I was stamped. "You want to see?" he asks. He points to a three sided mirror to the right of the den's door next to his wardrobe closets. I stand in front of the mirrors holding my collar open so I can see.

Taking up a space about three inches wide and six inches tall is a raised black imprint of exquisitely detailed smoke black fingers, positioned so they look like they are pressing into my chest. I have been branded with the Heavy.

Chapter Five

Abbot dismisses me from the hall. He tells me to eat as much as I can tonight and in the morning for breakfast, that I might need it for training tomorrow if he has time. Letting go of my collar, I pick up the pack from the chair I had been sitting in and walk out of the room to the elevator car. When I reach out to press the call button, my hands are unnervingly steady. My whole body feels like it's shaking, but my reflection in the polished surface of the elevator door is perfectly still.

Once I'm in the open air, I turn my feet towards the back gardens instead of to the Quad. Some time to process what has just happened, and not happened, is required before I can look anyone else in the eye. I'm overwhelmed with the desire to know what happens if I try to talk about Abbot and the hall. Given PG3456's feeling that I am weak and need to be coddled, it would be unwise to test my new tattoo in front of them. Finding a secluded spot isn't difficult this close to feast time. I only pass a boy and a girl sitting close together on a bench. They fly apart when they hear my step, and I can feel their eyes on my back when I pass them. I crawl under a large weeping cherry tree and try to slow my heart rate. If the tattoo is going to keep me from physically talking about the hall, it will most likely do it in an acutely painful way. Thinking about

Abbot and the hall certainly hasn't caused it to do anything. I've thought of nothing else since I was stamped.

I try first whispering Abbot's name. Nothing. And nothing would happen, as he lives among the rest of Chelon, he even wears a Banded cuff. Of course his Play Group would have to call him by his name. His existence and that he is an Unspoken aren't secrets. Next I whisper that I was in the Gratis Building tonight, again nothing happens. And again it's clear to me that these are things everyone already knows. I relax a little and start to say in a normal voice "The hall, my den," and the tattooed smoke fingers push hard into my chest and I am thrown backwards against the tree trunk, knocking the wind out of me. Trying to stay calm, waiting for my breath to return, it strikes me that this method is incredibly effective. It wasn't the impact with the tree that knocked the air out of my lungs, it was the push itself. You can't talk if you can't breathe.

Gradually, I am able to gasp in air, and I lay choking in the dirt for several minutes. Abbot was right. I don't like it. It feels like I am drowning with heavy chains wrapped around my chest. When PG3456 asks questions about my Service, I might be able to say my leader is Abbot and we are in the Gratis Building but that's all. I wonder if I could show them the black smoke fingers and if they would understand. Somehow I don't think it would be allowed.

Breathing normally again, I turn my attention to the pack. Unfastening the cords and clasps, the only thing I find is a leather bound notebook with a symbol embossed on the cover, a wooden case filled with colored pencils, and a jar of writing ink with a pen. I tilt the notebook so I can see the

43

symbol better. A swirl pattern circles around the soft leather, enclosing a hand. All the fingers of the hand are curled inward like a fist with only the thumb extended to the side. On the thumb is a carved ring. I can't make out the pattern on the ring; it's too detailed for the thick leather of the notebook. It sends an uneasy prickling feeling over my spine and I bury the notebook deep inside the pack again. I have a feeling that the smoky black fingers on my chest won't let me show PG3456 this either.

Suddenly, I don't want to be alone anymore. I scramble out from under the tree branches and start towards the Quad. The feast is already in full swing, the Keepers performing an over the top exhibition of dance and water art on the center stage. The feast tables, loaded with every kind of food imaginable, are set up along the edges of the courtyard. Dishes of sauces, complex desserts, and every kind of meat available are piled high on beautifully crafted etched orange and purple glass serving pieces. My stomach rumbles a deep appreciation for the smells drifting past. I'm starving. I load my plate with chunks of beef stewed in rice and tomatoes, yellow and green squash sliced into thin ribbons, and something that looks like yams cut into little star shapes.

I already have a mouth full of rice when I find PG3456 sitting at a table right in front of the stage. It's so loud this close to the performances I can't hear Harc welcoming me back to the group. I think Frehn says something about the yams because he takes one off my plate with his fork. Each of us take trips back to the feast tables for seconds, some of us even go for thirds. The Service entertainments swirl around the stage in a mass of color and sound.

When we can't eat anymore, Frehn grabs hold of my wrist and pulls me to the dance floor already crowded with other Play Groups. Soon Wex and Harc appear beside us and I see Doe dragging Merit out to join us. We dance until we are dizzy, sweating with exertion. I can't hear anything but the music of the strings and horns from the Architects now on stage above us. I push everything out of my mind. The Solace feels years in the past and the hall with Abbot and his pulsing tattoo doesn't feel foreboding in the least as I spin around the courtyard in Frehn's arms.

When the fiddles and pipes of the miners finally die away, Fauna Management is announced. Everyone clears the dance floor, the animals already being moved into position. Fauna Management is always the highlight of the feast night. Unless you are part of the Service, you don't get to interact with the animals much. All of the lines use them in some way, hauling and transport generally, but we almost never interact with them out of harness. The horses, muscles rippling under their lustrous coats, carry a special weight with us. While they comply with the trainers' commands, you get the feeling they only do it out of compassion. Like the horses know we are beasts of burden too.

The poultry is showcased first and they fly from one trainer to the other, wings whipping the air. A row of peacocks, tails spread wide, are guided up from the back of the stage. A dozen horses leap over the peacock line as sprays of fire sparks shoot up from the four corners of the dance floor. The crowd gasps, then applauds wildly. The trainers, dressed in long coats that spill over the sides of their horses, begin to move in high-stepping patterns across the dance floor. I glance at Merit. He could be one of those trainers in a few years. It seems impossible that our Service training starts in a matter of hours. Yesterday we were still thirteen, today we are fifteen. The Solace took our remaining childhood, our last years of freedom. Tomorrow we are adults.

Harc lays her hand on my shoulder and I know she is thinking the same thing I am. Polar opposites in every way, I never understood how she and Merit were always the closest pair within PG3456. Her strength seemed to count for both of them and his gentleness acted on her like a calming spell. They spoke without words somehow, the rest of us kept at a certain distance without being excluded.

I remember when Harc was in a rage over marks she received at the end of a Pedagogic year. Merit simply sat while the rest of us tried to calm her down so The Mothers wouldn't overhear.

We were completely unsuccessful, only making her eyes blaze. Once we gave up, Merit crept up to her, put his forehead on hers and just whispered something quietly. Then he walked away as she sank to her knees in the dirt, holding her head in her hands. Merit herded us away and when Harc rejoined us an hour or so later, she was completely calm. It was as if her tantrum never happened. I wished a hundred times while I was struggling and lost under the Heavy that I had known what he said to her. Perhaps it could have helped me.

Fauna Management ends their entertainment with a series of cross jumps with silk flags flying from the horses' harness and the trainers' hands. The streams of color blend together with the rapid movement. I can't take my eyes off the animal on the end of the row, his countless white spots on the sea of gray that makes up his coat are not like any other horse I have seen. The tip of his nose would come just to mine, I think. I'll never be close enough to him to know for sure. Merit will though and he can tell me.

The last line's entertainment approaches the stage, as the Healers always end the Oath of Service feast night. Their large string instruments have such low methodical tones, they sound like they are lamenting the pain and death that accompanies their Service. People trickle back out to the dance floor and just kind of sway around. It's mostly Banded couples now, but there are a few teenagers among them. PG3456 doesn't have the luxury of joining them. Un-Banded teenagers take a certain amount of risk when they parade their preferences during the Healers' songs. They risk feeling more for each other than The Mothers allow, and with that they are almost guaranteed a punishment.

The Mothers keep a low profile on feast days. Their presence is most certainly felt, but to a significantly less degree. They stand just outside the reach of the lights in the courtyard, always on the watch, ready to swoop down upon us when the time comes. But generally they keep out of sight. Which allows all of us to relax our formal friendships a little and just enjoy the celebration of the last night of childhood for the Play Groups who were assigned Services that morning.

47

PG3456 has been virtually shunned by the other Play Groups tonight- no one has stopped by our table as they would have before the Solace. I appear to be the only one who notices though, and even I don't mind. I pretend it's because they want to give us space to recover our group dynamic and not because we carry a stigma. And certainly not because I now wear the black diamond.

There are Unspoken here tonight, there must be. I sit up a little and begin to look at other Play Groups for the first time tonight. All the Services are represented in the entertainments, all of them except for the Unspoken of course, but they would attend the feast because they are part of their Play Groups. Yes. I see Abbot at a table not far from me, laughing with two men. And by the feast tables there is another man, younger than Abbot, with the distinctive haircut and his whole arm covered in weaving lines. On the dance floor a woman sways in time to the music with her Banded partner, her tattooed legs showing under her skirt when her partner spins her. I count twenty-seven in all. Including me, that's twenty-eight Unspoken.

That's a fraction of the forces in the other Services, which range from 100 to 1,000 people, the factories and keepers at the larger end of the scale and the teachers, architects and healers being at the low end. Even if some had already left the feast, it would still be an almost comically low number for a line that is supposed to serve a city of thousands. Less than thirty people couldn't possibly serve all of Chelon. Unless the Service was rarely needed. Like torture.

Chapter Six

The Healers are stepping down from the stage. The
feast is officially over and the normal order of subdued
obedience settles over everyone almost immediately. PG3456
starts back to our block, staying well within the crowd.

"Every time we go back to the common room, we must
be sure to search it carefully for anything The Mothers may
have left," Wex says to us under the cover of chatter around us.
"They may try to establish a feeling of safety in us. Once we
stop checking is most likely when they will place a device." We
all nod and smile as if he is talking about the performances.
"We won't talk about anything on the block tonight, but
tomorrow we will take an inventory of our services and what
we have observed." I feel the smoke black finger tattoo throb
on my chest. "Merit, you will be in the best position to find a
place to conceal a stockpile. The fields are too open but you
might be able to find a place in the stables or barns."

Merit agrees as we cross the threshold to our block. Our
talk turns to the feast and the anticipation of tomorrow's service
training. I don't speak, aside from the few times I am directly
applied to for an opinion. In a few minutes the bell tone
sounds, alerting us that power down is in ten minutes.

At that moment, something that makes me feel normal for the first time since the Solace began happens. We girls stand in a line in front of the fireplace and the boys walk down it, kissing each of us goodnight. We have said goodnight like this every night since we could walk. It was always my favorite part of the day. Armed with some return of our own routine that makes me feel safe, I no longer dread retiring to my solitary room.

I wash my face and get ready for bed, climbing into it just as the one minute warning bell sounds. The Mothers have cleaned my room and changed my sheets. The stale smell of imprisonment that dominated the room yesterday has been replaced with the crisp and cool feeling of outside. The window must have been opened for an airing and the blackout glass has been removed.

Something else has changed in this room, but I can't tell exactly what. Looking around slowly, I can see it's nothing to do with the furniture or the accessories. It's something strange though and it makes me uneasy. The slight buzz of the lights is silenced with power down. The Heavy steals over me again as I lie still, waiting for my eyes to adjust to the dark. I hear a little click in my door signaling that The Mother has turned the key and I am locked in again. This is also reassuring in a way. We have been locked in our rooms after power down since we were ten when we caught together on the common room floor in the middle of the night. I begin to see the shapes of my bookcase and desk as I get accustomed to the dark. Everything is the same. My new pack is on the back of the chair and the black box containing my uniform is on the desk. Everything is right where I left it, just straightened up. There's nothing missing or new. All the same, I'll have to start sweeping my room for devices as well.

And then I see it. On the ceiling directly over the door there is a painted hand with the fingers curled in like a fist, the thumb straight out to the side. The same design that's on my Service notebook. The symbol doesn't send shivers down my spine even though my body automatically convulses like it does. It has a soothing effect, as if it's to protect me rather than harm me. It reminds me of Abbot. Remembering that he is connected to the sign somehow allows me to shut my eyes and fall asleep.

#

I sit bolt upright in bed. My dreams were filled with Doe and Frehn screaming on the other side of a wall I could not break down. I'm drenched in sweat and heaving for breath. I look at the clock on the nightstand. It's 06:30 and time to get up anyway. I pull on a robe and go to my bathroom. I turn on the shower and try not to look at myself in the mirror. The sound of Doe screaming still echoes in my head. I try to burn it out by turning the water as hot as it will go.

After drying my hair I pile it up on the top of my head and dress in everyday clothes as instructed. I stuff the uniform in the pack and am just about to walk out of my room when I remember I have to wear the black diamond pin. I haven't seen it since I slammed it on the table yesterday afternoon. It's probably still there.

Merit is already in the common room, picking up his jade horse from the row of all our ornaments on the mantel. It's hung on a piece of leather string now and he ties it around his neck. He looks almost excited to get his hands on the animals.

"Morning," I say walking over to him.

He starts a little at the sound of my voice, but smiles at me. "It's going to take some getting used to, hearing other people's voices."

"I hold my breath every time I try to open my door," I say, "just in case it's not really over."

I see my black diamond in the middle of the row. Merit steps back to allow me to pick it up. I don't want to touch it. We stand there looking at it for a moment when Harc, Doe and Wex join us. They claim their own ornaments and are putting them on when Frehn's door flings open and he dances through it. The combination of his knees in the air and his uniform of orange overalls makes us all laugh.

"No one could possibly miss my magnificent body in these," he says, strutting across the room. The tight white shirt underneath the overalls is too small for him and doesn't have sleeves. "I will be the envy of Chelon at breakfast." He hangs the chain of emeralds, diamonds and coal around his neck and picks up the black diamond. He walks over and sticks it in my hair without ceremony. "Now," he says, "let's go eat."

His matter of fact way of picking up the thing the rest of us were all avoiding makes me feel childish. I put all my fears into an inanimate object, something that has no power, and I treated it like a venomous snake. If I start being afraid of things that cannot hurt me, it will only escalate my terror of things that actually can.

Grabbing our packs, we head to the canteen. After breakfast we will not see each other again until lunch. Because of the Solace, PG3456 has the advantage over the rest of the Play Groups from our year. The four hours spent in training this morning will be the longest forced separation for them. They will feel as if their families are being torn apart while PG3456 will be able to concentrate completely on our Services.

We devour our morning rations and make plans to meet up in the Quad before going to lunch. Then we walk our separate ways: Wex and Merit to the outer wall gates, Harc to the south to the rows of factories, Doe to the Healers' Building on the west side of the city, Frehn to the north where the tunnel to the mine entrance begins, and me to the northeast and the Gratis Building. Being this widespread is different from being locked away on our block. We aren't more than a few miles apart yet it feels like we are on the other side of the world from each other.

I'm buzzed through to the elevator with another Unspoken, a tall woman in her late fifties. Her tattoos seem to engulf her entire upper body. She looks down at me with a slight nod and we go our separate ways when we reach the hall. I unlock the door labeled 29 and step into my den. I shut the door behind me and lean my back on it, dropping my pack to the floor.

The den is just as I left it last night, the book Abbot assigned me still on the corner of the desk. I change into my uniform and stare at myself in the mirror. Between my black hair and the black suit with orange patches I look like an oriole.

Abbot said he would probably not have time to start my training until after lunch. I take this opportunity to explore my den further. The bookcase runs the length of the wall opposite to the wardrobe section. The desk is on the bookshelf side while the seating area spans the width of the room in front of it. A few feet behind the desk, an exercise mat takes up the remaining depth of the den. The back wall is covered in floor to ceiling mirrors. There are several lockers and when I explore these they contain hand towels, various free weights and exercise equipment. It's clear strength training is a major component of the Unspoken.

Coming back to the desk, I take up the book Abbot left for me, Elemental Behavior of The Human Body. Opting for the comfort of the sofa rather than the rigid desk chair, I gather my notebook, a lead pencil from the desk and curl up for a long morning of boring reading. I'm torn between being thankful for the solitude and annoyed at the waste of time. Anatomy is one of the basic subjects the Pedagogics teach.

The first few chapters are exactly what I expect, an elementary overview of the muscle groupings and how the different functions of the body are connected. Nothing I don't already know. I've been reading for what feels like forever, but when I look at the timepiece on the desk, there are still two hours before I can leave for lunch. Stretching and yawning, I decide to move to the desk, hoping it will keep me awake while I trudge through the book.

Putting the book down on its spine, it falls open to the middle of a chapter close to the end. There is a diagram of the nervous system on the page, only it's not marked the way I am used to. Instead of having each nerve labeled with its name, groups of nerves are bracketed together with strange terms written beside them. Exploroare, Detrudo, Sublevatio, Dominatio and others completely foreign to me fill the page. I flip the pages back to glance at the table of contents. After the first five chapters of the fundamentals I have already learned, the titles start looking interesting. The book is divided into three sections: the physical body which includes basic anatomy and how to accelerate the build up of muscle mass while keeping the body lean, a section devoted to the mind which looks like instructions on developing brain capacity and the last and largest section on the nervous system. The nervous system section isn't about how the different nerves control the body, it's about how to control the different nerves.

I flip back to the chart and start reading the paragraphs around it. "Isolate the Sublevatio nerve group and apply your intentional signal to activate the ink which marks them. The nerve group will send the ready signal to the brain and retrieve the action command, building up your weapon. With labored study, the Sublevatio weapon variations can be aimed with millimeter precision. Self control is essential. Activation of the Sublevatio nerve group is not recommended without the presence of a qualified trainer."

Weapons triggered by a thought? The Unspoken have weapons in their nervous systems and I will be trained to use them with my mind? This doesn't sound at all like the torture devices used by the five in black. They used knives and needles and poisons and who knows what else, but nothing that came out of their nervous system. I sit back in the desk chair and exhale.

"Didn't your Pedagogics teach you not to look ahead in your text books?"

I jump in my chair. Abbot is standing feet from my desk and I never even heard the den door open or close behind him.

"I-," my voice cracks.

"Forget it. Your impatience is a good sign. How far did you get before you skipped to the good stuff?"

"Just through most of the anatomy, things I already know."

"You got further than I did the first day. At least you are moderately obedient. Which surprises me. I half expected you not to show up today. Suit fit you fine?"

I actually hadn't thought about the suit fitting since I first pulled it out of the black box. It glided on with ease, no pulling or discomfort. It feels like a second skin.

"Perfectly," I say.

"They always do. Juwas never fails, remarkable since she hasn't laid eyes on you, or anyone for that matter. Guess that's why she's on the hall and not sewing for Chelon. Come on, I want to see about your stamina."

He leads me to the mats at the back of the room and puts me through a series of fast paced exercises that threaten to break my limbs, if my muscles don't burst into flames first. In between each weight set, squat count or crunches, he has me

56

run full speed from one side of the room to the other, slamming into the walls when I reach them.

The lamp flickers on the desk and Abbot cheerfully barks out, "Lunch!" as he rubs his hands together with anticipation. I collapse on the mats, trying to catch my breath. "Not hungry?" Abbot asks looking down at me.

"You go ahead," I wheeze, "I'll catch up."

He chuckles and tosses a towel down to me. As he walks out of my den I hear him call to another Unspoken to wait for him while he changes. I wipe my face and neck while I drag myself to the desk. It's ten minutes until lunch is served in the canteen, just enough time to change back into everyday clothes. Still breathing heavily, I peel off the black suit and leave it on the floor. Back in the clothes I came in, I step out into the hall and am immediately knocked to the floor by a man racing to the elevators.

"Oh, sorry! I forgot you were assigned 29," he says, "You alright?" He reaches out and offers a hand to help me up. I pretend not to notice it and pick myself up.

"Fine. Thanks," I say stiffly.

"I'm Zink," he says with huge smile, "And you're Keres of course."

"Yeah," I say rubbing my hip.

"Right," he says and scratches the back of his head, not sure what to say next.

I start moving toward the elevator and Zink follows. As we wait for the car to come back down, I get a good look at him in the reflection of the glossy walls. He is significantly younger than the other Unspoken I have seen so far- he would have to be in his early twenties. There are only two visible tattoos in his reflection, one just coming out of his shirt and up his neck and one around his left wrist under his Banded cuff.

"How long have you been on the hall?" I ask him to break the awkward silence.

"I just started my seventh year," he says. Then this is the boy I remember, the one who looked as perplexed as I felt, the one who didn't receive applause from the crowd either. And I feel closer to him immediately because of this. The elevator arrives and we step on.

"How long did it take you to get to the back of the book?" I ask.

"Oh, I really couldn't say."

"Well, how long did it take you to get used to talking to other Play Group members? I mean everyone on the hall so far has been so much older."

"That didn't take me long at all. Once I figured out we were all in the same boat so to speak, it became second nature to be at ease here."

"In the same boat?"

Zink curls his shoulders in as if he is trying to retract the words, "Well, I mean we are all in the same line of Service."

"And what line is that?" I ask as the elevator comes to a stop.

"That is something for which you are not yet ready to know," he says in exactly the same tone as Abbot did yesterday. He gives me a sly smile, jumps out of the elevator and runs out of the building. I assume he's going to meet his Banded partner and their Play Group. Seven years since he was assigned to the Unspoken, means that he was Banded just three years ago.

It's unnerving how nice, if a little maddening, everyone on the hall is. At least, it's unnerving how not intimidating they are. I almost wish they were ferocious. It would give me something to grab onto. Something I could be angry about. Something that would encourage the Heavy to push me under where I don't care what happens. Instead of wanting to crawl back to my round bed and wallow, I am wishing lunch was already over so I can go back to my den and finish reading that book. Maybe that's why Zink was running, he wanted to eat fast and get back on the hall.

What a change from the dread I felt this morning. My everyday clothes actually feel stiff after wearing my suit all morning. I find PG3456 already assembled on the Quad and we go into lunch. Doe tells us she has been given her first lesson in medicinal plants. Frehn spent the morning in a safety lecture and practicing emergency evacuations from the mines. "Turns out it's not Chelon orange on our uniforms, it's glow in the dark orange to make us easy to spot under a collapse or when the power goes out," he says.

They all look at me once their information is spent, and I can say nothing. Not even a noncommittal grunt.

"Well?" asks Harc with a note of impatience.

"I- can't-" I can feel the pressure from the smoke black fingers on my chest and gasp for air. Frehn whacks me on the back.

"Don't," says Doe, looking not at me, but at my chest. I've neglected to fasten the top button of my shirt. When I hunched in my shoulders trying to catch my breath, the top half of my tattoo was visible. I snatch at my collar and secure the button closed. Doe's eyes are wide with recognition, "Don't ask her anymore," she says in a high-pitched unnatural voice, "they could kill her."

Chapter Seven

I can hear my heartbeat in my ears and it drowns out everything else around me. I push myself away from the table, mumble something about excusing myself and start walking back to the Gratis Building. My tattoo is radiating heat but it isn't pushing the air out of my lungs anymore. They could kill me? My own death hadn't occurred to me; being trained to mutilate or kill others certainly crossed my mind and that was disturbing enough. I feel blindsided, tricked somehow.

Back in my den, I stand in the middle of the sitting area, hands behind my back waiting for Abbot. I don't even change back into my black suit. It's still in a crumpled pile on the floor. It's strange that The Mothers haven't been in to tidy up. They usually start in on a room as soon as you've left it.

The other Unspoken are returning from lunch now. I hear their footsteps and voices echoing in the hall. Standing in the center of the den, I clench my hands behind my back and set my feet in a wide stance. Setting my teeth, I tilt my chin in the air and wait. There's a knock on my door and I call, "It's open," in the calmest voice I can muster. Abbot opens the door and steps in. He looks me up and down and shuts the door.

"Well, let's have it," he says with a sigh.

"Could you kill me?" This is not how I wanted to start.

61

"Absolutely. But not the way you are thinking."

"With this tattoo, could you kill me?" I nearly scream yanking down my collar.

"No. But you could."

I can feel burning angry tears welling up. Of course I would cry now. Why can't I ever just stay calm?

"Sit down, Keres. You are steamrolling through a very complex arrangement and we have skipped a few key educational points. I should have anticipated you would not follow the prescribed training regimen."

"I'd rather stand," I say, keeping my feet planted. I have no desire to turn this into a cozy fireside chat, sharing confidences. Abbot shrugs and stretches himself out in one of the overstuffed chairs.

"That tattoo has a great deal of power because you have a great deal of power. Probably more than anyone on this hall," he begins. "We, everyone who was left with the black diamond, are marked from birth for this Service. Not by The Mothers or the Pedagogics, but by a series of circumstances that are not in anyone's control," he pauses, considering me. He props his left foot up on his right knee, "Within each of us, there is a certain level of power called intusmagus. In simple terms, it's the ability to control and contort our nervous systems into performing atypical functions."

"Those are not simple terms," I say.

Abbot curls in his fingers into a fist, leaving his thumb straight out. "I have a specific thought," he says. He puts his thumb over the swirl pattern tattoo on his neck, "and I tell a group of nerves to act on that thought," he traces the outline with his thumb and the ink begins to glow, "and I perform that thought," he flings out his hand, fingers spread wide, shooting light across the room, shattering the timepiece on the desk behind him.

I sit down. Abbot closes his hand again, drags his thumb over a tattoo on his exposed left ankle and sends a rush of air over his shoulder. The bits of timepiece whirl up and rejoin, the cracks glowing. "Repair isn't my best. Barely earned that one," he says apologetically, "Doesn't really matter, my role isn't about fixing the things I break."

My mouth is dry. "How-" I try to say but the words get stuck in my throat.

"That's what your training is for- you will learn how. It starts with understanding the human body as it is normally, for everyone else. Specifically how their nerves receive a signal, send it to the brain to interpret and the brain sends back instructions on how to react.

"Then you'll learn how our nervous systems work. You'll learn how to manipulate your thoughts and how to apply those to activate the ink. When the ink is active, it sends a message to a specific nerve group. That group sends a signal reaction to your brain. Your brain then sends the original intentional thought in the form of instructions back to the nerve group. The nerve group manifests that thought. You catch the manifestation in your hand and throw it to its destination. It all happens instantaneously. You'll start very simply, of course. Can't have you blowing up the entire hall in the first week."

"Not how you did it, how are you controlling me through this tattoo," I say.

"Oh, yes. That was your first question, wasn't it. I get so used to avoiding those. I'm not controlling you or your tattoo. You are."

"I would never choke the air out of my own lungs," I say angrily.

"Not intentionally. For now, your brain knows more than you do. It knows the importance of concealment."

"How does my mind know something I don't?"

"Because of the ink," Abbot says. "The ink used in our tattoos translates directions the nerves received into a physical manifestation. Without the ink, we have nothing more than what some term 'a quick mind.'"

"The ink tells my nerves to go see what my brain wants, my brain sends a command to the ink to make my lungs stop breathing?" Is this real life? It goes beyond my realm of belief.

"Yes, well, the ink in your guard tattoo sends a message to your brain that secrecy is imperative. Your brain then tells the nerve groups to use the ink to control breathing in your case. In my case it's a blinding pain behind my eyes. The brain and the ink will do whatever they have to in order to keep you from talking, or showing, anything that applies to intusmagus and the hall. And that includes killing you."

"Why didn't you tell me I could die? Why didn't you warn me? You baited me into testing it."

"There was no real danger, you didn't know anything to tell that would require permanent silence. Now, of course, the situation has taken a turn."

"Do all the tattoos act that way? I mean the ones on your neck and arms and everything, do they all conspire to kill you?"

"Only the one on the sternum acts as the guard. The tattoos in other places speak to specific nerve groups, which control a certain type of action. Didn't you read the back of the book this morning?"

The chart of different nerve groups bracketed together with odd names makes sense now. I picture the brackets around Abbot's body, they seem to group the varying patterns of ink that cover him.

"I saw the chart, but didn't read much."

"Well, knowledge is the key to understanding," he says with relish. "Get back to the book. You should be able to finish the section on the brain today. Tomorrow morning, we will continue strength training. And if you are a very good girl, I'll teach you a trick."

I want to ask what all this means for Chelon, what do we actually *do* for Service. So far, the Unspoken get strong and break things with their minds, or is it the nerves that do the actual breaking? Abbot is moving towards the door now.

"Why? Why are we able to do this and others aren't?" I ask as he puts his hand on the knob.

"That is something-" ·

"-for which I am not yet ready to know," I finish for him. Question and answer time is clearly over.

"You do learn fast," he says. "Refreshments are in the lefthand wardrobe. Reading is hard work."

Leaving me to the book, Abbot shuts the door behind him without a sound. I wonder vaguely how he does that when the empty, shiny hall would echo even a pin drop.

There's nothing left for me to do but read. The only way my questions will be answered is to follow instructions. Great. The thing I have the most trouble with is the thing I'll have to master first. However, being able to blow things to bits will be dead useful when PG3456 leaves Chelon. I have found my motivation, and I'll follow instructions to the letter now.

I skim over the first section of anatomy review. Once I'm satisfied there is no new information hidden in the paragraphs, I start to devour the mind power section. I read it through completely and then start reading it again. It's a wholly new concept to me. It brings new meaning to a phrase The Mothers use frequently when we are young. "Mind over matter!" they sing out when we struggled with something.

I'm so absorbed in the section that I miss the flickering of light on the desk, signaling the end of the day. Then someone is knocking on my door. "Come in," I say grudgingly. I just want to read.

"Just me," says Zink, opening the door. "Thought you might want to make the elevator ride back up a tradition." He trips on my black suit that is still on the floor. He picks it up and shakes it out, "The Mothers aren't going to clean up down here."

"Why not?" I'm disappointed by that. I haven't cleaned up after myself, well, ever.

"They don't come on the hall. I don't think they are allowed."

"Aren't allowed? Aren't they the ones who determine who is allowed to do anything? And if they aren't then the Absolutes are."

"Well, yes, for everyone else. But we are different, especially when we are down here," he says as he hangs up my uniform.

I watch him closely, not speaking. Asking questions seems to be the quickest way to not get answers down here so I just begin to clean up the desk.

"The hall and everything below us isn't exactly part of Chelon, so it's outside of The Mothers' jurisdiction. We are still citizens of the city, clearly, so we follow the rules. But it's more out of compassion for our Play Groups. Our actions still reflect on them and they are still governed completely by The Mothers."

"The Mothers can't touch us? Can't punish us I mean?" I ask before thinking.

"They sort of could before we were assigned Service, but not the way they could punish everyone else. I mean kids need discipline. But, no. They can't now," he shrugs.

And now it becomes clear why I was not visited by the five in black. The Mothers could not send them to me because I was marked from birth as an Unspoken and out of their control. And that is probably why PG3456 was often left to our own devices. My status and closeness with my Play Group undoubtedly drove them mad. I find a huge sense of satisfaction in that.

"But they can always control us through our Play Groups," he continues, "Same principle they use to keep everyone else in line: if you break a rule your whole Play Group is punished. Only in our case, they punish the Play Group more harshly because they can't touch us."

And the satisfaction is gone. "That's a reliable method," I say. I'm finished moving things around on the desk and my notebook is tucked away in my pack.

"Do you have a hard time, not talking about what you do here?" I ask him while I fumble around for my den keys.

"I did at first. I've still got scars from trying. But it gets easier the longer you are here. I've found a way to leave it all on the elevator. I leave my Play Group behind on the way down and I leave the hall on the way up."

I nod. It's something I will have to try if I'm going to be alive long enough to get my Play Group out of Chelon in one piece. "How do you do it?" I ask him.

"Well this helps a lot," he shows me a tattoo behind his ear. "It was my first, I mean the first I earned."

"What does it do?"

"It keeps things separate. It helps me focus on one thing when I need to and it allows me to let other things go. When I'm feeling particularly jumbled, I can use it to sort everything out and put my memories and thoughts away until I want them again."

"That sounds helpful."

"Want me to try it on you?"

"Oh- uh, no thanks," I stammer.

"It doesn't hurt. And you don't completely forget anything. You can just, I don't know how to explain it. It's like you can file your thoughts away, shut them in books and put them up on a shelf until you need them again," he says.

"Can you just make me put away the hall and nothing else?" I ask.

"It's up to you what you pack away. This just makes it easier to assemble what you want to think about and what you don't. It's totally alright."

It's totally not alright. What if he erases my mind? What if he can read my mind while he does whatever he is going to do? "Um, no thanks, not this time. I think I'll try keeping my mouth shut first." He looks crestfallen and I realize I've hurt his feelings. He has probably been aching to try helping someone for the past seven years. Everyone else on the hall would be so much more advanced than he, they wouldn't need his help. "Maybe tomorrow?" I say, "I just have to get used to the idea." He brightens up at that.

"Gotcha," he says, "I remember my first week. It was pretty terrifying."

"Oh, I'm not scared or anything," I suddenly have the need to be sure he understands I'm no coward.

"No, of course not," he says, mashing the call button for the elevator.

"I'm not," my voice has a whine to it. I might as well have stamped my foot, too.

The car arrives as Zink starts laughing. I huff and cross my arms. What am I doing?

"Come on, we will be late for dinner," he says, still laughing as he pulls me on the elevator. Once we reach the top lobby, he leaps out of the car and bolts out of the building.

Does he always leave the Gratis Building like this? I wonder if he runs to the hall the same way he runs from it.

I meet PG3456 at a table in the canteen. They are in deep conversation over the mashed potatoes and duck glazed with an orange sauce. I must find a way to balance my life underground with the one on the surface. Pushing everything from today to the back of my mind, I give my whole attention to the discussion Merit is leading about the animals.

"But I think my leader will have me with the horses tomorrow. She told me I showed promise already. They might let me start learning animal healing in a few months," he says, hardly containing his joy.

"That's great, Merit!" I say with genuine pleasure. He smiles at me, cheeks flushed with pride.

They all exchange information on their afternoons and I can actually pay attention. I even make a few contributions. When we finish dinner, our schedules indicate we should take part in one of the optional recreation activities on the Quad. Most of us are ready to be back in our common room though, away from everyone else. The day has been exhausting.

After searching the room three times for devices, we relax. "Alright," Wex says as he starts pulling out his notebook, "I'll start." He begins going down the list of notes he has made of things he noticed in the fields. Where the farming equipment is kept and which outbuildings are locked up at night. "I will be able to see just about every step in a growing season," he says, "I'll be rotated through the crops this year until they decide which one to put me on full time. I'm aiming for Experimental, that would be the most beneficial to us." Experimental encompasses the development and preparation of new food sources. Learning to identify new and different foods and how to cook them will be invaluable.

The others pull out their Service notebooks and read down their lists. After trying him at the coal seam for an hour, Frehn was reassigned to the transportation systems within the mines. "Apparently, my physique looked a little too menacing with a pick and jack hammer," he says in a raspy voice. I'm glad he won't be in the deepest places for hours at a time. He will be able to see light from time to time throughout the day.

Doe dealt with her first trauma case and says she noted everything that was done. She also has a book to study in her free time of medicinal plants and natural healing methods. In a few months, once she is proficient in the basics, she will be progressing to manufactured medicines. Those medicines are under a locking system that requires three different Healers to open. There will be no chance of adding anything from the Healers Building to our stockpile.

In the stables Merit learned some husbandry basics. His training will eventually cover prepping the meat for the kitchens, training the horses and eventually trapping the wild game that comes over the outer wall. "I'll be shoveling different types of manure for most of the first year though. Not a survival skill exactly, but it should be great exercise," he says hopefully, "And I found the perfect location for our stash. In our old hangout between the roofs of the horse barn. There's a corner that is only accessible if you pry up one of the loose shingles. I found it when my leader sent me to shoo the chickens to keep them from roosting up there. The space is large and dry and if Harc can rig some kind of fastener or lock that keeps the shingle in place unless we open it, everything will be completely safe."

Harc immediately says she has just the thing, she has already smuggled a set of magnets out of her factory. She can't explain how she got them in her pack with no one noticing, it happened so fast. She didn't even know why she was grabbing them before it was over. Her long fingers moved so smoothly and quickly that even she didn't see what they did. She begins to put a lock together for Merit while she runs down her findings. She was assigned to an electronics factory but will most likely be moved through several as demand from the other cities fluctuates. She should have access to thousands of items over the next few months. It's so loud and there are so many moving parts in the factories that no one can pay attention to anything but where their own hands and feet are, so it will be easy to pick up things here and there as long as she grabs from the discard piles. She'll wait and see if the magnets are noticed before she tries anything else.

That leaves me. And I can say nothing. No one looks to me or my pack where they must know my notebook is. Wex just gives us assignments for tomorrow, "Start paying attention to who you are serving with," he says, "they might not be accomplices but they could be allies when the time comes. None of us are with our Play Groups now and they will probably welcome a little friendliness, even from us."

I think of Zink. I don't think he would run. And I'm not sure that he would help either. But I'm also making judgments based on a total of ten minutes' conversation over the course of one day. Not much to go on.

Frehn pulls a fiddle out of his pack and begins to tune it. Our mouths drop as we stare at it in disbelief- we have never seen one this close before. Music has always been a feast occurrence, not something to even dream of outside a Service performance.

"What?" he asks in mock surprise, "Didn't I tell you I spent most of my afternoon learning? Hursh says I'm remarkable."

We pounce on him, demanding an explanation, "Since I'm traveling on the mine rails, I have to learn songs to communicate with the miners. Different songs let them know what part of the mine I'm in, where I'm going next, what I've got with me, when it's lunch time, quitting time and all that. I'm encouraged to practice in my free time."

"Well, let's hear something!" Doe cries, clapping her hands. While Frehn finishes tuning up, we all lean back into the cushions and get comfortable. This kind of treat is unparalleled and we are drooling in anticipation.

Frehn draws the bow across the stings and the fiddle emits a noise between a squawk and a groan. We all plug our ears with our fingers and shout in protest.

"Hursh definitely wasn't talking about your playing ability," I say, horrified.

"Well, what was she talking about then?" Frehn says, still trying to coax a single note off the fiddle.

"Probably your green eyes," chimes in Doe, "She thinks they're *remarkable*." She says the last word in a drawl as she clasps her hands and flutters her eyelashes.

"No, no, she had to be talking about Frehn's massive upper body strength," sings out Harc.

Frehn flexes, "I am pretty remarkable."

Wex launches a sofa pillow at him, hitting him in the face and we all burst into laughter.

Chapter Eight

The next morning, I change into my black suit the second I reach my den. Stretching while I wait for Abbot to turn up for the promised strength training, I look around the room for evidence of changes. Even though this is the only door I have the ability to lock, I still suspect others have keys as well. Nothing is out of place. I notice a thin layer of dust accumulating on the low table in front of the sofa. That would drive The Mothers to madness, Zink must be right. The Mothers can't enter the hall. I make a mental note to ask the Keepers in the Necessities Center for a lesson on cleaning and some supplies.

Abbot bangs on the door and opens it without waiting for my answer. Before he has even closed the door behind him, he begins to bark out a series of commands. "Ten pushups, run the mats five times, twenty squats, run the mats again!"

"Good morning to you too, Abbot," I grumble under my breath while getting into pushup position.

"I heard that," Abbot says, not looking up from the notebook he carries, "and if it was a good morning I would have said so. You aren't touching the floor with your chin, Keres. Start over."

Inwardly cursing him, I start the set of pushups again. While I'm obeying his instructions, he starts reciting the principles of muscle movement. He talks about how they are effected and affected by thoughts. I don't understand anything he says. Partly because the blood is pumping in my ears so I only catch one in three words and partly because the concept makes no sense to me. He puts me through my paces for over an hour before he allows me to stop.

"Did you finish the second section of your book?" he asks while I stretch to cool down.

"Yes, I was going over it a second time when I had to leave for dinner," I pant.

"Anything you didn't grasp?"

"Well, no, but there weren't any instructions on how to apply my thoughts. It just covered the principle of application."

As he makes a mark in his notebook he grunts at me to "wait here." He leaves the den for a few minutes and comes back pushing a large wooden contraption. There are red and white circles painted around a center black dot, like a target.

"I've got a bet with some of the others that you will be the first person in our history to earn a tattoo in the first month of training. So don't make me lose," he says, placing the target at the back of the den. "Now, watch me and pay attention."

Abbot curls his fingers under, making the now familiar thumb-out fist, "I'm envisioning picking up that target and moving it to the left." As his thumb moves across a patch of ink on his forearm, it swirls out of a looping pattern and into the image of a folded bird's wing. "Now, I'm telling the nerve group right here to get instructions from my brain on how to execute my thought." My eyes must be starting out of my head because he smirks at my expression. "And I take that action into my palm, then send it to the target." He flings out his hand, fingers spread wide. There's a rushing sound and the target neatly slides to the left a few feet.

"Your turn," Abbot says calmly.

I have no idea where to start. I have no ink on my forearm to use as a translator for my nerves. "We are practicing the principle only, Keres. Not the result. Start with movements," Abbot says stepping back and watching my reflection in the mirror behind the target.

I pull up one of the orange patches on the sleeve of my suit so that the same place on my arm where Abbot's folded wing tattoo is visible. I ball my fingers, thumb out, and imagine moving the target back to its starting place. Tracing some freckles on my forearm because I can't think of anything else to do, I force my entire body to hear what I want it to do, then I fling my hand out towards the target. Nothing happens.

"Good, your form is good. But you aren't talking to the nerve group." He walks back to the desk and retrieves the book. "This group here, isolate it. Send it the signal." He points at the bracket labeled *Commotio* that surrounds a group of nerves around deep branch of the radial artery.

And just how do I isolate things I can't even feel? I try to picture the bracket around my own arm and think of nothing but what is in that part of my body. I go through the motions again. As I trace the freckles, I can feel something inside my arm heat up and the palm of my hand becomes hot. When I fling out my fingers, a tiny puff of air and smoke appear. The target remains unmoved.

"Hexes on FIRE!" yells Abbot at the top of his voice, startling me off balance. "On the second try!" He continues jumping and swearing around the room in triumph.

"But nothing happened," I say when he calms down enough to just punch the air in jubilation.

"Nothing?!" He moves to within inches from my face, grasping my shoulders. "Didn't you feel the heat? See the smoke?" His eyes are searching mine.

"Well, yes, but it didn't do anything. The target is in the same place. I didn't even shake it."

"You don't have ink to translate the resulting action correctly so of course the target didn't move," he says in exasperation. "You just did what has taken everyone else on this hall months to build up to. You just threw your first magus."

I look at my hand, the palm is still red from the heat. "I think I need to reread that book," I say.

"Oh no, you are going to throw again. I'll get you that tattoo before lunch," Abbot says turning me around to face the target. "Again," he says.

I go though the movements again, this time thinking of just the nerves that are still warm inside my arm. This time, the smoke that shoots off my palm is dense and straight. The target still remains steady, but the smoke hits the outer ring and dissipates.

Abbot cannot contain himself any longer. He runs to the den door and flings it wide, yelling into the hall, "Zink!

Marum! Journer! Get in here!" He strides back across the room to me and says under his breath, "Just do exactly what you just did. Exactly." Zink, another man in his mid thirties, and the tall woman in her fifties I rode down the elevator with on the first day appear at the door.

"Watch her," Abbot says in a voice shaking with adrenaline. He nods at me and I think about nothing but the still burning nerves. Smoke again hits the target, this time one ring closer to the center. As the smoke is swirling across the face of the red and white rings, Abbot punches the air again. I turn and look at Zink, wanting to read some kind of explanation in his face. He just stares at the place where I hit the target, his mouth open.

Abbot slaps the woman on the back, "Well, Journer? Pay up!" Journer pulls a small envelope out of a pouch on her belt and hands it to him. He stuffs it in his own belt before crossing his arms over his chest in satisfaction.

"She'll pass my rank in a matter of months at this rate," Journer says. "Try her with the ink, Abbot. See if she can control it."

Abbot pulls the same metal stamp that gave me the black smoke finger tattoo on my chest out of his belt. He takes my arm and presses the stamp to the exposed skin that shows through the sleeve of my suit. Because I know what's coming, the pain only sends a tremor over me and I am able to stay on my feet this time. When he pulls the stamp away, they all crowd in to see my tattoo. It's in the shape of a fully extended pair of wings in blue ink that spread over a much larger space of skin than the stamp covered. Abbot grins with pride. "It looks like she took inspiration from mine," he says.

"What do you mean?" I ask.

Marum rubs his finger over my ink wings and says, "Everyone's tattoos are different, unique like a fingerprint. Once you begin to tap into the depths of intusmagus, you will start to clearly see other people's tattoo patterns morph into their actual shapes when they throw a magus. When we're stamped, the ink interprets how we envision the action of the nerve group it covers. Movement, in the case of this nerve group, makes you and Abbot both think of flight," he looks disapprovingly at Abbot. "Skipping around in the training I see."

Abbot shrugs him off, "She's my apprentice, I'll teach her in the order I see fit." He drops my arm and looks me in the eye, "Try it again, Keres."

I inhale sharply, envisioning the total destruction of the room if I can't control the ink. As if she reads my mind, Journer says, "It's only movement. You can't do any permanent damage. Zink can fix anything that breaks, it's one of his specialties."

Zink nods in agreement. The four of them step back and I face the target again. I can see their reflections in the mirror on the back wall and Abbot gives me an encouraging nod. The nerves have cooled off now and I can't feel them anymore. I try to imagine their lines and trace the wings with my thumb. When I fling my hand out, a tornado-like spiral of air bursts from my palm, knocking me backwards to the floor. The target is sent flying into the lockers, smashing to the ground in pieces.

My own amazement is overshadowed by the others' disbelief. They stand silently looking at the massive dent the impact left in the locker doors. Marum walks over to the splintered remains of the target and picks a piece up, "Better keep her on wood for a while, Abbot."

Chapter Nine

Abbot decides we better back up in our training and cover more of the principles before continuing practical application. The others leave us to our studies once Zink is able to pry his eyes off the wreckage. He smoothed the crater-like dents in the locker doors and restored the target before they left. Still, some pieces were splintered too finely to repair, leaving chunks of the target missing.

Abbot pulls charts and books down from the shelves and begins an agitated lecture on controlling thoughts. "You cannot have a general idea of what you want to do, you cannot be distracted, you must picture exactly what you want the magus to do before you throw it. For you especially, the slightest wrinkle in concentration can be deadly. The destruction that came out of you was the result of not keeping your whole attention on the desired result."

"I was nervous," I say, "You told me not to lose your bet for you, you called in an audience, and just shot my arm full of ink! Ink which, by the way, can kill me if I talk too much. What did you expect?"

"I expected you to follow directions and just move the target," Abbot holds his finger up to me in an accusing fashion. "You have got to show some measure of control over your thoughts. You've had enough practice with them over the last two years."

"That's not fair, Solace wasn't practice. It was torture."

"You don't know what torture is!" Abbot raises his voice and slams his fist on the chart in front of us. His Banded cuff tears the paper. I don't say anything. What can I say? He's right, I don't know what torture is. I wasn't the one visited by the five. I swallow. I hate being in the wrong. It makes obedience that much more impossible.

"Let's start again," Abbot says calmly. He adjusts the charts, bringing the elaborate diagram of the left arm forward so we can concentrate on the movement nerve group. "This group can be used to control movement. That's movement of objects, people, whatever. Your use of the group will depend on what your brain can handle," he says.

I must look confused because Abbot puts his hands to his temples and inhales deeply. Moving his arms to the table, he says, "We are just like everyone else in Chelon. We each have different abilities that others may not have. My Banded partner, Serees, has had her hands inside someone's chest cavity, pumping their heart with her fingers to keep them alive long enough to have an artificial valve installed. Crisum, another member of our Play Group, passes out cold when anyone so much as stubs a toe. That is why Serees is a Healer and Crisum is not. They have different talents.

"It's the same with us on the hall. Some of us have extraordinary talent with certain nerve groups. Some people can throw a magus that no one else has even heard of before.

83

Others are not able to pull out the slightest breeze from that same nerve group."

"Like fixing things for you and Zink," I say. "That's what Journer meant when she said it was his specialty."

"Exactly," Abbot nods. "Now, here's where you come in. No one who has ever walked this hall has done what you did this morning."

"Smashed a target to bits?" I ask.

"No. Thrown a magus on the second day. Not only did you throw, you annihilated. That kind of destruction should not have been possible without months of practice and education."

"So my talent is annihilation?" The direction of this conversation is not helping my sense of self worth.

"No. Your talent is overachieving."

"Overachiever isn't a word anyone would use to describe me."

"Arrogant, disobedient, flagrant, willful, impulsive. What about any of those?" Abbot shoots at me. "Shut up and pay attention to what I'm telling you."

My face is hot with embarrassment. All of those words and more have probably been used to describe me and it bothers me that he knows that.

"When was the last time you remember being hurt, Keres?" Abbot asks me.

"I've been to the Healers' Building a score of times."

"That's not what I asked. When was the last time you were hurt, broke a bone, had a cut or bruise that lasted more than a day?"

"I fell down two flights of stairs once."

"And you lived. Not only lived, but walked away. No broken bones and no bruises the next day."

"How do you know that?"

"You have been marked since birth, so naturally we have all watched you, protected you. You are our responsibility."

"Then why did you let The Mothers waste two years of my life in Solace?" I'm crying. No wonder everyone thinks I'm weak and unhinged.

"Because it was better to put you under the Heavy than let you bring the entire city of Chelon to its knees."

"You put me under the Heavy?" I'm screaming at the top of my lungs again. It was manufactured, it wasn't a lack of self will, it wasn't depression. It was thrust on me purposefully by Abbot. It's as if all the emotions I should have gone through over the last two years are fireballing out of control. Fluctuating between despair and elation over the last 48 hours has taken a toll on what little self-control I possess.

"Yes," Abbot says simply.

I begin to throw things indiscriminately. Books, desk accessories, decorations from the shelves, gym equipment, whatever I can lay my hands on. My eyes are blazing and I'm choking on screams. Each object my hands come in contact with becomes one of The Mothers, one of the five, Abbot for sending the smoke black fingers of the Heavy that kept me trapped under an ocean of depression, my Play Group for making plans without me. But it's not enough, nothing is alleviating the hatred I feel. When I make a move to draw my thumb across the wing tattoo, Abbot is instantly before me with my hands firmly locked in his.

"Never, ever in anger," he says quietly. "Rage as much as you need to, but you will never throw a magus in anger."

I jerk my hands and he lets them go, watching me closely. I stand in the middle of the wreckage, regret for my tantrum falling over me like a tidal wave. I wonder if Harc feels this way after her storms of temper. Is this what Merit tells her, never in anger? Because Abbot's words deflate me completely. I feel nothing but shame now.

Carefully, slowly, I try to put together words. "Why? Why would you try to destroy me like that?"

"You had to be controlled, Keres. Your actions were leading up to something much bigger than childish disobedience. You would have killed that Mother if you had been given the chance and for what? Because she slapped your friend for being smart? Hardly seems worth murder."

"Harc was just a child!"

"And so were you. A child on the verge of complete breakdown. You endangered the lives of your entire Play Group because of your lack of control. Righteous anger is still anger."

I sink to the floor among the things I have thrown around the room. "Never, ever in anger," I sigh out.

"And that is where I should have started you in training, with self control. I was over anxious to test your ability. I had hoped the Heavy had left you a little quieter."

"Is that what it was supposed to do?" I ask.

86

"It was supposed to keep you from more violent outbursts against The Mothers. It was supposed to separate you from your Play Group enough that you would feel less inclined to attack The Mothers on their behalf. It was supposed to keep you safe. In retrospect, it appears to have backfired."

"No kidding." I feel more rage against The Mothers, against the Unspoken, against my Play Group than I ever have.

"No use crying over spilt milk. The Heavy didn't bring forward anything that wasn't already there. We will just have a harder time breaking through than I had hoped. With the progress you showed this morning, it's not really so much a set back as it will be giving us- some pace."

"That's one way of looking at it," I say, trying to keep the sarcasm out of my voice. The light flickers on my desk.

"After lunch, go by the Necessities Center and get something to clean this place up. It's filthy," he says, looking around. "Then we can work out some of that aggression in sweat," he says while sauntering out of my den.

I have a brief internal battle between the desire to throttle Abbot and compunction. The guilt wins out and I change for lunch. Zink waits at my door when I walk out, ready to ride up with me. He mentions his hope for something with cheese for lunch, avoiding my eyes as much as I'm avoiding his. I manage to humble myself enough to ask him if he would mind stopping by my den after lunch to repair some things I broke. And while he agrees readily enough, his customary mad dash out of the building seems pointedly directed at me this time.

I meet Frehn on the way to the canteen, as the street to the mine entrance joins the one that leads to the Gratis Building just north of the Quad.

"Hey, Frehn," I say, trying to muster up some goodwill.

"You look like last week's refuse," he says without hesitation.

"Thanks," I answer, trying to smooth my hair.

"You've got something on your arm...oh. Never mind," he yanks his hand away from the place where my new wing tattoo is. I don't know what to say so I just keep running my fingers through my hair in an effort to straighten it out.

"Here," Frehn hands me a comb from his pocket. I can't help cracking a smile.

"You take a comb to the mines?" I ask, laughing.

"My rail car is crazy fast, I have to keep one on me if I'm going to stay presentable."

"How far are the mines from the entrance?"

"It has to be 20 miles at least. But it only takes five minutes on the bullet train. That's why we can get back to the canteen for lunch."

"Is that the train you conduct?"

"I wish, no I run a rail car. It's like a cart from the fields, but moved by electricity that runs through the rails. The bullet train is just like the ones the traders use to get to other cities, just an older, dirtier version."

We've watched those trains leave the platforms just outside the main gate of the outer wall. They are packed with electronics, fabrics, jewelry and coal for weeks leading up to a departure. Then one morning the traders show up outside the gates. The are put through the four checkpoints before boarding the train. When the train takes off, there's a woosh of .air that pushes up the walls of Chelon and down onto the group of kids watch through the gates. It only happens two or three times a year and never with any warning. The trains are just loaded throughout the year and whenever the traders arrive to escort the goods to other cities, that's when it happens. I've seen trains leave nearly empty and so loaded down that huge crates are tied to the backs of the cars. I doubt even The Mothers know in advance of the traders' arrival.

Frehn and I reach the canteen before the others, so we stake out a table. I find myself wishing I'd had the foresight to wear long sleeves today. Frehn can't stop looking at my tattoo.

"It's really beautiful," he says abruptly.

I devote myself to the pasta pockets stuffed with cheese.

"So we can talk about it, you just can't acknowledge it," he says, eyeing me. "That will make things easier."

"The sauce is really good today," I say.

"Excellent," he says stabbing four pieces of pasta forming one giant mouthful. "I'm starving."

"You're always starving," Merit says as the rest of PG3456 come up behind me.

"I'm a growing boy," Frehn says.

"Good thing our fifteenth year is more than halfway over. You won't fit in anything pretty soon," Harc says, placing her tray on the table. "Especially anything that has to go over your head."

"Nice, really nice. And here I am slaving away on that blasted fiddle to have something to entertain you all with tonight. You can just forget it now."

"I'm still trying," Wex says with a groan. "You'll have to slave long and hard before I listen to that monstrosity again."

"Don't pick on him," chirps Doe. "He's doing the best he can."

Frehn changes his expression of indignation to one of saintly innocence. "I am, as I do in everything put before me."

"Oh, eat your lunch," I say laughing. "No one is buying that, not even Doe." As I speak, I reach for my glass of water with my left hand. There is an audible gasp around the table.

"Isn't it nice?" Frehn says, "She still can't talk about it, but I found out that we can."

Doe is rigid in her chair, watching my chest.

"It's true, watch," he turns to me, "That's a really nice addition to your arm there, Keres. The floral pattern on the top part is especially artistic."

What floral pattern? I think. Trying to glance at my arm without anyone noticing. Yes, the blue extended wings have morphed into a complex circular pattern of dots and lines in a deep brown color with a flower leading at the top. It looks like the same style as all the other Unspoken tattoos I've seen.

I look up at Doe and see she is stiff with fear for my life. "Try the artichokes, Doe," I say trying to signal to her that I'm fine. "They are really good today."

I can see everyone release their tension.

"It's going to be a lot of fun talking about her like she's not here," says Wex with a wicked grin. "I can't wait for tonight."

Now I am in for it.

Chapter Ten

The muscles in my legs are on fire. Not even the cold
shower I took right after dinner has displaced the heat. Abbot's
method of working out my aggression in sweat has done more
than that. It has left me completely void of the ability to move
without painful reminders of my tantrum shooting through my
limbs. To add insult to injury, when he finally let me stretch to
cool down, he dropped a heavy volume on my stomach with
the command to "read it."

I don't know if he meant read it all tonight or what, but
I stuck it in my pack and brought it to the block. I also brought
my uniform because it was beginning to smell. The Keepers
showed me some cleaning technique basics when I told them
Abbot sent me for something to use on the dust gathering in my
place of Service. They seemed over anxious that I understand
their art perfectly before I left their hall with a fully stocked
bucket. Some of them even walked me to the building entrance
and waved me goodbye and good luck. Cleaning must be
harder than I imagine if I need a sendoff like that.

I have never washed anything before, but I figure
washing clothes can't be that different from washing me. I fill
the sink with hot water and add some of the soap the Keepers
packed in my bucket. I stick my suit in the water and swish it

around a little. It's got several hours worth of sweat trapped in the fabric so I just leave it to soak for a while. Grabbing Abbot's assigned reading and my notebook out of my pack, I head to the table in the common room.

Only Doe came back to the block with me after dinner as the others opted to join a field game on the Quad. Doe and I sit at opposite ends of the table and try to focus on our own work. She has a set of books in front of her that appear to cover everything from using plants for disinfecting cuts to performing complicated inner ear surgery. Looking down at my book, I discover Abbot has given me reading material on the management of emotions, several chapters on anger taking up the majority of the pages.

I suppress the desire to rip the book in half and try to remember that I have to get through this in order to move forward in my training. Being able to control my rage and perhaps even to have a serious discussion without bursting into tears might be helpful. So I press on through the chapters until the others come in from their game on the Quad.

Once we make three passes searching the room for anything The Mothers may have left, we settle down to a long discussion on other people's potential usefulness in our plan. After one day, it's clear that it is still far too early to tell if anyone will actually be valuable to us. But we certainly know who won't, and so far, that's everyone.

"It's going to be a lot more difficult than I thought to feel people out," Wex says, "I would not have guessed no one would respond to an open invitation to discuss The Mothers, even if it was completely harmless. I tried to ask someone if they thought The Mothers keep snacks in their headdresses as a joke and you would have thought I had suggested we team up to murder them."

"People aren't used to us, or us them. We've been away too long. I have no idea how to talk to anyone in Fauna Management," Merit says. "Besides, I've been thinking we should keep completely to ourselves. The more people who are familiar with us, the more likely they are to figure out what we are planning. And that will only lead to two results. Either they will inform on us or they will be visited by the five when we leave. Neither of those options are worth what little potential help they might offer."

Harc pipes up, "I'm with Merit. There's nothing anyone can do for us that we can't manage on our own. It will only make it harder to leave them behind when the time comes. We can't take everyone."

No. We can't take everyone. It would already be hard to walk away from Zink and Abbot, especially after today. Zink repaired everything I smashed without a single word of rebuke. He didn't even ask what happened. He helped put everything back on the shelves and set the den back in order. He even showed me how to clean without just moving the dust around. And I've only known him a couple of days. What's it going to be like in a few years when it's time to go over the outer wall? I don't want to leave Chelon anymore.

"Harc is right," I say. "We can't build up friendships with people and then leave them to The Mothers. Better not to know them. It will be easier to forget that way."

94

"Can we really just leave everyone behind? You know The Mothers will be so enraged that restrictions and punishments will increase tenfold," Doe whispers. "I don't know if I can do that."

"Think of what The Mothers did to you, Doe. Think what they did to us. Think what they are going to do to us in the years to come. Can you really stay?" Merit asks.

We all know the answer. We can't stay. Not even if it means increasing the suppression of everyone else in Chelon. We have to leave.

"If we all aren't going, then none of us go," says Wex.

Doe is silent for a few minutes, then says quietly, "Alright, we all go. But we do what we can to make it clear to The Mothers that no one else knew anything about it. If anyone uncovers the plan, we take them with us whether they want to go or not. I won't leave anyone to the five in black. I won't." Her eyes flash at Merit with a hard determination I have never seen in them before.

Before any of us can answer her, the bell tone for the common room door sounds and three Mothers bustle in. Apologizing for interrupting our free time, they begin fussing around the room. Straightening the mess from studying on the table and cleaning up the grass tracked in from the field game. It makes me uneasy, as The Mothers generally wait to execute the nightly clean up until after power down. They move into our rooms, smoothing and cleaning and even turning down the beds.

"Oh!" gasps one from my bathroom. "Oh! What have you been doing!" I leap to my feet, remembering I've left my suit to soak in the sink, fearing the dye has bled out or I used too much soap and suds have covered the floor.

When I see The Mother holding up my soggy suit between two fingers, I have to chew the inside of my cheek to keep from smiling at her dismay. She truly looks disgusted.

"I was doing a little laundry," I say with a shrug.

The other two Mothers are now at the bathroom door behind me. They raise such a noise over the scene, pushing past me to join their fellow at the sink, simpering over the mess.

"Oh, and it's black, too, such a nice piece of fabric!"

"And she's ruined it! Such a shame!"

"Perhaps we can take it to the laundry and wash it properly. Maybe steam?"

I start to feel the pressure on my chest. I want to snatch the suit out of their hands and yell at them to get out of my room. Just seeing them in possession of something that belongs to the hall, something that has nothing to do with them, something that was wholly free from association with them makes my blood run hot. I walk toward them slowly, forcing myself to stay in control. I firmly, but gently, take hold of the suit and remove it from their hands.

"Leave it alone," I say quietly. "I will take care of it. It's my responsibility."

Their eyes grow round and wide, staring at me as I wring the suit out and hang it over the shower door. They tuck their hands under their aprons and purse their lips.

"You are not permitted to wash things on your own, you don't know the first thing about the delicate fabrics," one of them says to me.

"Yes, Mother," I say while I spread out the legs and arms of the suit trying to pull the wrinkles out.

"You must put your clothes in the hamper, all of your clothes, even your Service uniforms."

"Yes, Mother."

"We will have to note your disobedience in your file of course."

"Yes, Mother." I barely keep the tremors of anger out of my voice. They are baiting me. I know they are. And it's working.

"Punishments in the morning. For now, off to bed. Power down will be soon."

"Yes, Mother."

They leave the bathroom in tight group and I let go of the suit leg. I have wrung it dry in my clinched fist.

The warning tone for power down sounds and I go to stand in our goodnight line. "Punishments in the morning. Be ready," I say to the room at large. "I'm sorry." Now it seems reckless to have brought the suit off the hall. I should have asked Zink where we have them laundered, do we really send them to The Mothers? It seemed improbable, the suit was made on the hall by an Unspoken, not by the Keepers in the Necessities Center like the everyday clothes or other Service uniforms.

Now we will be punished because I forgot the most basic rule of Chelon. We do not take care of ourselves. Being on the hall and under Abbot's training, I had forgotten that I still belong to Chelon and to my Play Group. And my Play Group belongs to The Mothers. My next tattoo better be that thought filing system that Zink offered to me the first day.

The next morning, I decide to find Zink's den and ask him how he earned that tattoo. After knocking on two wrong dens, he opens the third door I try, numbered 15. He stands aside to let me walk through into his den.

I pull up short- his den is nothing like mine or Abbot's. Ours are like cozy old libraries packed to the breaking point with books and nicknacks, Zink's is all smooth lines and clean surfaces. Where I have wood and supple fabrics, Zink has metal, glass and sleek upholstery.

"Yeah, it's a little different from yours isn't it?" he says.

"Just a little," I say.

"It was designed by my mentor, just like Abbot designed yours," he says.

"Abbot designed my den?" I'm startled by this, I can't imagine Abbot paying that much attention to anything like a room, let alone fill it with beautiful accessories and furniture.

"Yes, he gifted everything you have down here. Your den, each piece in it, your uniforms, equipment, everything. It's very expensive to be a mentor. Lucky new people don't turn up on the hall often. We would all be bankrupt."

"What does that mean, gifted?" That's a new word.

"He gave them to you. It's not like when The Mothers issue things that will have to be returned or traded in, whatever you have here is yours. Forever. A present."

"How can he do that? How does he have the right to give me anything?"

"He can do what he wants with his money. Just like anyone else," Zink shrugs.

Money. We can earn money by returning to Service for extra hours after dinner or on the 7th day of the week, which is the rest day. Money can also be earned if The Mothers post tasks that need to be completed which aren't assigned to a Service. Most people use what they earn to buy things needed to make ceremonial robes. They will have to make a set for each child they create, for Banding, and for Disengagement. I have never heard of anyone buying something and giving it to someone else for no reason other than that they can.

All of those things in my room I smashed were not assigned to me by The Mothers. They were presents given to me by Abbot. The surge of shame takes over me. He gave those beautiful and useful things to me and I smashed them to bits before his face. The cost must have been extraordinary. Nothing in my or Zink's room could have come from Chelon.

"Who do I give my uniforms to when they need cleaning?" I ask, trying to deflect the embarrassment I feel.

"Abbot didn't give you the tour?" Zink asks, grinning.

"No, I only know where his den is, my den and now yours. There's more?"

"Miles more, I'll ask Abbot if I can show you around after he's done with you. Better get back to your den or he'll think you slept in."

I take Zink's advice and return to my own den. Abbot is leaning next to the door waiting for me to unlock it. By the look on his face this isn't a good morning either.

"Sorry," I mumble, "I thought you had a key."

"You have the only key to your den. No one else has any reason to go inside but you."

Well that's comforting. Perhaps our stash would be safer in my den rather than under the barn roof. If it wasn't for a Keeper having to buzz us through the elevator.

Once inside, Abbot sinks into one of the chairs and I pull my still damp suit out of my pack.

"What did you do?" he asks, "Go swimming?"

"I washed it," I say with as much dignity as possible while I pull on the cold, wet suit.

Abbot lets a loud rolling laugh loose, "You didn't! Whatcha do? Stick it in the sink or wear it while you took a shower?"

"I soaked it in the sink. You never told me how to clean it. After two days of your training regiment, an unpleasant aroma was wafting off the fabric," I snap.

"Always my fault, isn't it? Well, I'm sorry. I've never been a mentor before. I forget you don't know what you don't know."

"Zink said he would take me on a tour, show me where everything is."

"Zink would say that."

"Well, can he?"

Abbot stands up, "I don't take issue to it. But my objective for the day is to make sure you can't walk without crying. Start running."

Chapter Eleven

When I am finally released from Abbot's insane training regimen, I hobble my way to the elevator, wincing with every step. Zink is already holding the door for me to drag myself through.

"Rough morning?"

"Abbot believes that he must crush my body to control my mind."

Zink chuckles, "I don't have a hard time believing that." He bolts when the doors open, leaving me to make my way slowly to the canteen. I start to look around for Frehn so I can lean on him. I bet it wouldn't take too much convincing to get him to carry my broken body all the way to lunch and back. But I don't see him on the streets leading to the canteen.

When I reach the Quad and look around for PG3456, I start to feel uneasy. There is a large crowd forming around the notice stand in front of the north residence compound. My heart sinks to my stomach as I walk slowly over, pushing my way through the people. On a poster with large letters reads: "PUNISHMENTS." There's nothing so unusual about that. Unless it's a Solace, punishments are announced this way. I scan the list of Play Groups, their crimes and consequences until I come to PG3456.

"PLAY GROUP 3456. ERROR- willful disobedience, direct insolence toward a Mother, disregard for the property of Chelon, misuse of facilities, and vandalizing assigned clothing. CONSEQUENCE- rack, 08:00 to 19:00."

The blood rushes from my head to my feet and back again. I feel heavy and sick. PG3456 has been chained to the rack for more than four hours while I have been safe on the hall. I race toward the Amendments Spire, hardly pausing when I knock several children over in my panicked movements.

A Mother greets me at the large double door entrance to the towering circular building, "And what can I do for you this morning, Keres dear?" she says in a voice as smooth as silk.

"I came for PG3456," I pant.

"I'm afraid that isn't possible, dear heart. They are learning from their mistakes."

"But it was my mistake. I washed the uniform," I say quickly, "It was me, not them."

"Oh, I hate to see you so upset, Keres dear," soothes The Mother, "You know, of course, that there are no individual actions of a Play Group and we all must take responsibility for each other."

"I take responsibility for theirs and mine, add me to the rack."

"No," coos The Mother biting her bottom lip, "Nooo, I'm afraid we can't do that. Go eat your lunch, baby lamb. You must be hungry."

"Can I at least see them? Speak to them?"

The Mother wavers a moment, "I think it would be good for you, dear. How wise you are." She motions for me to follow her. Pausing at a desk, she retrieves a group of keys and we walk deep into the building.

Making several turns so it feels like we have doubled back at least twice, we reach a door with a large iron double lock. The Mother turns to me, "Remember, dear, everything we do is for your own good. We want to help you be kind and obedient." She inserts two keys in the lock and turns them in opposite directions. The door swings open and I step into the dark room.

Stretched spread eagle by chains on the walls are Wex, Frehn, Merit, Doe and Harc. They are held upright by the iron shackles around their wrists, trickles of blood running down their forearms and mixing with beads of sweat.

"Look who it is, Doe," Harc says with ice in her voice, "Keres has come for a visit."

I can say nothing, struck mute by the sight. "Hello, Keres," whispers Doe.

"Now, don't be all dramatic," Frehn says in disgust. "We have made it through worse than this." He shifts on the wall and I can see braided whip marks on his bare chest. "It's only for the day, Keres, we will be back in the common room after dinner."

"I-" I start, "-so sorry-"

"It's nothing, we wondered where you were though, seeing as how you were the ultimate culprit in the greatest laundry scandal of the century," Frehn tries to say nonchalantly.

"Frehn dear, don't mock the seriousness of the actions that brought us these consequences," croons The Mother from the doorway. "You don't want to make us think we aren't learning from our mistakes."

"No, Mother," says Frehn and gives the chains on his legs a shake. "No, Mother. We wouldn't want that."

I move towards Doe who is limp with fatigue already, and they aren't halfway through the punishment yet. "Doe," I whisper, "do you need water?"

"No food, no water," sings out The Mother.

"They can't stay like this for seven more hours!" I cry.

"Certainly we can and will, we are learning," answers The Mother happily.

"Please, please," I begin to beg, the full force of the scene bursting on me, "please, rack me instead. They didn't do anything."

"It's time to go, Keres dear, you'll miss lunch!" The Mother begins to pull me from the room.

"No, no wait, let me clean their cuts, let me bring them something to drink!" I'm panicking now, and I can feel the tears welling again in my eyes. The Mother pulls me forcibly, and I am yanked off my feet and dragged from the room screaming, "I'm so sorry!" to my Play Group. Frehn's eyes narrowing is the only move made by any of them. The door slams and the iron keys click in the lock. I launch myself at the door and hang onto the handle, "Please, please!"

The Mother leaves me clinging to the door, tears rolling down my face, and she glides down the hall with her lavender tunic sweeping the floor behind her. Wex never lifted his head to look at me.

Abbot. I jump to my feet and race to the Gratis Building. Abbot will help me. Pressing against the elevator doors to make them open faster, I stumble across the hall to his door. I burst through into his den, eyes wild in panic, "Help me, please, Abbot!"

"We can finish this later, Marmet," Abbot says to a woman in the room with him as if I have only asked about the weather conditions. He hands a stack of rolled paper and a dusty book to Marmet and escorts her to the door, closing it behind her. "You didn't tell me that The Mothers caught you washing your suit," he says to me reproachfully.

"I didn't think they would react with a racking! I thought, I don't know what I thought. Maybe that we would have no recreational activities, or no dinner, or something. Abbot, you have to help them!"

"I can't, Keres, you know I can't," he says sadly. "Your Play Group is under their control. The Mothers can do what they think necessary," Abbot sits on the edge of his desk, "and what they think necessary is torture."

"Why can't I be racked with them? We should have been punished together, tell them to string me up with them!" I yell.

"I could, but it wouldn't do them any good."

"It would do me good," I sob. I fling my arms up to cover my face.

"They will be all right, you know. They will have dinner in your common room and they will go to sleep. They are not angry with you. They understand the system far better than you."

106

"You didn't see them, you didn't hear Harc." The memory of Harc's frostbitten voice echoes in my ears. "Wex didn't even look at me."

"And Harc would have been better served if she had followed Wex's example. What possessed you to go to them?"

"I wanted to- to help them." I stammer.

"For someone so smart, so powerful, you are inexplicably blind." Abbot scoffs. "Has nothing I said over the last two days sunk in? Do you comprehend nothing you read? Control your emotions, Keres. Do not act on impulse. Have a clear idea of what you want to accomplish before you fly into passions."

"I should have ignored their punishment? I should have gone to the canteen and eaten roasted beef flank while my friends were chained to the walls of the Amendments Spire, bleeding for my disobedience?"

"You are always in extremes, Keres! No, you should not have ignored their punishment. You should have made your block ready for their return tonight by stocking it with healing aids and food. Then you should have come to me calmly to see if I could do anything to lessen their sentence. By going to The Mothers in a fit of temper first, you gave them the power. Not only were they able to confirm that they have the ability to punish you with the mere idea of PG3456's consequence, they were able to show you results and watch your subsequent collapse. And now, PG3456 will probably suffer much more because you cannot control your anger. Now The Mothers will enjoy their victory and there is nothing I can do."

"Could you have helped them?"

"It's possible, I probably could have enforced a direct punishment to you and thereby lessening theirs. The Mothers aren't bound by our requests, but they do appreciate our importance to Chelon's survival."

"So I have made things worse, again."

"Yes."

"Abbot? Will you teach me how to separate my thoughts?"

"I thought you would never ask," Abbot sighs out his relief and stands up facing me, "This kind of magus isn't like an offensive or defensive pull, which relies solely on your intentional thought and the ink. Those have a tangible result. Anything to do with the mind, alternative sight, or searching are subject to a thousand factors. Where you are, who is near you, what you have at your immediate disposal. External factors can interfere with an intangible magus. That makes them extremely advanced magusi."

I nod even though I don't understand. I just want to forget PG3456's bloody arms trapped in chains. Abbot leads me to the mirrored wall at the back of his den. "Look at yourself. Picture your mind as a set of different sized shelves and drawers. Visualize all your knowledge and all your ideas as objects inside those cabinets." He raises his thumb and traces the ink behind his left ear. Then he passes his palm over his eyes and back to the base of his neck. "Now, take the object form of the thought you want to pack away, and place it in a drawer. Lock it up."

I can almost see the iron cuffs, sticky with blood. I go through the same motions as Abbot and leave my palm on the back of my neck. My vision goes out of focus and Abbot says, "Excellent. Now we will try it with ink." I feel the stinging pressure of the stamp behind my ear and try the movements again. This time when my vision blurs a room full of wardrobes and chests of drawers appears sharply before me. I can feel the iron cuffs in my hands as I pick them up from a round table in the center of the room. I place them in an old dusty wardrobe drawer. My reflection stares back at me a hundred times over in the moldy mirrors on the front of the wardrobes around the room. Standing there, looking around at the vast space, I brush the round table clean with my sleeve. The room slips out of focus and Abbot's den comes back into my line of sight. I feel less on the point of violence, able to think clearly about what my actions have meant to PG3456.

"I think I managed it," I say.

"It should be easy down here with no distractions. It will be much harder when you are in middle of something you need to set aside. Practice dissecting your thoughts tonight after power down. See if you can separate different elements of the same idea, concentrate on only one aspect at a time until you have the entire idea diagrammed in your mind."

I look at myself reflected on Abbot's back wall of mirrors. My hair is unkempt from the scene in the Amendments Spire and running across the city, and my eyes are still red from crying, but have lost the wild animal glint. I feel calm for the first time in years. I turn my head to the side and pull my ear forward so I can see the shape of my newest tattoo. There is a tree with crescent shaped green leaves and long tangled roots running the length of my ear.

"Thoughts take root in our minds, getting tangled together until we can no longer tell what is emotional and what is factual," Abbot tells me, pulling his own ear forward. His tattoo is already transforming back to its pattern form, but I catch a glimpse of a mass of wildflowers sprouting out of a human head before it is gone.

"Be careful how you use this, Keres. Don't become so reliant on it that you can't make a move without it. Thought separation is like a drug. Some of us can't sleep anymore without using it."

"I will, Abbot, thank you." I can see why- the clarity I have is unlike anything else I have felt. I feel almost free.

"I should go back to the block and get ready for PG3456's release," I tell Abbot. Although I am not sure what to do, I am fairly confident that I will figure it out when I get there.

"Let Zink show you around first. You have hours yet before they return. There are things here which will help you speed up their recovery. When you have seen everything, Zink will help you prepare for tonight. Healing is his primary objective, remember."

Chapter Twelve

"She's got the Dominato tattoo now," Abbot tells Zink
as soon as he opens the door, "At 18:30 go with her to collect
them. She'll need help getting them back to their block. Take
what you need." Zink nods assent. "Some of them may need
help putting it into perspective, do that for them," Abbot starts
walking back down the hall.

"I'll have to clear that with Journer," Zink says after
him.

"Already have, but do whatever lets you sleep at night,"
Abbot calls over his shoulder. "Just don't let them know that's
what you're doing."

"Obviously," Zink says under his breath. He turns and
looks at me. I feel strangely at ease. I can do nothing for
PG3456 until 18:30. When that time comes, I will be able to
act. Until then, I will keep the iron cuff locked in its wardrobe
drawer and concentrate on what the hall has to offer.

Zink picks up his pack and we walk down the hall. But
instead of pushing the call button as I anticipate, he stops at the
door numbered 49 just before the elevator. He places his palm
flat on a metal plate and pushes it open. On the wall directly in
front of the door is a large portrait of a group of twenty or so
people, strangely dressed with elaborate tattoos on every

visible part of their skin. They are gathered around a long table littered with books and maps. All around them, strewn on the floor and hanging on the walls, are peculiar artifacts- a bow made from a single horn from a large animal, crystal phials filled with different colored liquids, a silver sword and shield carved and studded with sapphires, a strange open ball made of different metal rings, a long spear with a jagged purple stone fixed in the top, several beautifully made knives and daggers and a large shallow golden bowl. For a long moment, I stare at the people's faces which betray sad and serious expressions.

Nudging me forward, Zink says, "Put your palm here," indicating a place on the wall to the left of the painting, "It will scan your hand in to the security bank. Now you'll be able to enter the Warren without an escort." We round the corner and I am confronted with another long hall. There are so many different kinds of materials used to create the Warren, it reminds me of a patchwork quilt. Colossal wooden beams support the ceiling in some places. Thick metal doors alternate with wooden ones. Scattered among a mass of concrete, patches of wood, packed dirt and sheets of metal are large stone stretches of floor. Footsteps echo around the walls as Unspokens go about their business. A musty smell of moist dirt seeps through the walls. I feel like a mole in a huge rabbit burrow.

"It's big down here, but everything is on a grid and all halls lead back to this main one so you can't get lost. It was built over several centuries so it's a little patched up," Zink says walking forward. "We just passed the combat training areas and down there is the food hall. There's a kitchen, cafeteria, and a couple of storage pantries. Across the way here is the med bay, additional training areas, and weapons development."

"Combat and weapons?" I ask as we pass the cross-section of halls with heavy iron doors. "Are we fighting someone?"

"That is something for which you are not yet ready to know," he says. At a glance to my expression he adds, "Give it time."

After several minutes we reach the last intersection of halls and turn down the righthand side. "You'll spend a lot of time here in the coming months. It's the oldest part of the Warren on this level." He pushes on a huge solid oak door on the left and we step inside.

The room is crammed with rows of shelves, each one tightly packed with books of all sizes. I walk forward, running my hand over the book spines, feeling the different leathers. "And I thought my shelves were full. What is all this?" I ask in awe.

"The Magus Library. Every magus ever thrown, the theory behind it and the different ink formulas used are explained in these books. I spent hours in here before I ever earned my first tattoo, but I wasn't on the accelerated training schedule you seem to be on."

Zink lets me wander for a long time, reading the titles, pulling books off the shelves, flipping through them and pouring over the diagrams. "I had no idea it was so complicated," I whisper.

"For most of us it is, extremely complicated. For you, it doesn't seem to be. You threw one before you even understood it, before you even knew what it was. It took me over a year to understand the theory and apply it for the first time. Come on, there's more."

I reluctantly close a book with a detailed illustration of a complicated ink mixture and its effects on a group of nerves in the upper right arm. Sliding the volume back on the shelf, I turn to Zink and let him lead me to the room next door. When he opens the door, my jaw drops in disbelief.

"Ink production," Zink tells me with a wave of his hand. "It's something I have no aptitude with so I can't tell you much about what happens in here."

A myriad of smells assault my olfactory senses when I enter the room. Boxes and jars of every shape and size are neatly stored on every inch of available surface. They are crammed full with what looks like herbs, plants, leaves, insect parts, body fluids, oils and all manner of minerals. I walk past two vast, solid looking tables in the center of the room. My eyes travel over the assorted bowls, mortar and pestles, writing ink stones, glass tubes and collections of knives, tongs and long-handled spoons that cover the surfaces. There is a sky blue concoction simmering over a small flame. It's as thick as wet mud and smells like the fertilizers used in the fields. I move away quickly after catching a whiff and gravitate towards the long wall on the right where hundreds of filled phials, systematically labeled, reside in a series of roughly carved, dark walnut cabinets with rippled glass doors.

"Marum is the lead inkest, so you'll have to ask him what everything is. All I know is that the ink available for my level of intusmagus is over here," indicating the fourth cabinet from the door. "I'm working my way through understanding them. Just finished with this one," he pulls a small phial filled with a glutinous substance the color of dying grass.

"What does it do?" I ask him.

"It's one of the healing agents- they work with the nerves on the legs and feet."

I slowly make my way down the row of ink, reading labels as I go. There is immense variation in colors and consistencies displayed in these glass phials, more ink than there were nerve groups in the first diagram I saw. At the end of the row, I come to a cabinet with solid wood and brass doors. When I try to open the doors, they won't budge.

"That's the experimental cabinet. Nothing in there is ready for application. It's kept locked to avoid a mistaken application."

"They are developing new inks?"

"Of course, we are always trying to evolve, trying to gain the advantage."

"Advantage over what?"

Zink only smiles and shakes his head. "Let me introduce you to Juwas."

He guides me out of the ink room and back down the hall through the intersection with the main hall. He bangs on a plank door with a boar's head knocker. A muffled voice answers and he opens it. The room is almost in complete darkness. Zink flicks on a light by the door and my eyes blink at the brightness.

Bolts of fabrics are littered all over the room, sewing machines, dressmaker dummies and dyes strewn everywhere.

In the back corner, hunched over a table, is the form of a woman slightly rocking with her back to us. Her grizzled dirty gray hair sticks up in every direction.

"Juwas, I brought you someone new," Zink cheerfully calls to her.

"Eh-" she grunts not turning around.

"Go on," Zink whispers to me, "Go say hello."

I'm not sure why I feel nervous. Something about the strangeness of Juwas' body posture, her methodical rocking motion, and her almost animal-like grunt make me feel like I'd be walking a tightrope across the floor to her. But I walk forward at Zink's push and say, "My name is Keres, Juwas. It's-uh- it's nice to meet you."

"Heh."

"Did you make my uniform? It fits me perfectly."

"Know it," Juwas croaks with the voice of a thousand bullfrogs.

"Well, um, thank you, I really do love it."

Juwas spins around in her chair fast, whipping up her head to look at me. Her face is like old cracked leather. Scarred and tough, while her solid, stark, milk-white eyes staring blankly at me make a bright, sickening contrast.

"Not to love. To use," she rasps. She makes a move to grab my arm; the leather fingerless gloves she wears have metal plates in the palms and I jump and shiver when their unnaturally cold surface touches my bare skin. Goosebumps travel up my arm, spreading quickly over my whole body.

116

"Yes, of course. I do use it," I look wildly at Zink who is grinning like an idiot in the middle of the room, twirling a piece of thick cotton cord in his fingers.

"Don't. Not yet. Will though," she lets go of my arm, nodding to herself. She turns back to the fabric she was working with, "This too. Yes. Before you go." Go? Go where? To this war we seem to be training for, to the enemy we are trying to gain the advantage on? Has she looked into my mind with her niveous white eyes? Has she seen my Play Group planning to escape Chelon? I look at Zink again and he starts to chuckle, unable to hold it in anymore.

"Alright, Juwas. We'll let you get back to work. Come on, Keres," he says, "I'll show you the laundry."

I trip over a long roll of fabric that bangs against my shins like it's made of iron and stumble out of the room. As soon as Zink pulls the door shut, we can hear Juwas let out a crackling roar of what I assume is laughter.

"Who is that?" I demand, embarrassed by my absurd reaction.

"I introduced you, that's Juwas. She makes all our uniforms from the fiber collection to the finished product."

"What's wrong with her?"

"Wrong with her? Oh, that. She's blind, did it to herself as a baby. When she rubbed her eyes for the first time, she burned out her irises."

"Oh, how awful!" I look back at the door with a feeling of pity mixed with nausea.

"Journer says that it's not that she is particularly strong in ability but that her hands are weak. She has normal hands, not like ours. It's like a birth defect, born marked for the Unspoken but not with the body to contain it. So they pulled her from The Mothers immediately and she's lived in the Warren ever since."

"Who raised her if she wasn't allowed to stay on the surface?"

"They all pitched in. People took turns staying with her until she was old enough to be alone. Someone developed the leather and steel palm covers that keep her from doing any additional damage, and someone taught her skills so she would be useful to others. But she doesn't need sewing to be useful. There's something in Juwas that's far beyond any of us- she sees without eyes."

"Like the future?" Please let it be the future and not into minds.

"Not exactly, no. The future isn't something you can just read like a book. There are too many external elements that shape it so it's impossible to know it. She can bend the present to look around the corner at the future. No one is really sure how much she sees, she's not very chatty."

"I gathered that." If Juwas can see to PG3456's escape, at least she won't be able to tell anyone else.

Zink shows me the laundry room and how to use the machines to clean my uniforms. Turns out, I wasn't too far off with my sink experiment. I was just missing the motion to drive the dirt and sweat out of the fabric. "Don't wash in the mornings, Juwas' apartment is right next door and the vibrations from the machines bother her. She sleeps late."

118

We pass through an expansive room with comfortable seating arrangements, table games and televisions, and come back out on the food hall. Zink shows me the kitchen and dining areas and then takes me to the med bay we passed earlier.

"Let's stock up now, for their release," he says.

We pass through a row of high narrow, rectangular beds with machines grouped around them and come to an open door at the back of the room.

"Right. We will need a disinfectant, numbing agents, bandages, maybe a clotter just in case." He is talking to himself more than to me as he pulls open compartments and stores various things in his pack. "One of your Play Group is training to be a Healer, right?"

"Yes, Doe is."

"Do you think she will be in any condition to help with the others?"

"I- I don't think so," I say, remembering her sunken eyes and blood-caked arms after only four hours of the rack doesn't leave me very hopeful.

"We will repair her first then. Listen, Keres. I'm going to have to throw magus to help them quickly. It is imperative to my life as well yours that your Play Group is not cognizant of anything."

"I don't think that will be an issue. When I saw them, only three showed any kind of sign of awareness that I was even in the room."

"That means nothing. Showing awareness also shows resistance. And it would not be wise to show too much resistance when racked."

Wex had figured that much out within days of being visited by the five in black. He knew to feign compliance in order to avoid further torture. Maybe Wex did not look at me because he was manipulating The Mother in the room. With every fiber of my being, I will that to be true.

"Zink, do you know anything about five elders dressed in black?"

Zink stops putting things into his pack. He stands frozen, his hand just touching on a jar of pink paste of the shelf.

"I do."

"Who are they?"

"They are torturers."

"Yes, I know that, but who are they? Are they Unspokens?"

He whirls around glaring at me, "Keres! No!"

"They wear black, Zink."

"And they live off the agony of others. They eat the screams of those they mutilate. Does that sound like something Abbot would be a part of? Does that sound like something I would do?"

"Training for war and striving for an advantage over our enemies doesn't exactly sound like we preparing to inflict joy."

"We are protection, Keres. We are here to save people."

"From what?" I say loudly, flinging out my hands. "We should be protecting people from The Mothers, from the five in black, and we are down here in secret underground lair, concocting ink potions and preparing for what? War? Uprising?"

"The Mothers are not our adversaries."

"They aren't our allies either."

"I cannot explain this to you-"

"Sure, absolutely, I'm not yet ready to know." I could kill him right now.

"I can't explain it because I am not yet ready to know either. In a lot of ways, you are already more advanced than I am. I may have more ink, but you have more power. You'll know our destiny before I do," he says resentfully.

"Does getting more ink mean I'll be closer to knowing what our purpose is?"

"Advancing deeper into understanding magus will give you the tools you need to be ready," Zink recites.

"Journer feed you that line?" I say cuttingly, then regret my sarcasm almost immediately. "I'm sorry. You are only trying to help."

"We need to get moving. We should go eat now. Food will not be a possibility once we retrieve PG3456; and we need the calories. It's going to be a long, painful night."

Chapter Thirteen

We perch on a counter in the kitchen methodically eating cans of chicken covered in a thick creamy sauce, trying to occupy our thoughts while waiting out these last few minutes. When the last dregs are gone, I watch Zink wash the dishes, making mental notes on how it is done.

Pushing back through the Warren door, we walk across the hall to Abbot's den. He and Journer are waiting for us with final instructions and advice for Zink.

"It's your first opportunity to use everything you have been building for the last seven years. Don't waste it," Journer tells Zink. "Trust your instincts, do what you can and nothing more."

"And remember to be back on your block before power down. There's no rule against your helping another Play Group, but don't flaunt it," Abbot tells him. "And you," turning to me, "remember it was your lack of forethought that got them in this position. And only you have the ability to keep it from happening again. The Mothers want to control you, not them. So let them." He hands me a pack, "I've put some things in there that will help them, some water and clear broth. When they have eaten that, give them the bread. Starvation won't have set in, not by a long shot, but it will be better to ease them back to food. They won't be used to going this long without eating."

I thank him as I sling the pack over my shoulder. Journer finishes giving Zink last minute advice and we begin our silent walk to the Amendments Spire on the other side of the city. The looming double doors come into view a few minutes before the scheduled release time. We wait, motionless.

"Will they unchain them at 19:00 or will they leave the building at 19:00?" I ask.

"They will come through the doors at release time. They are probably off the rack already. The Mothers will want time to kiss and coddle them when the punishment is over. As if that will make them forget who strung them up in the first place." Zink's eyes narrow and he makes a face as if a piece of foul smelling rancid meat has passed under his nose.

Picturing The Mothers swarming around PG3456 with rolls of gauze and making kissing noises through their puckered lips makes my stomach drop and my anger rise. I clench and unclench my fists at my sides, trying to remember what Abbot said. "Is there a magus for subduing anger?" I ask Zink.

"Emotions can't be controlled by anything but self-will, unfortunately."

"Somehow I figured that."

There is movement behind the pristine glass doors. "Get ready, don't rush up to them, wait for my signal," Zink says. He turns his back to the doors and nudges me to do the same. We melt into the small patch of birch trees to the right of the Spire and pretend to be deep in conversation. We hear the doors open, the sound of shoes dragging on the stone entrance, The Mothers cooing their special brand of counterfeit sympathy, and then the doors open and close again. I spin around and start towards them when Zink catches my arm, "No, wait."

I bite my lip and try to stand still but end up pacing the edge of the tree line like a caged cat. Merit, Wex and Harc are standing, leaning against the stair rails. Their wrists are sloppily bandaged and the blood has been cleaned off their arms. Doe is stretched limp on the stairs and Frehn's hands shake while he tries to lift her head off the ground. The door opens again and several Mothers spill out, pausing to stroke PG3456's hair. They shake their heads as they glide down the steps and up the road leading toward the main gate.

"Now, go!" Zink says urgently.

We race forward, Zink picks up Doe, cradling her in his arms and I hand flasks filled with water to the others. Zink is already walking towards the Quad and Wex struggles to follow.

"It's alright," I say to them, "His name is Zink, he is with me."

We follow behind Zink as he carries Doe through the gardens and tree parks, avoiding the roads. He has already laid Doe down on the sofa in our common room by the time the rest of us stagger through the door, Frehn and I supporting Merit between us. There are several patches removed from the legs of Zink's uniform and I can see his tattoos are still glowing. He has already been working on Doe.

"What's the matter with her?" I ask him.

"Well, they are all dehydrated and hungry. That's why their hands are shaking so badly. Heat up the soup on the fire, Keres, while I change the bandages."

While I stir the fire in the grate, Wex begins moving around the room feeling under the furniture.

"No, Wex, let me. You sit here and watch the soup," I say to him. He has no strength to argue, so he slumps against the hearth and drinks from his water flask slowly. I am crawling around feeling for devices under the table when Zink turns his head to watch me.

"What are you doing?" he asks.

"Looking for anything that might have been- uh- left for us," I say moving to the decorative wooden trim around the bedroom doors.

"There's a much easier way," he says standing. "Which one is your room, Keres?"

I jerk my head in the direction of my room and Zink stands. "Just give me a minute," he says walking across the common room towards my door. I turn back to Merit and start unwinding the bandage strips from his wrists. The Mothers have not used any ointment and the strip has clotted into the open cuts. He flinches while I try to slowly pull them off.

Zink is only in my room a fraction of a second. "All clear. It's rare that they do leave anything anyway. I think they prefer to speculate rather than eavesdrop, it allows for imagination to create a much more exciting reality." He moves to his pack and starts pulling out jars.

One of the cans of broth is boiling over, I reach around Wex to pull it off the fire. "Oh, sorry," he says trying to slide out of my way.

"It's fine, just keep drinking," I tell him. "Wex, I'm so sorry I did this,"

Wex lifts his chin, his eyes find mine and I feel a leaping sensation in my stomach, my knees threatening to give way to my weight. The side of his face close to the fire is illuminated with a warm glow, leaving the other side coldly dark. The outline of his square jaw and defined cheekbones is even more striking in this half light. I cannot look away. Something wonderfully hot steals up my neck and face. Wex turns towards Zink, breaking my gaze. "Thank you," he says to Zink. "I don't know how long it would have taken for us to get Doe back."

"She's far worse than the rest of you. Why? What happened?"

"I wouldn't stop baiting her about Keres," Harc says suddenly, like she's spitting nails. She hasn't moved since Wex helped her into the chair.

"Doe was upset that Keres wasn't racked with us. She was convinced that something much worse was happening to her. That Keres was being crushed or dying or something. After Keres came and left, Harc kept pushing Doe to admit that Keres is treated differently because of the black diamond. Doe-she had some kind of breakdown," Wex says between spoonfuls of hot broth.

Zink looks at me and looks back at Doe. She is twitching compulsively on the sofa. Zink finishes dressing her cuts and lifts her gently up again, "Which one is her room?"

"This way," I leap up and hold open the door for Zink to carry her through.

He lays her on the circular bed and turns to me, "Shut the door." Clicking the door softly behind me, I walk over to his side to look down at Doe. She looks like a tiny animal who has been swallowed and is now waiting to die in something much larger's round acidic stomach.

"Can you help her?"

"Yes, but there's something else happening here. I think she knows, Keres. I think she knows what we do."

"How can she? I never-"

"No, you couldn't of course. I think she must have seen Grainom."

"Who?"

"Grainom. A few days ago he tried to throw a magus when he thought he was alone on his block. His guard tattoo knew there was someone watching him and it reacted. He ended up in the Healers' Building before they could get him to the med bay in the Warren. Journer said there was so much blood on the floor, it actually rippled in waves when they walked through it to get to him. Doe must have seen it."

"She was agitated when she saw my guard. She told everyone to leave me alone, that the Unspoken could kill me with it."

Zink nods. "This might be harder than I thought. The others will be fine, they are just weak and tired. Their cuts aren't even that bad. But I'll have to help her."

"What can I do?"

"Go back out there and change their bandages, apply the disinfectant and the ointment in the blue jar I brought. Rewrap them and make sure they drink at least two flasks of water and finish the broth."

"Merit's bandages are stuck to his cuts, how-"

"Wet them, they will loosen up."

"What are you going to do to Doe?"

"Clear her mind, heal her wounds, try to soothe her fears. Her cuts are deep, she must have seriously fought against the shackles during her breakdown. Now go, the others will get restless if we are both in here too long. Wex looks like the protective type."

Closing the door behind me and leaving Zink blindfolding Doe, I bring a water flask over to Merit and start wetting down his bandages. I peel them up a little bit at a time, trying to keep the chicken and rice I ate an hour before in my stomach. The blood has congealed in hard amber-colored clumps that crackle when I pour the antiseptic over them. Merit avoids looking at me while I rewrap his wrists.

"Eat, Merit," I tell him, handing him a can of broth. He takes it from me and leans back in his chair, drained from the effort to hold back tears of pain.

I move on to Harc and repeat the wound cleaning process. Her muscles strain when I apply the ointment. "Thank you," she says through clenched teeth. I lean over as I stand up and kiss her forehead, tears are welling up in my eyes.

Wex holds out his arms to me and I am about to fall into them when I realize he's only asking me to redress his wounds. Grinding my teeth, I go to work removing the old bandage. His fingers wrap around my arm while I rest his wrist in my hand. "I know, Keres," he whispers so quietly I have to lean my ear to his mouth. "I know what you are."

My guard tattoo sears my chest like a branding iron. "I'm a child of Chelon, just like you," I say, pulling back. His fingers tighten, enclosing my wing tattoo and he shakes his head.

"No, you aren't. You are something unnatural."

My face contorts at his words and I can feel my heart pound against my ribcage. He thinks there is something wrong with me, that I am tainted, abnormal. Because of that, he will not want me. I am marked with the black diamond and therefore untouchable.

"And it's more important than ever that we leave Chelon," he whispers.

"All of us, including me?" I whisper back.

He nods and lets me finish wrapping his wrists.

Frehn already has his bandages off and sits down next to Wex. "My turn," he says. "And be gentle."

When I tuck the end of the new bandage around Frehn's wrist, Zink emerges from Doe's room. "She's sleeping now."

"Will she be alright?" Harc asks with a sharp edge in her voice.

"She'll be fine. She understands now what happened, that Keres is fine and that you were under too much stress, you didn't know what you were saying," Zink says coldly to Harc.

Tears roll down Harc's cheeks and she doubles over in the chair.

"You should be sorry," Wex says to her. "You gave in."

"Stop," Merit says, "Don't, Wex. It's not the time to reprimand. She's sorry, she knows what she said was out of line. Let it go."

Frehn stands and pulls his shirt over his head. "Got anything for these in your pack, Zink?" He shows the dark red and purple marks. "They sting like I got into a hornet's nest."

Zink tosses a green jar to me. I gingerly apply the orangish-brown paste inside it to Frehn's back and chest.

"I must have really ticked them off. They went to town with the whip" Frehn says with a sigh of satisfaction. "That feels great, Keres. You have good taste in friends."

A smile creeps across my face as I look around Frehn to Zink, who is making notes in his book. I catch his eye and he half smiles back.

"Alright," he says as he rips out a page, "These are instructions for the rest of the night. Change the dressings every two hours and reapply the ointment. Your cuts should be gone in the morning. Doe will need some more time, probably through tomorrow, so be sure you send her back to Service hours with a fresh set of bandages. She will remember everything, but have sort of a removed perspective on it. So don't treat her like she's breakable. That will only make it worse for her."

Wex stands and moves to shake Zink's hand. Zink seems surprised, but returns the grip warmly.

"See you in the morning, Keres," he says to me before leaving our residence block.

Left alone to manage PG3456's wounds, I refill the water flasks and cut up the bandages. After two hours, I change everyone's dressings again and divide up the remaining bandages and scoop out ointment into even clumps and place one set in each bathroom. Power down is in a few minutes and they will have to change their own through the night. I set the alarm on my clock for midnight and tell them I'll call them through the tubing network in the vents.

"How are we going to change Doe's?" Merit asks.

I look at my instructions from Zink, surely he had thought about this. "Zink says she will be fine until breakfast, he used a different salve on her that needs to cure overnight. I'm just supposed to change her in the morning," I say, breathing a sigh of relief. I suppose Merit could have squeezed through the vents like he did when we were in Solace, but I can't imagine him getting very far, as weak as he is. He was already underfed and the day without food and water has taken a serious toll on him.

We don't form our goodnight line when the warning tone sounds. It doesn't feel right without Doe. Instead we just go to our rooms and try to sleep until the first alarm goes off. I don't even hear The Mother coming by to lock our doors. Waking every two hours as directed, checking on each other through the vents, changing bandages, applying the torridly painful ointment, and trying to sleep in-between makes for a

131

restless night. Once, I hear Frehn screaming and Wex banging on the wall to wake him up. They talk to each other for a long time through the vents but I can't tell what they are saying. Only the mingled tones of their deep voices reverberating through the vents reach me.

The morning takes a long time to come. When The Mother finally comes to unlock my door, it is just before dawn. I slip out of my room and across to Doe's. She's still sleeping, but the creases of stress and worry between her eyes have smoothed out. I check her bandages. She had bled through them in the night. I carefully begin to change them when she wakes, eyes fluttering.

"Oh, hello," she says.

"Hi," I say back.

"They don't hurt like yesterday."

"That's good, Zink worked hard to be sure they got better fast."

"I like him."

"So do I."

She's quiet while I reapply the salve and rewrap the bandage.

"Think you can stand?"

"Oh, yes, I'm fine now. I'll be glad to get some breakfast though."

I leave her to get dressed and wait in the common room. Our ornaments of Service are lined up on the mantel as usual. The Mothers have straightened the common room, removing the snipped ends of gauze and cleaned the place where I wiped ointment off my hand and onto the sofa. I'm aching to get to

132

the hall and the Warren, to get away from anything The Mothers can touch.

PG3456 appears in the canteen as if nothing happened the day before. Doe's wrapped wrists aren't visible under her long sleeves. We eat and talk and leave for morning Service hours, carefully presenting a face of angelic repentance.

Frehn walks north through Chelon with me and when we part ways he rests his hand on my neck, giving it a squeeze. "We will be fine, Keres. Focus on what's in front of you."

On the elevator, I drag my thumb over the tree tattoo behind my ear. In my vision I pick up a crystal box with pewter corners off the round table and look inside. There is a rope made of different colors of silken cord. Five different knots are tied along its length. It's resting on a cushion of soft velvet. Looking around, I spot a robust looking trunk with iron bands and a series of complicated locks. I place the glass box inside the trunk and lock it safely as the elevator doors open. I step out of my vision and onto the hall.

I change into my suit and run through my training as if Abbot is there barking commands. The sweat pours off me in buckets as I surge through the exercises. I am focused on the muscle movements, thinking carefully about what each one looks like when I move it.

"Looks like you finally gained a little control."

I drop the barbell with a loud crash. It's disconcerting how Abbot can come and go without a sound.

"I have purpose now," I say.

"Don't we all," Abbot returns with a shot of venom. "Dry off, we have work to do."

133

I wash my face in the bathroom on the wardrobe wall. The tattoos across Abbot's forehead, the rough line of coarse stubble around his jaw, and his steely eyes all seem to stare through me as I walk back across the den to the mats.

"Let's work on harnessing Commotio." I stare at him blankly. "The movement group," he explains. "Retention isn't your thing is it? You must have read about Commotio four times in the first two days."

"It's been a rough first week."

"Always an excuse," he says dismissively. "Watch me." Abbot traces the ink design on his forearm with the thumb-out fist, and the pattern glows and morphs into the folded wing I saw two days ago. He gently opens his fingers, and a small whirling wind spins on his palm. "I thought it would be better to start with envisioning your out-of-control tornado as something small and manageable rather than trying to move targets again." He tosses the tiny whirlwind in the air and it fades instantly.

After a few tries, a broken lamp, a shattered model of the human heart, and splitting one of the overstuffed chairs down its middle, I manage it. Gazing at the miniature version of destruction pirouetting wildly around my hand, I feel totally in control for the first time in my life.

Chapter Fourteen

Over the next few weeks Abbot puts me through a punishing workout regime each morning. After lunch I spend the hours in the Magus Library or watching Marum brew inks. I work towards a thorough knowledge of the tattoos I already have, their inks and their abilities. Abbot is anxious that I move forward quickly but I still struggle with controlling the movement tattoo. While I am unfailingly able to throw the magus, it's hit or miss in application. Zink has started coming by my den half an hour before the lights flicker signaling dinner, just so he can repair the results of my study.

After weeks of exhausting practice, tears, and hair pulling, Abbot and I finally have a breakthrough. "Visualizing the desired result clearly doesn't work for you. You naturally jump from one thought to another without recognizing it. When you force yourself to concentrate on one thing, it becomes overly intense. All the rage and emotion you have built up inside is channeled to that one thought and things explode. You won't be able to use the mind-clearing tattoo each time you need to throw a magus. Your thoughts are getting tangled, tied up together, tripping over themselves in that rat's nest of a brain you have," Abbot tells me. "Let's try not concentrating on the intentional thought. Just for the fun of it. Skip the visualization part and just throw it."

So I look at the target, trace the wings tattoo, and fling out my hand, not forcing myself to think of a desired result. And it works. The target slides neatly to the left several inches. "Again," grunts Abbot. I repeat the process, and while I initially picture the target moving to the left, I don't force my mind to focus on it. I let my thoughts travel from one thing to the next. The target moves perfectly again. And again.

With my wings tattoo, I move every item in my den from the sofa to the tiny brass whirring instrument that sits on the bookshelf without disturbing so much as a dust cloud. Abbot huffs in mingled disgust and elation, "I should have seen this from the start. Being able to throw on the first day should have told me you would be long past having to use supreme concentration to control the result. Tomorrow morning we are skipping strength training. Go to the ink room and have Marum teach you how to brew ink for the Demoror group. We will use what you make for your next tattoo." He ambles out of my den. I can tell by the way he holds his head and the angle of his shoulders that he's proud of me. Well, if I were being honest, he's probably more proud of himself for finding the solution than my execution of it.

When I ride up the elevator with Zink, we clear our minds in unison with the Dominato tattoos behind our ears, leaving the hall and the Warren in the car as we surface. I feel so light, I take off running with Zink when the elevator opens. He looks over at me while I sprint by his side and laughs, "If you are gonna run, then RUN!" he yells. He increases his speed through the streets, nearly slamming into a knot of miners coming from the other side as we fly down the hill. Pulling up short, we lose our balance and fall backwards, trying to avoid a collision. Laughing, trying to pick ourselves and our packs up off the ground, unable to catch our breath, we give up entirely and roll around in the dirt in complete bliss. Frehn finds us that way a few minutes later and pulls us to our feet.

"Why is it that whenever I see you two together someone is always in a prostrate position?" he says, offering Zink his hand.

"Good fortune?" replies Zink, with an appreciative slap on the back for Frehn, he takes off running again.

Back in our common room, full of fresh game hen and greens, PG3456 searches for devices, then settles in for the evening. Harc shows off her latest acquisitions from the factories: a pair of scissors that only want sharpening and a box of scrap metal. Merit stuffs them in his pack to add to the stash under the roof of the horse barn in the morning.

"Teach us a song, Frehn," Wex says after the run down of our day's accomplishments is complete. Frehn has improved marginally on his fiddle over the last few weeks and insists we all pay homage to his hard work. Doe tucks her feet under herself in preparation for the night's entertainment, her big brown eyes trained on Frehn's hands while he tunes the instrument.

"I learned this today from one of the older guys on the granite track. There's a whole collection of underground songs that have been quietly passed down for hundreds of years, right under The Mothers' noses."

He draws his bow down across the strings and starts a simple, sanguine tune.

I, oh aye, toil away
Aye, oh I, yes all the day
Just to walk back to you
Only to get back to you

Aye, oh I, look up to the sky
I, oh aye, wish I could fly
Over the wall to get back to you
Only to get back to you

I, oh aye, push past purgatory
Aye, oh I, to sing out my story
So I can bring it back to you
Only to get back to you

Aye, oh I, have earned my sweet rest
I, oh aye, stopped my own chest
Only to get back to you
Only to get back to you

As Frehn's voice fades on the last stanza, I feel my heart sinking. It's the first love song I've ever heard, sung in Frehn's low, rich voice with the tapping of his foot to keep time. The melody was so upbeat we could have danced to it. And then it ended in pain and death. Just like everything else in Chelon.

"Are there more songs?" asks Doe from her corner of the sofa. "You said there was a collection."

"There are so many," Frehn says with excitement, "The miners sing them to keep pace with their picks. Bik, the old man who taught me this one, said that every Service has them, but it's the miners who have the most as The Mothers hardly ever go past the tunnel entrance. Running the rail car, I've picked up a lot of things I never knew before."

"Like what, for instance?" asks Merit.

"Like fifty or so years ago, they had to shut down one of the diamond tracks because they were inches from tunneling out of the mines."

Wex sits bolt upright. "Inches from tunneling out? To daylight?"

"Yep, Bik said there was a crack in the cave wall where the sun shines through. He wouldn't tell me where though."

I look at Wex and then Frehn. That could be our way out of Chelon. We can escape through the mines.

"I know what you're thinking, of course. And it might work if I was running the bullet train. We would be overtaken instantly if we tried to get through the mines on foot. If we could take the train, they would have to follow us in carts at best. We would have hours of lead time," Frehn says, looking at Wex.

"But getting to run the train would take some time, more time than I think we have. You have to be useless at everything else before they let you conduct the bullet. The woman who runs it now had her leg crushed in a collapse. The

Healers took it off, so now she sits in the front of the train because she can't do anything else for the Service."

"We'll have to find a workaround, is there a way to break the bullet so it can't chase us?" Wex's eyes are alive with planning, scheming.

"Maybe, but that will take a ridiculous amount of preplanning and probably outside help. I don't know anything about the bullet. I'm not even sure where the engine is, it's not in the front "

"Just keep your eyes open, there has to be a way. It's too perfect an exit not to be achievable." Wex leans back in the chair. I watch him from my place on the floor, I can tell he is living out our escape in his mind. His lips move slightly as he forms each step of the plan and I rest my chin in my hand and lose myself in studying his face. He is beautiful. Pensive and alert, his face is vivid with excitement. As if feeling my eyes on him, he looks down at me. I quickly change my focus to the book in front of me, hoping my hair covers my cheeks which are now flushed with embarrassment.

In our goodnight line, Wex's lips linger next to my cheek for a second longer than the night before. I can feel his breath on my ear and I shut my eyes and I lean into him just as he pulls away. I have to take a step to catch myself. Feeling cold and confused, like I missed the bottom step of the staircase, I shut myself in my room for the night.

It was your imagination, I tell myself as I pull on my pajamas. He did not pause or kiss my cheek any longer than he did Doe or Harc's. And even if he did, we cannot be anything more than what we are already. The Mothers would not stand

140

for that kind of affection before Banding. I will not lose control again and subject PG3456 to the Amendments Spire. This strange hungry feeling for Wex will have to be squashed. I start to drag my thumb over the tree tattoo behind my ear but stop, remembering forcibly what Abbot told me the day I earned it.

There are Unspoken who can't sleep without using it. They are addicted to putting their thoughts away the way some of the Healers are addicted to the pain numbing drugs kept in their building. Trying to blot out appalling sights of mangled bodies fresh from the Amendments Spire, in search of relief. They become so dependent on the drugs, they stop eating, choosing to shoot their veins full instead of their stomachs. They become thin and gaunt, their skin gathers and sags around their wrists and ankles in papery layers. I drop my hand to the bed and roll over. Pulling the covers over my head, I try to think of anything but the addicts and Wex.

The nightmares which follow center around Wex as a rawboned addict, racked and spewing blood, lethargic, with Juwas' milk-white eyes bulging from his head. I'm jolted awake by my own screams, my hair ringing wet with sweat. In the shower, I sink down to the tiled floor. His beaten, broken face appears before me every time I shut my eyes. So I cry wide-eyed, letting the hot water beat against them, stinging the vision of a broken Wex out of them.

Marum is already in the ink production room when I arrive in the Warren. He is flipping through several books at the far table and doesn't notice me when I enter. Coughing as if to clear my throat, I walk over to him. "Abbot said you would teach me brewing today."

"Yes," he says not looking up. "You'll start with a basic Demoror blend." He picks up a sheet of paper and holds it out to me, still not looking up, "Ink elements list, find them and then follow the directions. I'll take a look when you're finished."

I take the paper and walk to the other table where a clean set of bowls and instruments await me. *Tuber of elevated gastrodia* is the first item on the list. When I locate the right box, I gingerly pull out one of the bulbous roots. It looks like thick shed skin from some kind of prehistoric snake. When I've gathered camphor, logwood, powdered goat horn and others elements on the table, I set to work, carefully mincing the tuber. Following the instructions to the letter, I light the fire under the glass bowl and wait. The ink starts to thicken immediately and turns a grayish-purple color.

Marum walks over and sticks his pinkie finger in the bowl and takes a closer look sniffing. Then he flicks his tongue over the speck of ink on his fingertip. "Very good. It's salty-sweet just as it should be. Ready to try it?" he asks me.

"Should I get Abbot?" I ask uneasily.

"No need," he retrieves a brass case from the shelves, pulls out a thin glass tube and uncorks it. He tips the glass bowl of my ink and starts pouring it into the tube. There doesn't seem to be enough space in the tiny phial to hold all of the ink from the bowl, but every drop fits. Marum replaces the cork and hands me the tube of ink and the brass case. "Take these to Abbot, he'll show you how to use them. Naturally, I am not surprised your brewing ability is astounding. Thankfully it's easier for you to control than magus. Zink wasn't able to keep anything in the bowls, we went through several tables before I gave up trying to teach him. Well, we all have our métier of course. Still. Extraordinary." He moves back to his books as he speaks, "I am confident that you will not try anything beyond your means. This is one area of the Warren in which you will not need guidance. Brew what and when you like. I would discourage you from experimenting though. There are countless lethal combinations of even the most benign elements, many of which still remain undocumented."

When I knock on Abbot's den door, he opens it slightly and looks through the crack with one eye, "Oh it's you. Done already? I'm busy now. Go wait for me in your den. Read something," he says distractedly and slams the door in my face. A month ago, I would have been enraged by his rudeness. Today, I simply smile wryly and walk to my den. But instead of reading, I practice with the wing tattoo until Abbot bangs on the door.

"Let's see it," he says, throwing the door wide and holding out his hand for the phial of ink. He turns it over, holds it up to the light and shakes it. The ink doesn't slosh around the glass, it just churns at the bottom of the phial. "Outstanding," he smirks at me. "Marum pleased as punch was he?"

"Not really. He said I didn't need supervision though and told me I can't experiment."

"That would be the Marum version of ecstatic." Abbot leads me to my desk and unpacks the brass case. "This will be your stamp. You load the ink here," he turns a wheel and flips the top of a smooth hourglass-shaped stamp open. He uncorks the ink tube and slides it neatly upside down into the stamp, closes the lid and tightens the wheel. "Would you like to do the honors?" he asks, holding out the stamp to me.

I take it from him and place it on my upper arm, above my wings, and look at Abbot for confirmation. He nods and I press down, clicking the two levers on the sides of the stamp. A stabbing knife-like pain slashes through my arm. I drop the stamp in surprise.

"Hurts more when you do it yourself," Abbot says, peering at the new band of fishing net that travels the circumference of my upper arm.

"You could have warned me," I say, a sulky note hanging onto my words.

"That wouldn't have been much fun for me. Try it out," and he throws a movement magus which picks up one of the lockers, sending it back and forth across the mats. I run my thumb over the new ink and send out a wall of red light. It slams into the metal, encasing it, crumpling it.

"Ok. Ok. Now try it gently. Even Zink can't repair a thing that's been broken repeatedly," Abbot starts the mangled locker's movement again. I aim the magus a few feet in front of the locker, so it hits the stationary wall and not so the wall crashes into the moving locker.

"Much better," Abbot says. "Tomorrow, we'll go to the target range. You can work on stopping multiple objects at once. Should be fun for you. Keep your stamp and the ink in your belt- it stays on the hall. Oh, and there's a scavenging mission planned for two months from now, since we are running low on some of the ink elements. I want you to go."

144

"Scavenging? Outside the walls?" my insides jump at the idea, equally terrified and overjoyed at the prospect. I've never even talked to someone who has been on the other side of the outer wall.

"Can't get gorged lizard spleen on this side. Trip's after power down and we are always back before dawn."

My heart sinks to the pit of my stomach like a rock. "I'm locked in after power down, I can't go," I mumble.

"You think we mend broken stuff and can move things at will but can't unlock a simple door? Speaking of, Zink tells me I neglected to tell you something. Add it to my list of mentoring sins. The hand symbol painted above your door, an observant girl like you could not have missed it."

"I've seen it."

"That is an added layer of protection against those who would do you harm. The Mothers for example. That hand will show you anything that has happened in your room and the common room." He counts off on his hand, "The thumb will glow if you are being watched, the index finger if you are being listening to, middle finger if someone has taken anything, ring finger if something was left and the little finger if something was tampered with. Zink said you all were crawling around on the floor looking under chairs like simpletons," Abbot snickers uncontrollably at the mental image of us feeling around for devices.

"I'm glad I can provide so much amusement for you. Anything else have you 'forgotten' to tell me?" seething inwardly, I count to ten to stop myself from reaching out to yank the obnoxious canine tooth earring out of his earlobe.

"Eh, who can tell," he shrugs, still laughing, "Why don't you go to the Magus Library and read up on the different inks used on the Caesim and Furtim nerve groups. Let's see if you can brew some of the more complex inks by next week."

After dinner, Frehn and I join a round of quoits, a game of throwing rings of heavy rope around pegs for points, on the lawn next to the Quad while the rest of PG3456 lounges on the grass.

The weather is unseasonably cold, driving Nutriment Cultivation to force their way through the harvest at double speed as they try to beat the first frosts. Wex can hardly keep his eyes open through meals and stretches out of the sofa when we are on the block. Escape plans seem at a standstill for now, though Harc continues to add to our stash a little bit at a time. Merit has built a relationship with the horse trainers, gaining unrestricted access to the barn. Doe doesn't talk much about what goes on in the Healer's Building. Some days she comes back with her body in knots from tension, her face bloodless and drawn. Frehn and Wex watch her constantly, as all of PG3456 have given up worrying about me. Whatever they think is happening in the basement of the Gratis Building has been overshadowed by their anxiety for Doe and what she sees as a Healer.

I am poised to toss my last rope ring to clinch the game when I see them. Twenty Mothers are gliding up through the lawn, herding everyone towards the Quad. I drop the ring. Frehn and I bolt towards PG3456 a few feet away. In a clump, we walk ahead of The Mothers, clinging to each other as if life depends on it.

The Quad is already crowded with most of the population, while others are pouring out of the residence compounds in a steady stream. Doe's eyes are enormous with fear, so we keep her in the middle of us to prevent people from brushing against her. She looks like she'll go mad at any moment. It is several minutes before a Mother ascends the stage, hands folded under her white apron, face tight with anger. Everyone on the Quad falls immediately silent.

"Children," The Mother says and pauses, raising a handkerchief to dab at the corners of her eyes and then clutching it in front of her mouth as if she can't bear to continue, "Children, we have a brigand among us."

Chapter Fifteen

Merit's hand flinches in mine and I hear Doe breathe in sharply through her nose. Harc has been caught.

"Children," The Mother continues, openly weeping now though we can all see on the large television screens setup on either side of the stage that her eyes and handkerchief remain dry. "Theft is the greatest of all misdeeds, worse even than disobedience. It embodies deception, defiance, carelessness, and moral depravity. Don't worry, children, we will find the culprit. Be not afraid, your Mothers will protect you."

I exhale slowly. They don't yet know it's Harc.

"We must flush them out. Make them understand their wicked actions have brought suffering to everyone in Chelon. To help the sad wrongdoer see how their misdeeds have impacted all of the children of Chelon, all meal rations will be cut in half, and activities on the Quad will be suspended. Instead of enjoying your free hours after dinner each night, a Play Group will be selected to set an example of public learning. Every day the thief chooses to stay silent will increase the consequences tenfold. PG3420, come forward." As The Mother calls this Play Group, I can feel Harc lean forward as if to go with them. Wex catches the back of her shirt and whispers something in her ear.

They strap PG3420 into strange spiral hooks that hoist them up over golden pyramids on the stage. They hang suspended, straddling the razor sharp pyramid peaks, unable to move without the apexes cutting into their upper thighs. Everyone in the Quad stands transfixed, unable to look away. Merit and Wex both keep a strong hold on Harc's arms, whispering urgently and quietly through unmoving lips.

"We have no way of knowing if it was you."

"The Mother purposefully didn't say what was taken, or from where, to draw out everyone who might be guilty."

"You will jeopardize everything."

"Just keep still."

Doe sways a little when the first of the blood begins to stream down the pants leg of the man hanging over the far right pyramid. I slip my arm under hers to support her. Somewhere to my right a woman is sobbing uncontrollably. I hear Play Groups of the smaller children whimpering, clutching to Mothers' tunics and aprons, burying their faces in the folds. Fury builds up inside me with every anguished noise I hear.

There is a slight scuffle behind us, as a boy pulls on a girl's hand to hold her back. When I turn my head to look, her flashing green eyes meet mine for a split second and I am forcibly reminded of a wildcat we once saw trapped in the metal jaw traps that Fauna Management sets around the fields. The girl is savage with fear and anger and determination. She is in the same year as PG3456- I recognize her from the Oath of Service. I try to remember her line assignment. Keepers maybe?

149

"I did it, it was me!" she screams out, and the boy flings her hand away from him in disgust.

The crowd turns and moves away from her as she makes her way to the stage.

"Take them down, it was me," with the last word her voice falters. There's perfect silence as PG3420 is lowered to the ground. The Mother on stage hungrily watches the green-eyed girl walking up the steps towards her.

"And what did you take, Sotter dear? Tell us," she asks holding out her hands to grasp both of the girl's.

"I didn't know, I thought they were being thrown away."

"Never mind that, dear, tell us what you took."

"It was behind one of the fabric factories, it was a pair of scissors," the girl hangs her head and assumes the attitude of a naughty child caught taking more than the allotted sweets ration.

"Exactly so," The Mother says, twisting her hand around a lock of Sotter's hair then pulling up her chin so she can look into Sotter's face. "PG3453, come forward."

The boy who was holding her back makes a noise of contempt and leads the other four members of PG3453 through the crowd to the stage. Frehn grips my shoulder, digging his fingers in. I can't take my eyes from Sotter. Something strikes me about her posture. It is too perfectly submissive, too forced, too trained.

"PG3453, Sotter has shown great bravery in coming forward. You should all be proud to have her in your Play Group. Her clear repentance for taking something that did not belong to her endears her to us." The Mother smiles

150

sickeningly at Sotter and then turns to address the crowd, who are now straining for better views of Sotter and PG3453 projected on the screens. "Children, you should all thank Sotter for her honesty." A smattering of half-hearted applause rises up. "She has saved you all from these consequences," The Mother waves her hand at PG3420 who are still lying on the stage floor bound to the spiral hooks. "You are all released now, please continue with your schedules." The Mother tightens her grip on Sotter, pulling her into a side embrace.

Novices climb the stage to start untying PG3420. People hurry away towards the residence compounds, anxious to be out of sight of The Mothers. Younger children are sobbing now. The Mothers in charge of them carry them away, cradling their small heads, making shushing sounds to calm them. PG3456 stands where we are. Frehn's fingers feel like they have reached down to my collar bone.

"She serves with me," Harc tells us without moving her lips. "She was there when I took the scissors. I didn't think she saw me."

The Mother leads PG3453 off the stage. She talks to them a few minutes and sends them to their residence compound. The Mother then folds her hands under her apron and glides over to a cluster of other Mothers. They pull their heads down in fervent discussion.

As Sotter turns to close the residence compound door behind her, she looks across the Quad at us, the only people left in the courtyard. Frehn's fingernails are digging into my skin and his hand begins to shake, "It is. It's her," he gasps.

"Her who?" Wex asks him, alarmed.

"My twin," Frehn breathes.

"Inside, we can't talk here," Merit says quickly.

Back on our block, I drop Doe on the sofa and walk directly into my room, look up at the thumb's out fist painted above my door. All of the fingers remain dark. Returning to the common room I find Wex, Merit and Harc franticly turning furniture upside down. Frehn is wringing his hands and jumping around the room in nervous agitation. "It's fine, we are alone," I tell them. Everyone stops, mid-action to look at me. "The room is safe," I repeat.

"She must have something from the Unspoken that sweeps the room," Merit says. "Secrecy has to be a big part of whatever they do, they would need some way to be sure they have it."

Everyone accepts this and they sit down, except Frehn, who resumes the odd nervous jumping around the room. "She's got the same eyes," he says to the ceiling.

"Tell us what you know, Harc," Wex says to her.

"Sotter is in the factories with me, she and I have been assigned to the same row. So she is always nearby, no matter what building or machine we are on that day. I was taking out a roll of fabric clippings to the incinerator when I saw the scissors on the ground by the steps. I dropped the fabric and pretended to adjust my shoe and slipped the scissors up my pants leg. When I picked the fabric up again, she was just coming back from dropping her clippings roll in the incinerator. I didn't think she saw anything."

"I guess she did. Any reason why she would say it was her who took them?" Wex asks in a troubled voice.

"None, I keep to myself. It's too loud to get chummy with each other anyway."

At this Frehn lets out a strangled noise somewhere between a yell and a squeak. We all turn to him.

"She knew already. She knew she was my twin."

"How could she, Frehn? It hardly seems possible that she could know without you knowing too." Harc says.

"I don't know, but she must. That's why she took the blame. She must have known that if you were caught it meant I would be punished again. And given our history with consequences and Keres being what she is, Sotter knew that whatever punishment was handed down- it would be carried out in the Amendments Spire at best or by the five at worst. If she took the blame, PG3453 would get a light consequence, go without something for a while because they haven't been on the corrections list for years. It's the only thing that makes sense. She knew. She knew she could help me." Frehn slumps in a chair and puts his head in his hands. "I have a blood sister. Her name is Sotter," he says to himself as if trying to make the unreal real.

I feel an unreasonable jealousy swish around in my stomach. He has a family, someone outside of PG3456. Frehn will try connecting with her now, try to build a relationship. And where will that leave us? Our plans to escape?

"PG3453 will have to come with us," Doe says from her corner of the sofa.

"What?!" Harc almost shouts in surprise.

"Sotter knows," Doe says simply. "She saw you take the scissors and who knows what else. She knows we are planning something and has probably guessed escape. If she knows, then PG3453 knows. And they have to come with us. I won't leave them to the five in black," Doe says in a deadly calm way that makes me feel like ice water has been dumped over my head.

"Even if she hasn't figured it out, we can't very well leave her now that we know she's Frehn's twin." Wex says with a resigned sigh. "Doe's right. They have to come. The only question is how do we get them out? We can't ask them to join us, what if they report us to The Mothers?"

"Leave it to me, I'll manage it," Frehn says firmly.

Wex looks at him appraisingly and nods. Then he stretches out on the sofa, resting his head in Doe's lap. She smoothes the worry lines between his eyes with the tips of her fingers while Merit and Harc have a whispered conversation in the window seat. The jealousy I felt for Frehn transfers instantly to Doe. Wex chose her to comfort him.

Frehn paces the room, muttering disjointed words like "Sotter, sister, eyes, twin, escape, sacrificed." I go to my room, impatient with the entire situation. Resentment of Frehn's newfound blood connection, envy of Doe being chosen by Wex, anger at The Mothers' constant reminders of supreme power, and uneasiness for what PG3453 will undergo because one of them chose to step forward to save her brother.

I try to imagine myself in Sotter's place, but I can't begin to understand what it means to have a brother, a bloodline. A family. It's easy to picture myself sacrificing my safety for any one of the members of my Play Group but it's much harder to imagine myself doing it for someone I don't know. Would I have stepped forward for Abbot or Zink?

Possibly. I hope I would. But our situations are so different. As members of the Unspoken service, we are immune. And safe.

I strip down to my underclothes, tossing the skirt and top in the hamper. Standing in front of my full-length mirror I look at my tattoos. I have four now: the Heavy, the wings, the tree, and the net. There are a hundred ways that these limited ink patterns could have stopped the scene on the Quad. I could have moved the golden pyramids, could have lifted PG3420 to safety, I could have stopped Sotter from going forward. I could have cleared Harc's mind to keep her from the waging the internal war between remaining still to protect PG3456 and our plans and speaking out to protect the entire city. Instead I am forced to hide my abilities and live with the guilt that I stood there and watched people suffer, watched people be tortured. And I did nothing.

The next morning when I press my hand to the metal plate on the Warren door, an unfamiliar voice calls my name. I turn and see a short woman just stepping off the elevator. The sides of her head are shaved, with ink covering every exposed inch of skin above her shoulders. The strip of dark brown hair running down the center of her skull and halfway down her back is arranged in hundreds of tiny braids that start at the roots. Different colored beads randomly secured through her braids click together as she walks towards me. She looks like an eccentric, tiny bird.

"Abbot tells me you are joining us on the scavenge," she says, as her voice spills out of her like she's a cup left under the tap too long and is rapidly overflowing.

155

"He said he wanted me to go. I assumed he had to get clearance before it was official."

"Clearance? From whom? Abbot's your mentor," she looks at me quizzically. "My name is Loshee."

"Nice to meet you."

"Same. Listen, you don't know who I am do you?"

"Abbot doesn't tell me much. He enjoys seeing the results of ignorance."

A grin spreads across Loshee's face, "That's Abbot alright. His greatest source of joy is watching others squirm. I'm the weapons builder. I design and construct everything we use." She seems to search my face for some sign of awe but finds nothing. She makes a movement with her hands indicating dismissal, "You'll be impressed when you see them. Which is now actually. I've been asked to fit you out and train you for the scavenge."

"Fit me out?"

"Each weapon is as unique as the user. Just like our tattoos, in point of fact. Let me change and I'll meet you on the weapons hall." Loshee disappears in a den while I continue to press my way through to the Warren.

Loshee's cocky, bubbly personality might have struck me differently if the day hadn't already started out so strangely. Instead of going straight to breakfast, PG3456 ran to the consequence board in front of the north residence compound to see what Sotter's confession earned PG3453. We read the notice poster four times before we realized PG3453 was not listed. They were not receiving a punishment. At least not today. Occasionally, The Mothers take some time deciding on a consequence, which delays the notice a day or two. But it's rare, as in the case of PG3456's Solace.

After I replace a few books on the shelves in the Magus Library, I meet Loshee just entering the weapons hall.

"I hear you throw already. Which probably accounts for Abbot sending you to me so soon. I usually don't get my weapons on newbies until the sixth or seventh year," Loshee babbles as she unlocks a door, "You must be a beast. How many do you have?"

"What? Oh, um three, not including the guard."

"If I don't have control over it, I don't include it," she flings her bulging pack and armful of papers onto a table and moves towards a rack holding a number of long spears and tall bows. "I'll start with showing you mine. Then we'll test you out on some of the other types and see what fits you." She grabs a long staff with twisted copper and brass plating running the length of the wooden shaft. At one end, a glass orb with blue smoke trapped inside is secured in a swirl of metal shaped like leaves, on the other end is a dingy blade. She spins the staff in her hands and several of her tattoos begin to glow and morph to their true shapes, while the smoke in the orb end churns and thickens. Loshee makes a jab with the spear while dropping to one knee, her other leg kicked out in the direction of the thrust. An audible sizzling sound accompanies the three blots of blue electricity that shoot out of the orb, hitting the target on each side and in the dead center, exploding it in a shower of sparks. Loshee flicks a piece of lint off her knee, casually throws a repairing magus from the tattoo on her ankle at the target and

157

jumps to her feet. I can feel my bottom jaw hanging open and snap it shut with a click of my teeth.

"Now are you impressed?" she asks me.

"Very."

"It is pretty flashy. But then, so am I," she says, tossing her hundreds of minute braids and rattling her beads.

"How did you do that without touching your ink?"

"A weapon is built for a specific person. My staff, like all the weapons, is infused with a unique ink blend allowing it to interact with just me. When the owner of a weapon holds it, it responds to the intentional thought. When your mind sends a magus to the designated nerve group, the weapon pulls it away. It throws the magus like it's an incredibly powerful extension of your palm. Like a lightning rod, only controllable. Intelligent. Let's try some on you, see what fits."

We walk to the rack and she has me spin spears, thrash sickles, fire arrows from different-shaped bows, jab the air with a pair of sai, swing swords, axes, and spiked iron balls attached to sticks with iron chains. Loshee lets me wield each weapon for less than a minute before yanking it out of my hands and thrusting a new one at me. She's visibly frustrated, but I can't tell why. All the weapons feel the same to me, foreign but not unnatural. When she pulls a particularly menacing sickly green colored scythe from my hands almost the second I close my fingers around it, she flings it across the room in contempt. Propping her hands on her hips, she blows a huff of air at a braid that's fallen across her face.

"Is something supposed to be happening?" I ask her. "Am I doing something wrong?"

158

"No, no. I mean yes," she answers waving both her hands as she walks in circles around me. She stops abruptly and pulls my wrists up to her face, inspecting them. "It's worth a shot I guess," she mumbles to herself, then to me she says, "Stay put. We are going to try something." She leaves the room and returns with a square wooden box. "I've been working on these for a while now. But I wasn't sure who would be able to manage them. They will pull forcefully straight from the wrists and there aren't many people on the hall who could withstand that kind of continued drain in combat. These are just the prototypes, mind. So don't turn up your nose. I'll build your own impressively gorgeous set to your specifications," she says while she opens the box and shows me two small crossbows resting on pegs inside. She takes one out and rests it on the top of my wrist and hand, buckling one of the leather straps around my thumb and wrist and another around my knuckles. The crossbow is about seven inches wide and six inches from the prod apex to the back of the stock. Loshee's prototype looks like it's made from discarded scrap, a mash up of bits of metal and wood that look as if only Loshee's sheer willpower hold them together.

"Well, go on, give it a try," she says giving me a push toward the target.

"There aren't any arrows to shoot."

"Don't necessarily need them with these. But I'll make you some bolts if you're stuck on the idea. Try it."

I stretch out my arm with the crossbow attached and punch the air awkwardly. I feel the inside of my arm heat up as the bow string quivers ever so slightly.

159

"Hot Hexes. That's the one!" Loshee cries. She rips the buckles loose and tosses the tiny crossbow back in the box with its mate. She wears an expression of supreme smugness while she takes measurements of my body. She can't reach the top of my head so I hold the tape for her.

"Now, let's see what kind of magus you can really throw. Target range is across the hall." She leads the way, kicking open the door with her boot. I get the feeling she likes to create a lot of noise to make herself seem larger than she is in reality. She would crash through the forest to scare away dangerous predators who would interpret her smallness as a sign of easy prey. In the target range, stalls are set up across the back wall, but I don't see any wooden targets. Loshee positions me in the center of the opposite wall. "Don't think, just throw. Ready? Go!" she yells and stomps a green button on the floor.

I hear a noise like gears creaking and look around the stalls- suddenly a huge wild boar is barreling towards me, tossing its tusks and snorting madly through its flaring nostrils. Panic takes over, and without thinking I drag my thumb over the fishing net band tattoo and throw a red wall at the boar. It slams into it and dissipates into a thin mist. I turn to look at Loshee in alarm. She is leaning against an empty weapons rack with her arms crossed, smirking. "Not awful, but you are already sweating."

I brush my sleeve across my forehead in frustration. Why does everyone down here get such a kick out of watching me tailspin into hysteria? A pack of wolves is bearing down on me now, their fangs dripping with a sticky yellow foam. I pull my thumb over the wings on my forearm and throw a whirling tornado which sweeps them aside like so many dry leaves. As soon as their mist fades, out of the corner of my eye I see a jungle cat stalking me. Instead of sending a wall from my net tattoo, I imagine sending a tight web of steel threads that dig into the ground, snaring the cat. Then, I immediately turn to fire off a magus that picks up a fellow Unspoken, who is about to be disemboweled by the claws of an enormous bear. I follow that closely with a red light box which falls over the bear, trapping it.

Loshee steps on a red button next to the green one on the floor and the clicking, grinding gear noise slows to a stop. "Not bad. I thought the last one would trip you up, not being sure how you felt about the rest of us and all." She eyes me critically. "Least I know your instinct is to save."

My instinct is to save, I chant repeatedly in my head while I brew inks that afternoon. I knew instantly, almost without looking, that the person dressed in black with the strange spiked hair was friend and not foe. That they should be saved. Do I feel like I belong here? With these people? I search my feelings, probing them for tender spots of like or aversion and find nothing that convinces me either way. The only irrefutable thing is the knowledge and skill I am gaining. But even as I think about the important role I will be able to play once we escape Chelon and The Mothers, a black thought slips over my satisfaction. How will I keep the Heavy from pressing all the air out of me when I am forced to throw a lifesaving magus? How do I avoid dying when I try to save my friends?

Chapter Sixteen

When we were in our eleventh year, Doe contracted
harshpox. She was taken from our residence block to be
quarantined in the Healers' Building. With only the five of us
left, we felt off-balance, empty and intensely alone. The
Healers told us to prepare ourselves, that Doe was near death.
If she died, her body would be taken to the other side of the
outer wall, burned in the pit, and her ashes buried between the
trees that surround Chelon. We would not be allowed to see
her. The natural death of a child is uncommon, but not unheard
of. There are eight or nine Play Groups who lost a member to
disease or in an accident during Service hours. Without a full
set of six members, the odd one out was simply not Banded
when they entered their eighteenth year. If death is a judgment,
a punishment, the entire Play Group is executed on the Quad in
front of the population. It's called an Extinguishment, with the
offender always the last to be put to death, so they may watch
what their actions brought to their Play Group members. Public
slaughter is an extreme rarity, but the most recent occurrence is
never too far out of living memory to make it feel impossible.

Doe was kept away from us for a little longer than two
weeks. During that time we roamed the residence compound,
the Quad, through Pedagogics lectures without purpose, like

ghosts of ourselves, aimless like lambs who have been separated from the herd. It wasn't that Doe was a group leader, or even that her voice was needed to propel us forward through the days. I suppose we would have reacted the same way if any one of us were removed from the group, because each of us is a keystone in our functioning arc. Remove a keystone and the arc crumbles. Remove one of us and the whole group falls.

Today, I look at the five members of PG3456 as we wait in line at the Necessities Center. We have our fifteenth year clothes in large laundry sacks which we sit on, waiting for the annual clothing trade out to begin. Harc has taken on a nervous, involuntary jerking motion whenever a Mother appears. It looks unnatural on her, like it belongs to Doe or Merit more than to her. She hasn't tried to take anything else from the factories, choosing to keep her head down instead. I hope she is at least learning how to weave fabrics. We will need clothing on the outside, as we aren't used to having pants and shirts wear out, and someone will need to know how to repair or replace them. Harc is the only one of us in a position to learn anything in that line. She has kept a haggard expression since Sotter stepped forward to take the blame for her theft of the scissors. Harc's face remains pinched, as if she's continuously thinking of that moment, trying to go back to it and step forward herself. But even she knows it would have done no good. Sotter's Play Group finally appeared on the corrections board with a punishment of halved food rations for a week. Nothing that holds a candle to what would have happened to PG3456 if Harc had confessed.

163

In the weeks that followed, Frehn was able to not only talk to Sotter, but her entire Play Group. He starts games on the Recreational Fields with other PGs and PG3453 joins in. They are able to talk frequently without attracting the attention of The Mothers. Still, the twelve of us avoid being involved in the same activity- it would be strange if PG3453 started eating with us in the canteen, for instance. But on the fields or during free time when other members of groups are interacting at the same time, we blend in.

"Why have us get in line so early if they aren't going to start the trade-in on time?" Frehn says in frustration, peering around me to the front of the line. I know he wants to meet Poy and Revvim from PG3453 on the Quad for a game of cards.

"I think they have started, there's just a problem," Doe says. "There are Mothers up there now."

"Someone must have lost something. Well, pull them out of the line and let the rest of us move," Frehn says.

A few minutes later, The Mothers come gliding down the line. A PG is trailing behind them, heads hung, laundry bags on their backs. The line begins to inch along and we make it to the Clothier Counter an hour or so later.

"Bag, ticket," says the Keeper behind the counter.

I hand mine over and the Keeper counts each item, inspecting it carefully. She makes a note and pins it to my bag, then hands me a new bag with a list of contents sewn onto a fabric tag.

"Next in line," she calls out.

We all make it through the trade-in without incident, the Keeper never even glancing at any of our faces. She seems intent on getting each of us through the trade-in quickly so she can pull down the counter shutters and block everyone out.

We haul our clothes for the sixteenth year of our lives back to the block and unpack. I carefully tack the fabric list in the closet to be sure I keep track of every item. I saw a Play Group bullwhipped once because one of the boys lost a handkerchief while playing in the fields. Ever since then, I have checked my clothing list each night before going to bed to be sure I still have everything assigned to me.

Once everything is put away and after glancing at the painted hand above my door, I wander back in the common room and fling myself into a chair. Play Groups aged fifteen through seventeen were released from Service for the afternoon so we could attend trade in, so we have hours to kill before dinner. Going back to the Warren isn't an option after being dismissed. Neither is joining a game on the Recreational Fields- it is too cold this time of year and there's no snow covering the ground yet to provide seasonal activities. The card game Frehn has planned under the heat lamps on the Quad feels like dull work.

Wex comes out of his room and sits at my feet, resting his arm over my legs.

"Is it safe?" he asks me.

"Huh? Oh, yes, the room is clean," I answer, the weight of his arm demanding my whole attention.

He sighs with contentment and leans his head back against the arm of the chair, "There are definite drawbacks of you being an Unspoken, but that trick is not one of them. Not

165

having to worry that we've missed something in our search is almost a balance to not knowing what you do all day."

I can say nothing. My hand is millimeters from his head and I want to sink my fingers into his thick hair, running them through over and over.

"I've started a map," Wex starts again, "of everything I can see through the outer wall and everything I can pick up from the leaders who load the trains. They've talked to the traders you now. Actually talked to people form outside of Chelon. Harc is working on one for the inner wall of Chelon. I think the best thing to do, once we get out, is follow the river up to the mountains. Best to stick close to a clean water source."

Sure, whatever, just don't move.

"That opens us up to a lot of problems though. It will make us dangerously easy to follow and track. But I don't know who they would send after us once we get past a certain distance. Somehow, I can't picture The Mothers coming after us, and the five in black are too old," Wex trails off, his fingers playing with the embellishments on my pants cuff.

"Unless that's what the Unspoken are for," Harc says from her door.

I look up at her, startled, and Wex withdraws his arm. I want to pull it back across my legs and fling a magus to push Harc back into her room, slamming the door in her face.

"You think that's what the Unspoken Service is? To bring people back?" Wex asks her incredulously. "Doesn't seem like it would be worth the effort to have a whole Service for something that only happens once every sixty years."

"No, I think they do all The Mothers' dirty work," Harc replies, avoiding my eye.

"And what exactly would be considered dirty work to a Mother?" I shoot at her, feeling a warning shove from the Heavy as the words leave my mouth.

"Chasing people down, for starters. Making sure we have no options but to obey is another. Maybe teaching The Mothers everything they know about torture, building their torture devices, perhaps. That's why you aren't punished with us, because your Service taught them everything they know," she spits the words out like they are hot embers and they burn me like fire.

"No, The Mothers do their own chasing," Merit says, coming through his bedroom door. "Five horses are kept bridled and saddled at all times just in case someone makes it out. There are hidden doors in every part of the outer wall they can use to get out quickly and cut the runners off no matter how or where someone escapes. One of the people who works the chickens remembers the last Play Group who was Extinguished. He remembers seeing The Mothers galloping off on horseback, their tunics flying behind them. He said it looked like they rode straight through the wall by the stream. He never saw the door open, but he heard the scream of the girl as she was caught. Said it felt like her screams echoed all through the valley for hours afterwards. When The Mothers brought her back, she was tied to a pole between two horses, legs and arms bound, swinging like she was a trussed pig." Merit shivers at the grisly image his words created.

"If they don't give chase, if they don't help The Mothers, then what exactly do the Unspoken do? I've paid harsh penalties for Keres's mistakes and I have the right to know why she doesn't pay right along with us," Harc's face is bloodless, and her gray hair swings as she turns her head quickly to look at me. She looks wild and unearthly. "Well? What? Oh, but I forgot. That pretty picture on your chest saves you from having to tell us anything, doesn't it?" she says with a sneer. I've never seen her turn on one of us before. I never imagined her anger could be directed towards one of us. She is shaking with barely suppressed rage. She is poised, ready to lunge at me.

I shift in my chair to ready myself for her when Wex puts his arm over my legs again, pressing me down into the cushion.

"I do not serve with The Mothers," I say quietly, testing the Heavy tattoo. "I do not serve The Mothers," scorching anger boils up my chest and neck at the idea that a member of my own Play Group could think of me not only working against them but working in tandem with The Mothers. Working with sadistic, fear drinking, pain sucking, inhuman demons. Zink's anger at me for asking the same question of him during my tour of the Warren is before me, the devastating mortification mixing with the anger. Their joint heat singes my cheeks. "I have no control over what they do. To you or to me."

"What about what they don't do to you, Keres? Do you have control over that?"

I fling Wex's arm off my legs and burst out of the chair. I'm an inch from Harc's face, ready to claw at her eyes. For an

168

instant, I see The Mother who drew blood when she slapped Harc's thirteen year old face. Surprised and shaken, I stumble backwards and gasp out, "If one of us falls, so fall we all."

Harc takes a step back too, her hands on either side of her head, gripping her hair. Frehn and Doe have flung opened their bedroom doors at the noise we are making.

"I'm- so sorry," Harc says as her body starts to shake with sobs. "I have- no idea- I don't understand- something is wrong with me!" she cries out. She drops and curls up in a ball on the floor, violently beating her head and hands on the wooden planks. The hair around her face is wet with tears almost instantly. All my anger abruptly changes to pity. I sink to the floor with her and put my arms around her, trying to keep her from the horrible self-inflicted pain. Her head rests on my shoulder. Doe crawls over to us and leans her own head on Harc's back. We sit on the floor, crying together while the boys stand over us. They look at each other, half afraid of our tears and half relieved to have avoided a fight. For now, at least.

The next day, I wait for Abbot outside his den for over an hour before I give up and turn to laundry instead. After starting the machine, I walk into the hall again, unsure what to do next. Juwas' toady cackle reaches out through her sewing room door across the hall. I walk over to it and knock, her answering mumble tells me to come in. I don't flip on the light at the door as Zink did, choosing instead to pick my way through the maze of fabrics and materials on the floor by the light of the single heating lamp at the far end of the room.

"It's me, Juwas," I say when I'm within touching distance of her work table.

"Know it," she answers.

"What are you working on?" I ask, dropping to my knees to be closer to her level.

"Eh," she grunts, fingering the stretchy fabric and holding it out for me to see.

I cast around for something to talk about, something to catch her interest, "Do you know a lot about fabrics, Juwas?"

"Do," she nods.

"Do you have a favorite?"

Without turning her head, she points to several bolts of leather propped up in the corner.

"You like the leather best? Why?"

"Alive. Better with ink."

"The fabric makes a difference in throwing magus?"

Juwas snickers a strangled sort of laugh at my question, "Does." She bends over her fabric again and cuts a shape out with a knife blade and no pattern. I watch her piece together a sleeve in silence. There is so much I want to ask Juwas, but I bite the questions back. It's not easy to ask difficult questions when I'm not receiving any encouragement on the straightforward ones.

"Mothers are angry," she says abruptly in what passes for a conversational tone. Did she read my mind?

"Aren't they always angry?" I ask with hesitation.

"Angry at you."

"Why?"

"Unbreakable, don't like it."

"I don't understand."

Juwas turns, drops her work on the table in an impatient gesture and swivels in her seat to face me. Her white eyes reflect the low light of the heat lamp, they look like they are made of red glass. The effect is grotesque. "Gonna work on you hard. Gotta break you. Only way. Break your Play Group first." The effort to expel that many words at once seems to take its toll on her, and her shoulders heave while she catches her breath.

"Why have they got to break me, Juwas?" I whisper, reaching out for her hand. She grasps it hard and pulls me in close, putting my ear next to her mouth. The sound of her wet rattle breathing breaks me out in a cold sweat. I force myself not to pull away when her hot breath burns my ear.

"You the Catalyst."

Chapter Seventeen

"Been looking all over for you," Abbot says, grabbing my arm and pulling me up. "You've skipped out on physical training for three days in a row. You're gonna regret that." He drags me across the sewing room and throws a short combination of greeting and goodbye to Juwas, who grunts incoherently in return.

"What does she mean, the Catalyst? What is that?" I ask Abbot, walking double time to keep up with him.

"Juwas doesn't always know what she's saying."

"That's not what Zink says."

"Zink doesn't know any more about the situation than you do," Abbot snaps back. "Juwas isn't right. Her body can't contain or control her intusmagus, her brain has been addled by her power because it can't keep up."

"Seems fine to me. Slight speech problem maybe, but if you overlook her inability to put a subject and a predicate in one sentence, she's not that hard to understand."

Abbot pulls up short and faces me, pointing a finger straight at me. "You have no idea what Juwas has been through, what she goes through every single day. Do not treat her lightly."

"I wasn't trying to make fun of her," I say in a quiet voice, "Not at all, I was just saying that she seems to know a lot more than she can express."

"Girl, you may have just uttered the wisest words ever spoken. Now, run the mats until I say you can stop," he almost shoves me through my den door.

During the last few weeks, I have focused on brewing ink and stamping new tattoos on my skin. When they aren't in use, my entire left arm is covered in one long connecting ornamentation that stretches from my fingers to the base of my neck. The most beautiful of the individual tattoos is the image of a woman's profile that covers the tip of my shoulder. Her long hair whirls around behind her, spreading across my collar bone and wraps around the left side of the Heavy tattoo on my sternum. She represents the Detrudo group, which acts as a powerful force push.

I also have a pair of magpies wrapped around my wrist and joined at the beaks, for finding objects. There's a green vine wrapping around the upper part of my forearm, which throws a gripping magus that allows me to hold things as well as feel their textures. The one I have had the most difficulty learning to control is the Contortio group. The spinning blades design of ink above my fishing net band sends out a vortex of sucking whirling power. I put the target range out of commission with it last week. Loshee said the repairs could take a month or more. I damaged the generation mechanism below the floor with the downward drawing force.

Learning to control and throw different magus in rapid succession had taken the place of physical training for several days running. Loshee had suggested that I start in the combat simulators today, a scavenge scenario to better prepare me for the trip in a few nights' time. Evidently, Abbot has other ideas. My thigh muscles scream in protest as I slam into the lockers on my thirtieth lap across the mats. Gasping for air, I push off and start back to the other side.

"That's enough," Abbot says from his perch on my desk. "You can lift weights now."

"Thanks so much," I say, turning towards the weight bench.

"While you are lifting, I'll tell you a story."

"Even better."

"Once upon a time,"

I stop pressing the barbell away from my chest and look at him with a raised eyebrow.

"Fine. About forty years ago, the morning after a scavenge, an Unspoken in his second year of Service told his Play Group about a beautiful lake he had seen on the other side of the outer wall. He talked about it with such indiscretion that he was overheard by a much younger Play Group. One of the little girls in the group lost her head with the desire to see that lake. One day, she was so consumed with yearning, she slipped in-between the iron bars of the wall and blindly walked away in search of the cool blue water. The Mothers pursued her of course and brought her back. Within hours of her retrieval, her entire Play Group was hacked to death with an axe blade, legs cut off first to emphasize their crime was an attempt at escape. The girl went mad before the second person's legs were amputated and she screamed about the lake like it was some kind of promised land, a safe refuge, through the entire Extinguishing. Until she was forever silenced with a final swing of the axe."

My stomach churns, my heart feels as though it's somewhere at the bottom of my lower intestines, my upper lip curls back in preparation to retch on the floor, and my vision is nothing but blur.

Swimming, oscillating blur. The man who works the chickens saw her, strung up like a trussed pig between The Mothers' horses. "Why-" I start and find I'm unable to ask.

"Why did I tell you this? Because when we go on the scavenge, you will see that lake and much more. Because you need reminding beforehand. Everything we do, everything we work towards affects everyone on the surface. We cannot relax our guard, even for a blink of an eye. That Unspoken said nothing that caused his Guard tattoo to react, yet his words resulted in the deaths of six children. And he has had to live with that knowledge for forty years. The Mothers will go to any lengths to break us, to beat us into submission. To prove that they are the ones in control of Chelon. Nothing is out of their reach. Remember that." Abbot stops talking abruptly. He says nothing else for several minutes and I see his throat move as he swallows hard, his eyes over-bright as he slides off my desk and leaves my den. I sit for a long time on the weight bench, head buried in my hands.

I leave the hall for lunch with conflicting desires. I want more than anything to puts my hands on PG3456, to touch them and know that they are still warm with life. And I want to hide deep in the Warren and never see the surface or The

Mothers again. My need to see PG3456 wins out and I change into my everyday clothes again. Zink is waiting for me at my den door. "You look green, feeling alright?" he asks with concern in his voice.

"Fine, Abbot just-" I don't want to talk about what Abbot told me. "He just ran me hard is all."

Zink looks at me, I can tell he doesn't buy my story, but thankfully he doesn't question me. In the elevator, we throw the thought-clearing magus together. I fall against the wall of the car once I have locked the bloody axe in a small safe and pushed it into a dark corner of my mind. I could cry with both despair and relief now that the little girl's screams are no longer reverberating around the forefront of my thoughts.

Frehn catches up with me at the fork. He knows something is intensely wrong but he simply kisses my forehead and takes my hand, running it through his arm and we walk silently to the canteen. PG3456 eats quietly and retreats to the little knot of evergreen trees just north of the Quad. The trees provide some protection from the cold wind that's whipping down from the mountains.

"They are trying to break me through each of you in turn," I spill out in a rush, teeth chattering against the cold. "They will prey on each of you to teach me I can still be controlled. I promise you now," I look into each of their eyes, "I promise each of you right now, I will never put you at risk. I will do nothing to anger them. I will be submissive and passive."

"Keres, we know," Merit says as he reaches his gloved hand out to grab my arm, giving me a slight shake. "We know."

"But you don't, we haven't been alive long enough to know what they are capable of! We have to stop planning. I cannot let you risk more- more torture- or death."

"That's our choice, not yours," Harc says. "And we choose to risk everything in order to gain freedom. I know you can do nothing to help us now, but you will on the other side when we are out from under them. I just have to remember that when the doubts The Mothers have planted in me try to take over," she smiles weakly at me and presses her icy lips to my cheek. We squeeze each others' hands and return to our Services for the afternoon. I feel sick with fear for their safety and for my sanity.

Loshee greets me when the elevator doors open to the hall. "Hiya! We are gonna infuse your weapon with ink today!" she chirps, beads clicking. She follows me to my den, chatting wildly about the ink blend she developed specifically for my weapon. While I change, she prattles on, touching everything she can reach on my bookshelves. I have long since removed all the orange patches from the top half of the uniform, leaving my tattoos fully exposed through the openings. Behind my reflection in the mirror I watch Loshee hop from one foot to the other in an effort to make me hurry. The second I have fastened the last buckle on my boots, she yanks me to my feet and drags me to ink production.

"Right, here's the list and instructions. You start in on it and I'll run and get the wristbows." She bounds out of the room, leaving me to start collecting the components. Asafetida, clove, benzoin, dogbane, fenugreek, borage, patchouli and blue beetle antenna are just the top third of the enormous list. The instructions look more complex than any I have seen in the Magus Library. Loshee returns, holding a sleek dark mahogany case with a hammered steel band around it. She whips around the room getting the remaining elements and approaches me holding out an empty bowl with a notch in one side and a wide lip on the opposite rim. She pulls out a small golden dagger from her belt and reaches for my arm. I step back from her in surprise.

"What are you doing?" I squeak wildly.

"How else do you think the wristbows are going to know they belong to you? Gotta give up some of that sweet, sweet blood, Keres. Come on, Marigold won't hurt cha," she says, brandishing the golden dagger.

"You named your knife?" I ask incredulously, still keeping my distance.

"When they have personalities all their own, they end up naming themselves. Now come on, you're wasting time."

I approach her cautiously. Loshee takes my arm and rests my elbow on the lip of the bowl so my wrist crosses to a notch in opposite side. She traces Marigold's tip down the center of my arm once, then makes the cut on the second pass. I wince with the pain and turn my head so I don't have to see my blood spilling over the sides of the cut into the bowl. Loshee counts to eleven then passes the back side of Marigold over the cut and it instantly closes, leaving a long scabby scar that travels from my wrist to the crook of my elbow.

Loshee tips my blood from the bowl into a phial and jams a cork in the top. "Perfect, got everything right at hand now. Start with step one there on the middle of the page," she says, jabbing at the paper with Marigold's hilt. My first assessment that the ink brew was complex turns out to be a gross misjudgment. I have to reread each line of the instructions several times aloud before I understand it. I take the extra precaution of making sure Loshee hasn't lost interest in my movements before I make any attempt at carrying out a step. Two and a half hours later I tip the phial of my own blood into the bowl and stir. Red steam erupts from the liquid, giving off a sulfuric smell.

"Finally," Loshee breathes. She brings the wooden case around the table to me and slides the center of the steel band to the left, releasing the clasp. She opens the dark wooden lid and I let out a gasp. Sitting on a perfectly formed cushion of emerald green velvet is a matching set of silver and mahogany wristbows: the prod made of solid silver shaped into two thin, wide-spread wings, the stock carved and embellished like the body of a dragon, complete with emerald eyes.

"Go on, put them in the ink," Loshee says with a little shake of the box.

I gingerly pick them up, running my fingers over every inch of them, before slowly dipping them into the ink. When I let the second one drop to the bottom of the bowl, the ink turns golden, then green, and begins to boil rapidly even though the fire underneath it is still turned low. The ink level starts receding and I quickly bend down to look at the bottom of the bowl. "Loshee, the bowl must have cracked!" I exclaim with urgent concern.

"The wristbows are just soaking it up, Keres. Relax," she says.

"Oh," I say, straightening up. "Well good, because Marigold wasn't going to cut me again." I run my hand over the place where the cut was made. It's completely smooth now, no scab and no scar.

The strings on the wristbows snap as the last dregs of ink disappear into the stock.

"They are all yours now," Loshee says.

I reach in the bowl and pull them out. I can feel a quick, even pulsing through the wood, exactly like a heartbeat. Like my heartbeat. "Loshee, they are beautiful. Thank you."

"They are one of my better looking babies, yes. Very pretty. And deceptively powerful. Sound like someone you know?" she cocks her head quizzically at me.

I'm sure she is talking about me, but I don't answer. I strap the wristbows to the tops of my hands and wiggle my fingers. "Perfect fit. I'll still be able to do just about anything with them on."

"Including throwing magus, that's why I left the palms open." She turns back to the box and pulls out two small clutches of tiny arrows, "There are your bolts, in case you want to fire off something you can see. They are just like regular bow arrows, just smaller." She loops the clutches to each side of my belt and stands back to admire me. "Stand up straight. Try to look menacing."

I drop a foot behind me and pull my shoulders back, chin tucked a little into my neck, and clench my fists, slightly bowing out my elbows.

"Very nice. What a pretty picture of a warrior you make," Loshee laughs. "Let's go try em out, wanna?"

Chapter Eighteen

Loshee stands me in the ready vestibule right in front of the simulator door just off the main hall.

"The door will open as soon as I run the program. Zink is going through it with you. He could use the practice." She starts climbing the stairs to the control nest at the top of the room, spotting Zink just as he enters the ready vestibule. "Here he is! Keep each other company while I set the course," she says as Zink walks up to me carrying a short sword with a golden hilt designed like a snake that curls around his hand and a shield attached to his arm. His legs, which stick out from under the shield, are completely bare. Ink envelopes everything from the tops of his feet up to the edges of his tight shorts. I had always thought of Zink as a slow learner because I had only ever seen the two or three tattoos on his upper body, but his lower limbs are just as tightly patterned as any of the other Unspokens' upper torsos.

"Quit staring at my legs, Keres. You're embarrassing yourself," Zink teases, waving his sword hand to get my attention.

"Sorry, I'm just surprised," I stammer.

"That I have legs?"

"That you have ink."

"They are all for healing and protection. I can't seem to master the concept of offensive magus," he says, shuffling his bizarre shoes that expose the ink over the tops of his feet.

"I don't have anything except for an arm and shoulder," I say, squatting down to have a closer look at his legs. The ink wraps all the way around them, and I resist the urge to run a finger along the patterns to see what they do.

"Uh, Keres. Could you stop?"

"What?" I look up at him to see an expression of extreme discomfort. He squirms under my gaze.

"Looking at my legs like that. It's weird."

"Right. Sure," I blush as I stand up. "See what Loshee made me?" I say, thrusting my wristbows under his nose in an attempt to alleviate his discomfort and my embarrassment.

He admires them for a minute, then says, as if to reassure me, "Juwas is making pants for me ya know. They just aren't ready yet. I don't want to wear these," he says, pulling at the tight shorts.

"Of course. Who would want to run through a combat simulator in their underwear?" I say with a wink.

He turns bright red and tries to make his shield cover as much of his lower half as possible, but the corners of his mouth twitch as he fights a smile.

"You should be preparing for battle, not thinking about what I'm wearing," he says, utterly failing at a half-hearted attempt to be serious.

"Or not wearing," I say, laughing.

As we double over in laughter, the combat simulator doors slide open with a scraping noise and a rumbling bang.

Instantly, we are in battle stance and step over the threshold. I know the simulator is running a program based on past scavenges, but this realistic atmosphere is not what I was expecting. It's not grinding gears and smoke of the target range, but solid wood and stone. A rocky forest blanketed in thick snow greets us, icicles hanging from the trees. The air is dry and cold. We can see our breath forming little frosty clouds. The snow crunches under our feet and I can hear birds in the trees. Moonlight bounces off the ice, making everything sparkle. It's smoke and mirrors I know, but it's breathtaking how beautiful the world is. Zink prods me forward and we walk carefully into the trees, trying to muffle our footfall.

Our objective is to retrieve a plant root marked on our map and get back to the doors, unhurt and within a certain amount of time. I use the magpies tattooed around my wrist to throw a guide to the roots' location. The bird that springs from my palm flies straight forward, banks toward the right, then goes out of sight. Zink and I keep our weapons at the ready and follow in the direction of the magpie.

We walk uninterrupted for what feels like hours, building the tension to an absolute breaking point. Our muscles go taut with every change in wind direction, every new sound or smell. I can see the outlines of Zink's calves and thigh muscles flexing in the blueish light cast by the moon. The movement makes his tattoos look alive. I have to constantly force myself to look around me instead of down at his legs. Just when we spot my glowing magus magpie a hundred yards away pecking around some brown stocks with curled-in yellow leaves shooting up through the snow, Zink drops to the ground with a hard thud. I whirl around on the spot, aiming my wristbows wildly, looking for whatever hit Zink.

"Are you hurt?" I ask, panting, not taking my eyes off the trees.

"No, it was huge though. What was it?" he stands up and we put our backs together, still raking the trees with our eyes. A slight movement just inside my line of peripheral vision makes me jerk my wristbows on the spot.

"There, behind that elm," I say.

"I have something over here too," he whispers back.

"Wait for them to come at us? Or should be go after them?"

"Well, it didn't hurt me. I guess we move on? Why kill something that just wants to mess with us?" he says.

While I can't deny his logic, I also can't shake the feeling that this is a bad choice. But I nod in agreement, since he has been doing this longer than me. Wristbows still locked on the spot where I saw movement, we slowly back away from the area. We inch our way to the brown stocks and the magpie magus dissipates in a wisp of smoke. "I'll cover, you collect," I tell Zink.

He kneels down in the snow, his bare knees disappearing in the fluffy white banks, and starts to dig around the brown stocks carefully. I do not take my eyes off the woods surrounding us, my heart beating in triple overtime while the strings on my wristbows mimic its quick pace. I hear a snort to my left and swing around, winding up a force push magus, when my eyes land on a tiny pink piglet. For a moment I want to lower my arms and coo at his sweet wiggly nose and curly tail. In that fraction of a second, the piglet's mother comes rampaging down the slope, sending snow and rocks flying in all directions. She is the size of a horse, wiry hair bristling all over her body, and black tusks as long as an elephant's. I step in front of Zink, put aside the force push, not wanting to hurt the piglet, and pull out a metal cage of red light from the fishing net tattoo on my arm, trapping the mother and piglet together. At the same time, Zink has switched positions and is now sitting with the soles of his feet pressed together, his hands hovering above the tattoos on his thighs.

"I can set up a shield but it will make it impossible for you to fire at anything," he says. "It will also make it hard to leave once we are ready, especially if the animals hang around."

"It's fine, I have it. Just get the roots and let's go." The mother boar is ramming into the walls of my cage and I have no idea how permanent it is. It hadn't occurred to me that my magus would ever need to last more than a few minutes. The red light of the cage begins to flash each time the boar slams into it. The squeals of the piglet are starting to cut deeply into my brain. It sounds like a human infant in pain.

There's a savage yell from the right and I turn away from the boar to see a group of people dressed in whites and reds running across the riverbed fifty yards off, their spears and long handle axes raised. "Zink!" I scream, "Send a shield to the boar!" and I fire a vortex from my wristbow into the river, creating a whirlpool in the water, and they stagger backwards to avoid falling in. At the same time I throw a Commotio magus that lifts the frontrunners of the group, knocking them

185

into the back of the pack. While in the air, one of the men hurls his long axe in our direction. I drag my thumb quickly over the vine tattoo and fling out my hand. The magus grips the axe midair. I can feel its weight and smooth ivory handle in my hand, even though it's still hanging twenty feet off the ground. I fling it aside with a gesture and it lodges itself deeply into a boulder. From the wristbows, I send a dozen red light ropes that tie the group of attackers together.

"We have to move. I have no idea how long that will hold them," I look down at Zink. He is in some kind of a trance, his hands resting on his knees, palms upturned, holding the roots. The tied men are yelling in a strange language and spitting, trying to struggle free from their rope prison. I kick Zink with my boot and scream at him, "Get up! We have to move!" He lurches to one side as my boot makes contact with his hip and the roots fall from their place in his open palms. I recognize the tuber-like root with a cluster of tiny fibers at the end and shriek in terror, "You didn't let them touch your bare palms! Zink!"

We have been scavenging black henbane. It has a powerful sleeping aid among its many uses. If you touch the roots of the plant with your bare skin, it can send you into a coma-like state. I swear at the top of my lungs and throw another red light cage at the boar, this one solid so I can't hear the piglet's squeals. I send another set of ropes at the group of attackers who are now red in the face with yelling and straining against my ropes.

I rip an orange patch off the leg of my suit and use it to pick up the roots, wrap them carefully, and store them in my pack. Pulling my thumb over the wings tattoo, I lift Zink off the snow and painstakingly guide him through the trees in front of me. I have to get him to the med bay before the oil from the black henbane roots seeps too far into his system. He could be out for weeks if he doesn't die first. I hear footsteps running up behind me. The white and red men have broken free and are pursuing us at an alarming rate. I put Zink on the ground, cover him with a red light box and throw a Vermen magus just in time to grip a spear, narrowly stopping it from entering my eye socket. I block axes and spears frantically until I can pull up a strong enough Detrudo magus to force the pack backwards, allowing me space to throw another round of ropes, this time accompanied by a red light cage. Breathing heavily, I use the ink to pick Zink up again and I keep moving back towards the door.

In my panic, I've forgotten I am in a fabricated world. Forcing myself to calm down, I am able to pick our way through the trees at a faster pace, and we reach the door in a matter of minutes. As soon as I lay my hand on the panel, the woods and all its sounds and smells melt away. Only an empty shell of a cavernous concrete room is left.

I look up at the sound of applause. A large crowd of Unspoken look down from the control nest window built into the upper half of the room. Some are whooping and some look contemplative. I spot Abbot who gives me an approving sort of nod while he rubs his sandpapery chin. Journer is standing beside him, talking to another woman who is gesturing excitedly.

187

"Thanks for the save. Glad you didn't leave me behind," Zink says.

I whip around and see him standing, apparently in excellent health. "What did you go and touch the roots for? Couldn't you tell it was black henbane?" I say at him with disgust, "You nearly got us killed."

"Had to, those were my instructions. And we were perfectly safe. It's just a simulator, Keres. Nothing was real, not even the roots. As evidenced by my instant recovery," he does a little pirouette on the spot.

Feeling idiotic, I start unbuckling my wristbows. Loshee jumps the last few stairs from the control nest and starts punching the air in front of her in imitation of me using the wristbows. "Pew! Pew! Fantastic, like you were born with them!" she cries out, her voice higher than ever with excitement. "Like they were perfect extensions of your own arms! If I hadn't seen it with my own eyes, I would never have believed you throw magus like that with them. Consecutive and everything!" She is bouncing around me in circles now, then she jabs at Zink, "Bet you were itching to show her what you have, weren't ya? Bet it was hard not taking the lead!"

"Not having any pants and knowing the entire hall was watching us kinda made taking the lead a back burner thought for me, Loshee. But when Keres kicked me, I have to say the idea crossed my mind." Zink says with a laugh, rubbing his hip, which no doubt is starting to show a bruise the size of my boot.

"Abbot says you should wait in your den for him, Keres. He has to attend the debriefing but wants to see you before dinner," Journer tells me as she descends the stairs with a large group of Unspokens. She pats my shoulder as she passes me, "Good job in there." She beckons to Zink and they leave the ready vestibule together. Loshee takes another punch at him and he dodges it, still laughing.

"Good kid, that Zink," she says with her hand on her hips. "Nice legs too," cocking her head to the side as she watches him walk down the hall.

"Loshee!" I cry in amazement.

"Shut up, at least I didn't crawl all over the floor to look at them."

"I was looking at the ink, not his legs!"

"Riiiight."

My face is bright red, and I can feel the blush spreading from my neck to my forehead. Zink is at least seven years older than I am and definitely not in my Play Group. That makes him off limits, completely. But whose rule is that? The Mothers'? Does that make it invalid down here? Loshee sure seems to think so. And what about Wex? Frehn? I have never thought of Merit as anything but Merit, but Wex and Frehn have both commanded a restless, hungry feeling in the pit of my stomach. Am I starting to think of Zink the same way?

I carefully wipe down the two wristbows, place them in their box and carry it back to my den. Attraction and a freakish craving surge around inside of me. There is nothing I can do to satisfy or squelch it. For as long as I remain inside the double walls of Chelon, The Mothers control that aspect of my life. "I have got to get out of here," I say to my reflection in my wardrobe mirror. "This feeling is going to burn a hole straight through me."

Curling up on the sofa with a book on the components of ink used for the Furtim nerve group, I settle in to rest while I wait for Abbot. The Furtim group, which controls stealth, is the last one to earn before I complete the left side of my upper torso. Its location on the neck means it will be the first one that will be visible to everyone at all times. Once I earn it, I will stop wearing the black diamond over my left ear and start developing my hairstyle.

I'm ashamed to admit my excitement over this step, even to myself. I have devoted hours of free time sketching designs that will be known as my signature style. Loshee's shaved head and braids are a little too extreme for my taste and Journer's sweeping brown up-do with spirals of different metals spun in feels too tame. Now that I have the dragon wristbows, I'm leaning towards something tribal. Maybe something centering around a clip made to look likes wings or a claw.

Abbot thumps my book with his thumb and forefinger, making me jump so violently I fall off the sofa. "Remember when you used to knock?" I ask him, struggling to regain some dignity.

"Remember when you used to show me some respect?" he says.

"No, actually. I don't remember that."

"Oh, right. That was fear. I'll pretend it was reverence to spare my sensitive feelings. Ready to hear what the Doyens had to say about your performance?"

"The Doy-whats?"

"Doyens, supreme masters of intusmagus. The respected head advisors in the Warren for lack of a better way to explain them."

"What did they say?"

"A lot of nonsense. To sum up, they were impressed. Impressed you chose not to kill anything, even those who would have killed you. I think it was foolish not to bash their heads in with rocks when you had the chance, but my opinion doesn't count for much with some of the Doyens. You did do a few things that roused my interest and, dare I say, admiration."

"What was that?"

"The rapidity with which you threw. You didn't throw unless you were forced. You showed careful thought. You didn't miss a target. You accomplished the goal and you managed to kick Zink all in the same simulation."

I grin at him, "That was my favorite part too."

"You showed a particular zeal at that moment," Abbot chuckles. "The Doyens say you're more than ready to go on a scavenge, not that I needed their approval. Your movements are my business and mine alone. But it's always gratifying to have one's choices ratified." He picks up the book I was holding when he entered the room, "Furtim already? I hadn't realized you were that far along. I'll have to schedule your Bridging soon."

"Bridging?"

"Ceremony that officially promotes you to the next level on intusmagus. The first one typically happens when an apprentice bridges ink from one side of the body to the other. Depends on how they learn. There are many stages of

Bridging, all of which lead up to the highest level of Doyen. I'll arrange it for a day or two after we get back from the scavenge. You should be ready by then." The light blinks on the desk, signaling the end of the day. "Brew the ink for the Furtim group in the morning and I'll stamp you. Placement of ink on the neck, face and head can be problematic. We should probably talk about that sometime."

Chapter Nineteen

Two nights later, about thirty minutes after The
Mother's key clicks my door locked for the night, I hear
movement in the common room, and the handle of my door
begins to move slightly. A light pulses in the painted fist above
my door. The pinkie finger is glowing, signaling something in
our block has been tampered with. I slip out of bed and crouch
behind it, my heart pounding in my ears. I'm not sure why I'm
hiding. There's nowhere to go, no way to escape. I rack my
brain for something I have done to anger The Mothers,
anything that would call for the five in black to come to our
block. Are they here to force me to watch PG3456 tortured?
The door slowly opens and I'm about to scream when I see
Loshee's shaved head and strip of braids outlined in the dark.

"You could have told me it was tonight," I hiss at her.

"Did I scare ya?" she whispers back.

I grunt in reply and start pulling off my pajamas to get
dressed. "Not at all, I just don't have my suit with me. I left it in
my den," I say looking around for something appropriate to
wear in the ice cold dead of night.

"Gotcha covered," she replies as she tosses me a
wrapped bundle. "Juwas sends her compliments. You'll be
happy to know she finished Zink's pants too."

I unwrap the bundle to reveal a small knot of fabric loaded down with leather straps. Holding up the top, the straps seem to keep the fabric with gaping holes attached to the body. There certainly isn't enough actual shirt to stay on under its own power. "I'll freeze to death in this!" I say.

"Think Juwas didn't cover her bases? Wait until I tell her what little faith you have in her abilities. Just put the thing on and let's go. We will be late. Besides, there's a cloak in there."

Untangling the buckles and straps, I manage to get the new suit on without much struggle and I drape the cape around my shoulders. I pile my hair on the top of my head and shove the black diamond pin over my left ear on the way out of the common room door. As I follow closely behind Loshee, I don't recognize anything. In the fifteen and a half years I have lived in this building and traveled these halls, I have never once seen it in the dark. The city streets are stranger still. Every plant, building, and statue leers menacingly out at me from shadows.

We don't head north towards the Gratis Building, instead making our way due east to the checkpoint arch that looms imposingly over the first of two main gates leading to the outside world. Abbot, Zink, Journer and an older woman with snow-white hair I remember from the control nest after the simulation are waiting for us.

"This is Statric, Keres. She's leading the scavenge," Loshee says to me.

"Nice to have you with us, Keres. After your performance in the simulator, I'm confident you will be a valuable asset this evening," Statric says to me in a voice as

194

smooth as heavy cream. Her hair arrangement of three buns arcing across the top of her head like a crown doesn't distract from the long vertical scar that cuts her face perfectly in half. It travels down the center of her nose from far back under her hair line and ends in a deep X shape directly above her larynx. I suppress a shudder, thinking about what could possibly cause a scar like that.

"Thank you for the opportunity," I say to her. This seems to have been the right thing to say, as Statric smiles warmly at me and begins to arrange the packs. Abbot just rolls his eyes.

"Everyone ready? It's time to depart. Thank you for retrieving Keres, Loshee." Statric says. She looks up at the arch and waves a hand signal, a light blinks in a window, and the first gate opens enough to let us walk through single file. We walk across the huge holding yard, leaving Loshee under the arch, towards the second gate while the first one is closing behind us. Statric raises her hand to signal again, a light blinks in another window and the outer wall gate moans in protest. We pass through the opening and I find myself standing outside of Chelon for the first time in my life. Adrenaline blazes through me like a bullet train and I have to clench a strap on my suit to keep my hands from shaking. We walk across the rail tracks and into the thick woods on the other side.

I'm in the middle of the group, right behind Zink and in front of Abbot when I realize none of us have our weapons. I turn my head to say something to Abbot, when he puts his finger to his lips, signaling for me to stay quiet. We walk for several minutes, single file and silent. My nerves are on edge.

Even though the trees are close, knowing I am not contained by walls is making it difficult not to bolt for the mountains.

Our group comes to a stop and I lean out of the line to see around Zink. In the middle of a clearing is another Unspoken, leaning against a hitching post with six horses tied to it.

"Are we going to ride?" I say excitedly to Abbot.

"Yes, now be quiet."

The Unspoken unties a set of reins and holds them out to me. I walk to him silently and take them from him. My eyes travel the thin strip of leather up to the horse's nose, then to his eyes and over his body. He is the dappled gray horse from Fauna Management's entertainment at the Oath of Service feast night. I was right, the tip of his soft pink nose does just come to mine. I run my hand over his face and down his neck, instantly matching my breath to his.

"Whenever you're ready, Keres," Abbot says, already mounted on a solid black stallion that towers over my dapple gray. "We are here to wait on you."

I shoot a quick look of unabashed loathing at him and walk to the side of the dapple gray, unsure how to climb up in the saddle. The Unspoken who was waiting with the horses comes up behind me and shows me how to put my foot in the stirrup and swing my body over the saddle. "Thanks, uh-" I start to say, realizing I don't know his name.

"Holden," he supplies while looking down at his feet.

"Thanks, Holden," I settle into the saddle and grip the reins.

"Zink, if you would please," Statric says.

Zink touches a space of ink on his right thigh, sending a flow of sparkly gray smoke around the horses' hooves. Holden mounts the chestnut mare on my left and taps the rear flank of my horse with his hand. I hang onto the saddle horn for dear life, jerked backwards by the forceful takeoff. The landscape around me whips by in a creamy blur of greens and browns. I think we cross several rivers but I can't be certain. Zink and Journer ride in front of me. Zink's back is pitched slightly forward, one arm hanging relaxed at his side. He is completely at his ease on horseback, traveling faster than a bullet train. From my right, Abbot looks over at me and throws back his head laughing. My eyebrows furrowed, I press my lips together and grip the saddle tightly with my thighs and loosen my hold on the horn. I try to emulate Zink's posture, but keep both hands on the reins, resting them on the horn just in case I have to hang on tightly again.

The horses begin to slow an hour later as the edge of the woods rises on the horizon. When Journer and Zink part in front of me, I have to clap my hand over my mouth to keep from exclaiming. It's the most beautiful thing I have ever seen: a vast blue lake, the water sparkling like a thousand sapphires and diamonds in the moonlight, surrounded by a green field studded with patches of yellow and purple flowers. Rising up from the water, in the dead center of the lake is a figure of a man holding a trumpet to his mouth. Surrounding him are giant stone fish with the faces of birds, all of them spewing water from their open beaks. The air is crisp and dry. A soft breeze ripples the water and makes the flowers nod.

"Dismount, Keres, and get your weapons out of the saddlebag," Abbot commands me.

I slide off the saddle into Holden's outstretched hands and turn to the saddlebags to pull out my wristbows. Buckling them in place, I slowly spin on the spot, looking all around me. This place feels like magic.

"Watch where you step, Keres. Don't tread on the yellow flowers. They release a poisonous powder when you press the petals," Zink tells me as we drop the reins in the grass, leaving the horses to graze and catch their breath.

Statric gives us instructions on what we are to scavenge and we separate into three groups- Journer with Zink, Holden with Statric and Abbot with me. We don't spread out past the clearing, keeping each other within earshot and clear view. Abbot and I make our way to the lakeshore and look around for signs of sliver wheat growing under the soft sand. Abbot spots the oily bubbles popping through the ground first and has me dig around them with the silver trowel in my belt. He stands over me, his long bow primed, while I'm hunched over. I carefully make a trench around the bubbles so the sliver wheat can't escape when I scoop them up from the bottom. Sliding the plug of sand surrounding the sliver wheat into a bag from my belt, I move to the next patch of bubbles and repeat the process. Abbot keeps one leg touching my back throughout, swiveling his body around, watching the edge of the woods. Once, I feel his leg go stiff and I freeze, trowel poised in mid air, but he relaxes almost immediately and I press on. When I have collected seven plugs of sliver wheat, I stand and stretch my back taut.

A popping, snapping noise sounds like a shot and echoes around the clearing. Abbot swings around, pulling the string of his bow back so his hand is smashed against his cheek. I throw out my arms, aiming my wristbows at the sound as it travels from one side of the woods to the other. In the corner of my eye, Zink and Journer, who are out in the open, have flattened themselves to the ground. Holden has bolted to the horses, grabbing their reins and throwing a purple dome magus over all of them. Statric stands tall but very still, waiting for the popping sound to stop moving. My eyes are wide, as Abbot's breathing is heavy, waiting for something to appear.

The popping and snapping continues bouncing off the trees and the stone fountain in the middle of the lake, until I think I'll go mad trying to follow it. I'm about to scream at Abbot that I want to take cover somewhere, that it's insane to stand out in the open waiting to be attacked, when the noise starts moving through the woods and away from us. A silence even more disconcerting than the snapping settles over the clearing. Statric turns slowly in her spot, looking towards the sky. I follow her gaze and my mouth drops open. The entire coal black sky is dotted with millions of tiny white lights that blink on and off subtly.

"What are those, Abbot?" I whisper in awe.

"Stars," he answers just as quietly. We learn about stars in Pedagogics of course, but I have never seen them. The lights on the Chelon streets and buildings are so bright they white out the night sky and our windows are blacked out after power down. Nothing I have ever read or any picture I have seen in books compares to the enormity of the open sky overhead. I feel small and light. If I lift my feet to walk I'm sure I will fall upwards into the endless night.

"It's alright," Statric calls to us smoothly, "They've moved on. Has everyone gathered their elements?" We nod. "Excellent, please mount up. We have two additional locations to reach tonight."

Abbot pulls me forward, and we jog back to the horses. I secure the bags of sliver wheat in the saddlebags and let Holden help me mount again. Zink throws the sparkly gray smoke magus and we are flying through the woods once more. Stopping at a small creek to scrape up strips of purple spotted moss, we encounter nothing. The gurgling of the water spilling over the rocks makes a soothing noise that travels over the night air.

When we slow to our final stop, we are a few feet from a ring of smooth trees about eight feet tall. Their trunks and branches make them look like tall dancing women that have been frozen for all time in their fluid poses. Long lines of gracefully poised branches, their leaves flowing like hair, the dancing trees sway gently. A soft humming noise comes from somewhere in their trunks. A patch of white cone-shaped clusters of meadowsweet grows in the center of their eternal dancing circle. I start to dismount when Abbot grabs my arm, "No, let Statric."

Statric hands her horse's reins to Holden and dismounts in one swift movement. She walks silently to the circle of trees and holds her hands wide apart. After a pause, she steps deferentially in between two of the dancing women. She snips each flower cluster and smells it deeply before laying them carefully in a box lined with silk, as if they were alive. She makes an exaggerated effort to show visible appreciation of each cutting. When she backs out of the circle, she takes the exact path she used when she entered, and bows low once she is clear of the trees.

She remounts and we slowly walk the horses away from the tree circle. Statric makes sure it is out of sight before we break into a gallop again. We have been traveling at a breakneck speed for twenty or so minutes on the way back to Chelon when Holden is suddenly snatched upward off his mare, his boot grazing my face as he flails wildly. I scream and pull back on the reins. Abbot's glowing green arrow is already in the trees searching for Holden. I trace my Demoror tattoo and cast a wide net over the area, hoping to trap whatever took Holden. Statric and Journer are climbing the tree, jumping from limb to limb, chasing him down. The horses snort and stomp at the unexpected stop. There is too much noise. I can't hear what Journer is saying. Abbot sends another arrow high into the trees; it's answered with a sharp, high-pitched bark and something races down the tree trunk towards us. A beast springs off the trunk with colossal haunches as Zink pulls his short sword from its sheath. He jabs it straight at the mass of matted brown fur. Just before his sword enters the horrific animal's chest, it splits into three separate blades which glow blue, green and purple. Zink pulls his sword out and turns the creature over on its back.

"Hecate," he tells Abbot, then in answer to my quizzical look, "Climbing wolf."

201

"Better burn it before its mate finds the corpse," Abbot says. Zink drags the animal a few feet away from the horses and Abbot lights it on fire with the ink between his eyes. The body of the hecate burns to ashes instantly.

I turn my head upward, combing the branches for any sign of Holden and the others.

"Over there," Zink says, pointing to a tree about ten feet away. Journer and Statric are helping Holden negotiate the last of the branches, his neck and shoulder are spurting blood between his fingers.

"Zink, he needs you," Journer says urgently.

Zink is already at their sides, helping the convulsing Holden to lie on the ground.

"All that blood is invitation to dinner," Abbot says under his breath. "Statric, help me set up a wide shield." Abbot hands the horse reins to me and walks in a circle around us with Statric throwing magus with both hands, building a large shelter around us.

Zink sits with the bottoms of his feet pressed together. The new pants Juwas has made for him billow out, exposing his entire leg on two sides. His hands move rapidly over his thighs and calves, his entire lower body glowing as the ink morphs from patterns into their real images. I watch the flesh on Holden's neck slide back into place, the blood surging from his wound subsides and his body relaxes. Zink works over him for several tense minutes before he rubs his palms. "It was deep, very deep. I got the muscle back though. He shouldn't scar much. You got him down just in time."

I am surprised to see tears in Statric's eyes. She blots at them with the back of her hand and bends down over Holden. "Do you think you're able to ride now?" she asks him gently.

"With you? Always," he answers, opening his eyes to look at her. Statric leans further into him and kisses him tenderly on the mouth. I look away quickly, not understanding what I just saw. Even if they were Banded, a display of affection like that in front of all of us is bordering on vulgarity.

Abbot steps around me and helps Holden to his feet. Abbot lifts Holden onto the saddle right behind Statric. Holden wraps his arms around Statric's waist and rests his head on her shoulder. She takes his chestnut mare's reins in one hand while holding on to her own horse's with the other. The rest of us mount and Journer takes down the shield with a wave of her hand. Statric turns to look at me, "Was it you who threw the net?"

"Yes, I didn't know what else to do," I try to explain, knowing that my inept attempt to help must have gotten in their way as they fought through the trees.

"It was exactly right. A second later or an inch shorter and Holden-" her voice fails her and she reaches out to pat my leg. "Thank you," she mouths to me, Holden's head still resting on her shoulder. I grasp her hand in mine and the horses start galloping back to Chelon.

#

Still riding high on nervous energy built up from the scavenge, I persuade PG3456 to go sledding with me that

203

evening after dinner. I spent most of the morning and afternoon catching up on sleep on the sofa in my den. Abbot asked for some sketches of ideas for my hairstyle to use while he works out the details of my Bridging ceremony. Curled up in the overstuffed chairs, Zink and I went through my notebook and picked three of our favorites to present to Abbot.

The snow that has accumulated over the last two weeks is thick and soft, perfect for the blades of the sleds. In the last hours of daylight, we race down the hills until our faces are raw with cold and our lips chapped from smiling. We are, for a moment, seven years old again. The greatest tragedy we knew was going to bed without dinner.

Trudging back to the block, Frehn's arm laced through mine suddenly goes rigid. I look up and see PG3453 walking towards their residence compound, Sotter trailing them by a few feet.

When they cross our path, her open pack drops off her shoulder, spilling its contents in the snow. She hurries to shove the books and papers back inside while she waves her Play Group on. She doesn't look in our direction, and quickly runs to catch up with PG3453. Before we reach the spot Sotter's pack fell, Frehn leans down to adjust his shoe and switches sides of the road with me. He walks firmly the rest of the way to our residence compound, pressing his boots deep into the snow. Once inside the doors, he bends down to adjust his shoe again, mumbling, "Six weeks old and the laces are already fraying on these boots."

We change our wet coats and pants for pajamas, then meet in the common room to warm our hands around the crackling fire. Wex raises an eyebrow at Frehn and they both turn to look at me.

"There's nothing here, it's clean," I tell them. Looking up at the painted thumbs-out-fist over my door has become instinct now. Except for last night when Loshee picked the lock on my door, the fingers have always remained dark and black. But I never leave my bedroom without looking up at it.

Frehn looks back to Wex, "Poy will be able to do it. She's a Keeper assigned to mechanics. She's willing."

A wide grin spreads over Wex's face, "That's one hurdle cleared then."

"Which one is Poy?" asks Harc with narrowed eyes.

"The tallest girl in PG3453, red hair. She can disable the bullet train to the mines."

Merit's eyes dance at this news, "And you said she's willing? They will come with us?"

"Pretty eager to, I'd say," Frehn answers rubbing his hands close to the flames and putting them to Doe's cheeks. Each member of PG3453 has interacted with at least one of us by now. Poy and I have met in the Keepers' building when I needed to replenish my cleaning bucket supplies. We walked through the halls together and have been distantly friendly ever since. Revvim has raced across the icy river against Frehn and me half a dozen times. He and Frehn are like copies of each other and a handful to keep in order. Impossible to keep on task and always building private jokes together.

"I've been moved from shoveling manure," Merit says suddenly, almost shyly.

"What are you doing now, Merit?" I ask, waiting for the worst.

"Training horses to harness."

The room explodes as we all react to this bombshell. Harc tackles him with an engulfing hug and Frehn thumps him on the back. Doe claps her hands and squeals while Wex and I whoop in excitement.

"How did you move up so fast?" Wex asks him when we calm down enough to hear each other.

"A girl from PG3442 got demoted, rumor is she tried to eat the horses' carrots and sugar because her rations were cut by The Mothers. So my leader suggested they give me a shot. I started this afternoon."

Harc is radiant as she beams at Merit with unembarrassed pride. She clutches his hand in both of hers, perched on her knees, drinking in his every word. He flicks his eyes up to her face as he talks, reading her reactions. I lean back into Frehn and watch them together. I know nothing about love, nothing about passion for someone else. But twice in twenty-four hours, I have seen both.

Chapter Twenty

When I return to my den after lunch the next day, I find
Juwas standing in the middle of the room with copious
amounts of plush fabrics draped over her arms.

"Dress you," Juwas says as I walk towards her.

"Is this another suit, Juwas? I've only worn the new one
once. I don't think I'm ready for an upgrade."

"Nuh," she grunts back, holding up a flowing length of
soft white velvet. The edge she displays to me has thousands of
minute glass beads sewn in designs around the hem.
"Bridging," she says, pushing me towards the wardrobe area.

I take off my everyday clothes and she slips a long sky
blue dress over my head. The left shoulder is cut away and the
sleeves open at the tops of my arms, the fabric brushing the
floor. It's clearly been designed to leave each of my tattoos
perfectly exposed. Juwas covers the blue dress with the white
velvet cape trimmed in beads. She pins it shut with a ring clasp,
her milk-white eyes pointed everywhere but at her hands.

"Down, can't reach," Juwas rasps, holding out a hair
brush. I kneel down just as I did months ago in my stiff silk
robes, waiting for The Mother to collect me for the Oath of
Service. Juwas pulls my hair down and brushes it, leaving it to
fall around my face and down my back. In the mirror in front

of me, I take in the white cape contrasting with my cascading black hair, like a bed of coal on snow, the length of velvet pooling behind me. My eyes rest on the ring clasp attached to the collar of the cape. An enameled hand with the palm facing up crosses the diameter of the silver circle. The fingers curl over, gripping the opposite edge. A gold swirling leaf pattern is embedded in the circumference of the circle. Juwas finishes brushing my hair and runs her hands down it to be sure it's smooth, then secures the black diamond pin over my left ear. That done, she starts to shuffle towards the door.

"Thank you, Juwas," I call after her.

She replies with an indiscernible noise as she leaves the den and Abbot enters. Abbot stops short, looking at me kneeling on the floor before the mirror. His eyes rest for a moment on my hair as a mournful expression rolls across his face.

"They're ready," he says after he has cleared his throat. He holds a hand out to me and I take it, getting to my feet. He leads me through the Warren door and down the hall. We stop at a set of large arched doors I've passed countless times but never been through. Zink told me once they only opened to a meeting room.

"Remember to breathe and don't lock your knees," Abbot says to me, then he raises his fist to bang on the door. It silently opens allowing us to enter, my white cape trailing behind like an icy waterfall.

The room is dimly lit with large candles on pillars outlining the aisle Abbot leads me down. Unspoken stand just out of their eerie light, bodies visible but faces hidden in dark shadow. I look towards the ceiling as we walk slowly through the candles and see a mass of woodwork beams, arching like a ribcage across the entire room. Abbot steps to the side when we reach the end of the aisle, leaving me in the center to face a moat of water surrounding a two-tiered dais. A bridge connects the floor of the room to the dais where three Unspoken stand in a triangle. They must be the Doyens- all of them have ink across their lined necks and faces.

"I give you Keres," Abbot says in a clear, obsequious voice that echoes off the concave ceiling. His voice, the reverent tone and his perfect posture make me more ill at ease than the crowd does, the eldritch candlelight or the triangle of wizened Doyens.

"Does she come with will?" the Doyen in the center asks.

"She does," Abbot responds.

"Does she come with knowledge?"

"She does."

"Does she come with hope?"

"She does."

"Let her cross."

Abbot puts his hands out and helps me across the bridge and then to kneel on the first tier of the dais.

"Keres, you have walked across the bridge which spans the gap of knowledge. Walk with us now, across primordial rites of passage," the Doyen says as she signals to someone standing just out of sight.

A woman steps towards me from the left of the Doyen triangle, holding a tray laden with pins, combs, and different-sized rods. She rests it before me and begins to run her fingers through my hair, arranging it, as the Doyen in the center continues.

"We are the Tutelas, the keepers of Great Secrets. We desire only to protect the ancient knowledge of our ancestors. And though we are burdened with this great and terrible knowledge, we have control over but one thing. Ourselves. The abilities bestowed on our bodies is a gift, a curse, and a heavy responsibility. Our race is tied with an unbreakable cord to the duties of our charge. By protecting the Great Secrets, we ultimately protect the human race." The Doyen in the center turns to the one on her left. He steps forward and places a large silver ring on my head and the woman arranging my hair begins to wrap curls and braids around it.

"It is not our aim to seek power. It is not our goal to gain dominance. We remain underground, untouched and unspoken by those uninitiated. We live by two words-Secretum et Sacrificio."

"Secretum et Sacrifico," repeats the entire room of Unspoken in unison, their voices loud and teeming with passion.

"Secrecy and Sacrifice," the Doyen lifts her arms and a hundred candles flare up, flooding the room with light. The Doyen on the right steps forward and holds out two silver feet that look like they belonged to a huge bird-reptile crossbreed. The claws extended as if they are about to rip apart prey. He leans over me and fastens them to the ring, clamping it to my hair.

"Keres, step into the light," the Doyen beckons me to the center of the top tier of the dais. Abbot helps me stand again and walks forward with me, my hand gripped in his. As I turn to face the crowd of Unspoken- the crowd of Tutelas- the cape swirling around my feet, a beam of light creates a perfect circle of white on the dark floor, engulfing me and sending the rest of the dais into darkness.

"And so begins the New World," the Doyen says. All three of them step back so Abbot and I are the only people in the light. Abbot holds my hand high, then brings it to his lips. He kisses it while sliding a silver ring with a center line of golden leaves over my thumb, then swings my hand up over my head again. The crowd erupts into tumultuous applause. The noise is deafening, reverberating across the ribcage ceiling and echoing down the walls. When I look into the faces of the forty or fifty Tutelas, I read joy and pride and relief and- maybe hope? I wonder if Zink received the same treatment at his Bridging. Something isn't right about the looks in their eyes. Some seem as if they are alive for the first time, others are swimming in anxiety. It doesn't feel like a simple rite of passage ceremony anymore. It feels like a hero's welcome. A savior's greeting.

Abbot leads me out of the room, almighty cheers and deafening applause on either side of the aisle. The door shuts behind us, silencing everything. My face feels flushed with the rush of emotions and I put my hands to my cheeks. The silver ring is cold against my chin.

"Come on, let's get you off the Warren before the masses unleash and everyone wants a piece of you," Abbot says. He has dropped the reverent attitude he held during the ceremony and is back in his rough manner as if nothing happened.

"Is everyone's like..." I ask him breathlessly as I try to keep pace with him. The weight of the dress and cape slow me down. I've become used to wearing suits with light or little material. This velvet feels like it is as heavy as I am.

"That was a little, uh, embellished. And it's not usual for the entire Warren to turn up at these."

"Is it because I'm the Catalyst, like Juwas says?"

Abbot doesn't answer me and we reach my den. I stand, draped in a cape and dress that look like they are from another time, and stare at him stubbornly waiting for his reply.

"Abbot, please," I say in a low thick voice, tears pricking at my eyes. "Please. What is it that I am expected to do?"

"Secretum et Sacrificio. That is something for which you are not yet ready to know," he says heavily. "They should not have treated your Bridging like you were a sacrificial lamb," he says with a hiss.

"I- what? Sacrifice? Are they going to sacrifice me? Kill me?" I squeak in disbelief.

"No, no, nothing so simple."

"What then...am I never to know what it is I'm supposed to be?"

Abbot looks, his eyes drowning in a deep well of wretchedness, "These are things that would destroy you," he whispers. "Things far beyond The Mothers, things far beyond the torture they inflict. It's coming, Keres. But not now, not yet. You have too much to learn first."

"What can I do, Abbot? What can I do to get there?" I plead. I have to know what I am. What is happening to me? How does being the Catalyst impact our escape? It becomes instantly and excruciatingly clear to me. It means that not only The Mothers will pursue us, but all the Tutelas as well. And if that's true, then I am endangering PG3456 and PG3453 by going with them. They would never outrun the Unspoken. We would be brought back, and they would be turned over to The Mothers and undoubtedly killed in a intensely public and immensely heinous way. I would be protected from death of course, since I am the Catalyst. I will be forced to live like a horrible hybrid of Abbot and Juwas, imprisoned in the Warren with the knowledge that my own actions brought the death of eleven innocent people, friends I love with my whole self.

I will have to help them escape, then go underground in the Warren. It's better to be sequestered by choice than by force. I can help Juwas and live here until my ultimate destiny as the Catalyst is fulfilled, whatever it is. Then I will either join them on the outside or be dead. Either is preferable to this awful purgatory of ignorance and doubt.

"Keep learning," Abbot says simply, roughly. "We can start with containing the magus in your palm without holding your fingers over it. It's high time you stopped throwing like a child with training wheels. But first, change. We have training."

My hour of being the white cape clad savior of the Unspoken is gone. Abbot barks at me through the bathroom door as I buckle the last straps of my new suit, the Bridging dress on the floor.

#

At dinner a few weeks after my Bridging, Wex's leg bounces nervously. Under the table, I put my hand on his knee to steady it and opt to leave it there when it works. And because I like the way it feels. Who knows how much longer I will be able to touch him before they make their escape. I push the thought away and look across the table to see Frehn, who is openly staring at my neck. Ever since I was stamped with the Furtim tattoo, a beautiful fox whose bushy tail wraps down my neck and weaves into the woman's hair on my shoulder, I have caught both Frehn and Wex gaping at it with their lips parted and their eyes glazed over. It's like the swirling paisley pattern the fox becomes when not in use holds both Wex and Frehn in a trance. I tug the collar of my shirt up to cover some of the pattern and try to break Frehn's gaze.

As soon as I do, he shakes his head a little and says, "Learned a new song today." That's enough to get everyone to wolf down the rest of their sweet potatoes and head quickly to the block. Once secured in our common room, Wex pulls out a dozen tiny envelopes from his boots and holds them out to Merit with quivering hands.

"Seeds, to add to the stash," Wex says.

"How-" begins Harc, her eyes wide with alarm.

"Just one from each pack in storage," he quickly reassures her. "Took me three months to get them all. There is

214

no way for them to find out. We don't count the seeds, just weigh them. And I made sure that each pack weighed the same. I hid mine under a board in the storage room so if they were missed, they could have just fallen through the cracks in the floor. But no one noticed they were gone, even after the inventory check last week. So I thought it was safe to get them out."

Merit presses the thin envelopes between the pages of his notebook and stores them in his pack. "The only thing we are missing from the stash is something to protect us," he says, "and that will have to wait until we are on the outside, I guess." He glances furtively at me and I realize they are all counting on me to keep them alive when we go over the wall. And I can't do that if I've gone underground in the Warren. Rocks in the pit of my stomach are becoming a consistent feeling for me. Every time the plan comes up, which is every night lately, my internal organs contract into wicked shapes. I will just have to find a way to get them weapons, real ones, before they escape. If Poy was able to find a way to disable the bullet train, then I can find a way to protect them.

As Frehn tunes up, Doe sits at his feet with a Healer's book, and Harc and Merit arrange the fire. My heart skips a beat when Wex touches my arm and nods over to the other side of the room. I follow him to the window seat, feeling Frehn's eyes watching us. Sitting down, I look up at Wex expectantly, a nervous smile on my lips.

"You seem to have new tattoos every day now," he says, touching my newest pattern on my right wrist. It was the last one I needed to complete my right arm sleeve. Tomorrow I am

215

supposed to finally start working on different throwing
techniques. Abbot wavers between wanting me covered in as
much ink as possible and learning to escalate my ability with
each nerve group.

Wex's fingers travel to my neck and he moves them
over my fox tattoo as if he's trying to smooth the wrinkles out
of his bed sheets. The hair on the back of my neck stands
straight up. Frehn begins to play in the background but Wex
and I stay on the window seat, his hand on my neck.

I'll meet you under the tall corn stalks
Away from those who watch
I'll meet you under the towering stair
Away from he who sleeps
I'll meet you under the heavy cart there
Away from she who weeps

"Frehn's right, they are pretty. He says they are
intoxicating. Soft on you somehow. I can't stop looking at
them. Or you." I'm breathing short, shallow breaths. The rocks
in my stomach have turned into birds which are beating their
wings rapidly around.

Come to me under the blanket of dark
Where I will fold you deep
Come to me under the guise of light
Where I'll shelter you for keeps
Come to me under under the eyes of Might
Where I will hold you tight

"When we leave here, Keres, I want to start a new life. A new civilization. With all twelve of us going, we can start a new city together. One that's ruled by just compassion, establish a rotating council as a government, each one of us having a vote in all the decisions," he says, moving both his hands to cup my face.

Meet me under the tributary floor
Where we will yearn no more
Meet me under the layer of wood
Where our pain can be withstood
Meet me under the cold earthen mound
Where we can sleep a-crowned

He lowers his voice to a whisper, "Except for Banding. I want to choose who I'm Banded to, Keres, don't you?" He leans his head close to mine, his breath is warm and buttery like the sweet potatoes we had for dinner. Something hot burns through my chest and throat and I close my eyes as his nose comes so close to mine it's no longer in focus.

The common room door tone sounds and two Mothers bustle in, one with plates of marshmallows and chocolate and the other with skewers. Wex had leapt up at the sound so fast, he was at the fireplace before the door even opened, leaving me leaning forward slightly with my eyes shut and lips extended. Blazing hexes, how do they always know the perfect moment to interrupt?

"A little late night treat for you, dears!" trills a Mother waving her skewers. "We thought it would be so fun for you to roast them in your fires on such a cold night."

"Thank you, Mother," Harc says sweetly.

"Oh, yes, thank you!" everyone choruses.

The Mothers arrange the plates and skewers around the fireplace and give a long list of reminders not to get burned, not to drop anything on the rugs, and not to eat too much. They go around the room straightening pillows and books while Harc and Frehn make an effort to start roasting the marshmallows in apparent raptures. Wex keeps his back to me in the window seat.

"Keres, dear, don't you want a treat?" one of The Mothers says while she rearranges the cushions around me and turns on the lamp.

I jump up with a, "thank you," and a quick, "yes, please," and hurry over to the fireplace to join Harc in ooing and ahing over the chocolate. When The Mothers finally leave the common room, we put down the skewers and Frehn picks up his fiddle again. All of us exhale in collective relief. No reasons to watch the notice board for punishments in the morning.

Doe curls around Frehn's feet, Merit and Harc sit on the hearth so close to each other you couldn't shove a piece of paper between them. Wex sinks onto the floor. He reaches up putting his hand in mine and pulls me down into his lap encircling me with his arms, his nose tickling the little curls of hair around my ear. I lean into him listening to Frehn's song, smelling the toasted marshmallows and watching Doe sway to the music as she gazes up at Frehn. What was I thinking when I decided to let them go without me? There aren't five people on earth more important to me than the ones in this room. I am the only one who can protect them- from The Mothers, from the Unspoken if they follow us, from the strange creatures in the woods- from everything. Even if they escape The Mothers, they wouldn't last two days against beasts like the hecates. Catalyst or not, there's no way I'm sending them to face their deaths alone. If we die, we die together. And it won't be at the hands of The Mothers.

Chapter Twenty-One

In the Warren the next morning, I head straight for the target range. Loshee is already there practicing with her staff against an unending stream of overlarge barrel-chested dogs. I watch her quietly from the door until the run is over. Her braids swing as though caught up in a crosswind. For someone so small, she covers a huge amount of space between magus throws. Spinning and flipping as if war is a dance performance, she twists and bends creating beautiful lines with her body as different colors of light leave her palms and staff. The lights of magus explode like fireworks when they come in contact with their targets. She's using more flash than force, but if her targets are human, they will be transfixed by her movement. Just as I am now.

The last dog erupts in a shower of fire and purple sparks as Loshee's magus hits it in the chest. The force of impact sends a wind around the room, and it grinds across my forehead like hot sand.

"Hiya," Loshee says, straightening up. Her eyes change from wild to teasing the instant she sees me in the door. "Saw your Play Group at breakfast this morning."

"I didn't see you," I answer.

"That's because you were looking too closely at someone else, someone with biceps the size of tree trunks. How did you get all the luck landing in a PG with two out of three guys who are drool-worthy?"

"Uh-" I stumble over words trying to think of something to say. It's common knowledge that Wex and Frehn are the envy of every girl in our year. They wish Wex and Frehn were in their Play Groups so they would have a chance at being Banded to them, but that's as far as any talk goes.

"They are just kids, of course. But the chances of them going backwards up the ugly pipe are next to nil. By the time they are eighteen, I'll be shocked if someone hasn't gotten a handful."

My entire face and neck have to be beet red. Embarrassment from partially understanding her meaning covers me in confusion. I fumble with my wristbows, trying to buckle and unbuckle them at the same time. Loshee eyes me attentively for a moment.

"Listen," she starts, "just because The Mothers dictate who we are Banded to, doesn't mean we aren't all feeling the same things. And a Banded partner who is forced on me is not stopping me from noticing, and acting, on what I feel. Same goes for most everyone." She shrugs, "Just gotta be sure they don't catch on."

"You mean, you kiss boys you aren't Banded to? Who aren't even in your Play Group?" My mind is reeling. The only real kiss I have ever gotten resulted in a two year solitary confinement. Frehn kisses me all the time on the cheek and hands. He's been paying more attention to me since I have

221

started gathering ink. Each time his lips come in contact with my skin, I break out in goosebumps.

Loshee just laughs and grabs my wrists to fix the mess I've made of the straps. "Keres, open your eyes. The Mothers can't control what anyone thinks and feels, just our actions when we get caught. So we don't get caught. Tree Trunk Arms serves in the mines right? Listen to some of his stories and songs sometime. Really listen. They'll tell you everything you need to know. All set," she gives my hip a pat, "Let's see what you can do with two arms of ink. Try combining multiple nerve groups for one magus to send through the wristbows or send one magus pull through both wristbows at the same time, see what that gets ya."

Loshee pushes me to the limit in combinations and tumbling around the room to keep from being hit by oncoming targets. She shows me how to throw magus mid-somersault while blocking advancing targets. By noon I am able to throw various combinations of magus. One of my favorites from the day is the sharp curved knives which cover the target in a thick layer of ice, created by pulling from the double blade dagger tattoo on my lower right arm and from the face blowing snow and frost on my upper arm.

Walking to the canteen for lunch, I become acutely aware of people. I have never looked beyond PG3456 before. Our group was enough for me, enough for each of us. Now, as I walk the streets of Chelon, it is apparent that we are the exception rather than the rule. Pairs of men and women covertly hold hands and touch each other, others simply look on in a daze. Girls and women giggle to their friends as men walk by and smile at them. When a Mother comes into sight, everyone in the vicinity instantly, seamlessly melds into their groups of six. As The Mother passes on, the pretense is dropped and everyone relaxes back into cross-Play Group interaction.

"What are you looking at, Keres?" Frehn has come up beside me without my noticing.

"People. I've never really seen them before."

"I can tell you anything you want to know. I've been watching them my whole life." And he has, looking for his twin. He was always watching people while looking for Sotter.

"Do they actually have friends outside of their Play Groups?"

"All the time."

"Why don't we?"

"Don't need to, we got lucky. We are the best looking PG in the city. We are also the most intelligent. We all get along. We don't need to find stimulation outside of the six of us."

"Stimulation?"

"Keres, do we need to have the procreation talk again? You see a boy has a-"

"NO!" I say loudly, with firm decision, "I mean, no. No, I don't need to hear about procreation again."

"Do you want to know about kissing?" his voice is low and intensely deep all of a sudden.

"I-" I don't know what to say. My palms are clammy and Frehn is exceptionally close to me. "I do, yes. But not about the way Banded partners go about it. I mean, do people truly kiss each other outside of their own PG? Have you?"

Frehn pulls me behind a building into a clump of thick trees and swings me around so my back is against an elm. He leans one hand on the trunk and sort of purrs in my ear, "Maybe."

"Why? Why not just kiss us? I can't even imagine what The Mothers would do if they caught you with someone outside our Play Group. At least if it was Harc or Doe or me, it would be a simple, straightforward, non-painful, consequence. I mean, you'll be Banded to one of us eventually and you'll have to kiss us then."

"Maybe none of you have wanted to kiss me yet. Maybe somebody else did. Maybe I wanted a kiss so badly, I couldn't say no," his voice turns to gravel and I can smell the mine on him, sweat and rock. The gold dust on his neck glimmers a little in the late afternoon sun. His mouth is as close to mine as Wex's was last night.

"Don't you love Doe?" I ask.

"More than anything."

"Then why are you kissing other girls?"

"Because she doesn't love me. Not that way. She idolizes me like one of the ancient gods and that's not what I want, godlike as I am."

"What do you want? Assuming you have a choice."

"Someone strong. Someone with fire for blood. Someone fragile. Someone who looks at me with starving eyes. Someone who can put me in my place. Someone with a tattoo I'm dying to taste."

224

"Frehn?"

"Keres?" his bottom lip brushes against mine as he says my name.

"Do you want to kiss me?"

"More than anything."

"You'll have to catch me first," I duck quickly out from under his arm and run at top speed towards the Quad. I hear him curse as I take off. Frehn chasing me, his laughter mingling with mine as I slam into Wex, just emerging from the canteen to look for us.

"There you are, we've got a table on the far end," he says, pointing. "What's so funny?"

"Nothing," Frehn and I say together, trying to stifle giggles.

Wex looks at us suspiciously, but as he is about to open his mouth to say something, a pack of Mothers glides up to the canteen and Wex is forced to hold the door for them with a polite smile. Frehn and I follow them in, Wex hot on our heels. Sitting at the table between Doe and Merit, directly across from Wex, I can feel his foot tapping against my shoe. He's nervous about something. Frehn is deep in conversation with Harc about the prospect of a netball game against PG3453 that evening, winking when he catches my eye. I grin and turn my attention to the bowl of shellfish and vegetable stew on my tray. I feel almost giddy looking at this new world of interaction that has opened before me.

I meet Zink on the way back to the hall after lunch. I ask him what he thinks of Loshee on our way down in the elevator. I want to know if this notion of love and desire is something that only people like Loshee and Frehn know, the people who are confident in who they are, the ones who know how they fit into the makeup of Chelon.

"She's just after some fun. Her Banded partner is not a nice guy I hear and she doesn't get a lot of support from her Play Group, so it's understandable," he says offhandedly. Thinking about Loshee being Banded and therefore possibly already having a child makes my stomach clench. I can't picture her as part of anything but the weapons hall. Loshee as anything but a hyperactive humming bird armed to the teeth is unimaginable.

"She's harmless, just likes to talk. But I wouldn't be on the receiving end of her staff for anything in the world. Journer tried to get her to help me with the offensive magus like Abbot has you doing, but I wouldn't go near her alone. She wanted to go hand-to-hand with me, so to speak," he says ending in a laugh. Zink savors the memory of hand-to-hand combat with Loshee for the rest of the ride down, a sly smile perched on his lips. His mouth works like he is rolling the image of Loshee around on his tongue, tasting every aspect of her.

Abbot is waiting for me in my den with a stack of books and charts on the desk. While I'm changing, I can hear him bang nails as he starts hanging the charts around the walls.

"Time to take off those training wheels, Keres," he announces when I open the bathroom door.

"I'm ready."

"You aren't, but that's neither here nor there," he scoffs. "Your body is in the best shape it can be now, so it's time we caught your throwing up to speed. An intusmagus should be in complete control at all times. Over your emotions, over your power, over every aspect of throwing magus. We all start by learning to pull a magus with our thumbs, holding it in our palms with four fingers until we are ready to throw it. Right?"

"Yes,"

"That was rhetorical, don't interrupt. Now that your body has caught up to your ability, we can start pulling magus with fingertips. They are harder to control than the thumb because they are more sensitive and they are further away from the palm." He is pointing to different parts of the charts as he talks. He assumes I'm following every word. I, however, am completely lost.

"You trace the tattoos with your thumb to activate the ink, with the fingertips you brush over the ink, flicking the magus up to your palm. Watch me." Abbot brushes the ink on his arm lightly with his fingers and a set of glowing black throwing knives shoot from his palm into the center of the practice target at the back of the room. "It's the same principle as pulling the magus through your weapon. We are applying that to our fingertips instead." he says moving around the desk.

"I'm not even sure how I do that," I say.

"Doesn't matter. Point is, you can do it. So you can do this. Magus becomes weaker as it travel through the thumb and is held in the palm. The longer it spends between the ink and the target, the less effective it becomes. And milliseconds count tenfold. With the fingers, you flick it up in its raw form and throw it twice as fast. Downside is-"

"There's always a downside," I interrupt.

Abbot glares at me, "Downside is, it burns twice as hot."

"I can handle pain," I say, squaring my shoulders.

"Let's hope so," he says, more to himself than to me.

I move to the center of the room and try brushing a Contundo magus off my right shoulder.

"Fingertips only, Keres, you aren't cleaning crumbs off your sweater," Abbot says, pinching the bridge of his nose.

I try again, this time lightly grazing the absolute ends of my fingers across the snake that winds around my shoulder. As my palm comes up, a jet of dense green and brown smoke shoots forward wrapping around the target, crushing it in two. At the same time, I fall to the floor pressing my hand to the still-glowing ink. Something must have gone wrong, my shoulder feels like it's burning from the inside out. I expect my hand to be bloody, even coated in pus, when I pull it away, but there's nothing on it. Abbot nudges my head and holds out a wet cloth to me.

"It's cold," he says.

I press the icy cloth to my blistering shoulder and bite my lip to keep from whimpering.

"Tried to warn you."

"You said twice. That was a lot more than twice," I say tremulously.

"I may have misspoke."

"Misspoke or misled?"

"Same thing."

Unbelievable. "Does it hurt less the more you do it? Like getting stamped?" I ask hopefully.

"Nope. Like red hot irons every time," he says with satisfaction. "Sometimes more, depending on the magus. You just learn to deal with it. Seven months ago, the burn would have spread through your whole body, not just the nerve group you used. Muscle mass acts like a firewall, keeps the heat from spreading. When you've finished 'handling the pain,' Keres, I'm ready to watch you try again."

I struggle to my feet, inwardly cursing his unknown mother for giving birth to him, and begin again. I alternate between different nerve groups this time and allow the Contundo group to cool off. As my body burns internally, my suit starts to cool down. The fabric begins to feel like soothing aloe and ice against my raging skin. The hotter my skin becomes, the more comfortable the suit feels against it. I make a mental note to kiss Juwas' feet before sunset.

Alternating magus and applying the icy cloth, I practice for hours while Abbot directs me. He shouts orders to correct my form, peppered with the occasional word of praise. I am able to throw a magus from every one of my tattoos in quick succession before we stop for the day. Pouring sweat, I catch my reflection on the way to the bathroom and pause. My body is actually smoking. Every bit of ink is glowing, curling gray smoke winding upwards from my exposed skin. In the dim light of the den I look like a chunk of lava cooling off. I sizzle when the cold water from the shower hits my body, washing the faint smell of burnt flesh down the drain.

#

A few days later, Wex and I are the only ones who stay for the game of Viking on the slushy lawn after dinner. I'm jumpy from the long day of pulling magus with my fingertips. Pain still echoes around my body, and I need to relieve the tension built up in my muscles. Wex stays with me when the others protest against the cold. We are well into early spring and the melting snow and ice make everything damp and uncomfortable.

"That's all your shields down!" Wex calls to the two members of PG3460 across the field, and he takes aim for the king block in the center. He launches his wooden battle axe game piece in a perfect underhanded arc, knocking the king block neatly over to one side. We trot out to the center of the pitch to shake hands with our opponents, then gather our packs from the nearby benches.

"Good throw," I say to Wex, taking a long drought of water from my bottle.

"Thanks, not bad yourself. Except, of course, that unfortunate overthrow that nearly took out the girl."

"Don't know my own strength I guess."

"I find that hard to believe."

I keep my eyes on my shoes as we walk across the recreational field to our residence compound.

"Let's walk a little, ok?" he says to me as we reach the compound's glass doors.

"Ok," I say uneasily.

"We have another hour of light and I'm not ready to go in yet." He leads me in an about-face and we walk towards the back gardens, past the flower-shaped Pedagogics building and

230

into the rows of early blooming cherry trees. I hold my hand out to brush the low hanging branches, sending a shower of light pink petals over us as we walk.

"Keres, I think we are close to being ready."

I stop mid-step, "For what?"

"To leave," he says, lowering his voice to something below a whisper.

"Oh, right," I say, walking again. I'm not sure what I thought he meant, but whatever it was, I am relieved that it was something else entirely.

"We have enough food for the first three months, seeds to plant when we get far enough away to set up a temporary camp, vessels to hold and purify water, Harc's factory odds and ends to help build shelter, Doe's knowledge of healing, Merit is working on a plan to get horses out. He found the door in the outer wall over the river yesterday."

"He did?"

"Told me when we were taking inventory of the stash. And PG3453 has finished with their side of the plan. Poy has a way to disarm the bullet train. Drim, Flast and Som have worked out a brilliant diversion for The Mothers to give us extra time. We just need to work out the timing."

"Great," I say trying to sound pleased.

"There's really only one thing keeping us from moving."

"What's that?"

"You."

"Me? But I'm ready!"

Wex shakes his head, "You aren't. You are less ready every day. The more ink you have, the more attached to your

Service you become. We all see it. You don't want to leave anymore."

"I do want to leave. I just don't know if I can." The black smoke fingers of my guard tattoo press into my chest, signaling the need for caution.

"Doe says they will pursue you. She thinks they will kill anything that gets in the way to get you back. But she won't say how she knows. Healers learn a lot of things in their building, I imagine the Unspoken get sick and hurt too."

I say nothing at first and break a branch of blossoms off a tree as we pass, twirling the stick in my hand.

"I'm not leaving you." I say.

"And if they chase you?"

"I will run faster."

Wex grabs my shoulder to stop me from walking forward and whirls me around, looking straight into my eyes.

"Are you ready to risk that? Risk being killed for your friends, by your friends? There's no pretending that we can do this without you. And there's no pretending that you don't care for them the same way you care for us. But we will not survive on the outside without some kind of protection, and I think that's what you've been learning under the Gratis Building," he searches my eyes looking for an assent. I stare straight into his, willing him to understand. *I have been learning to protect, I will be essential to your survival. But I will also exponentially increase the danger for everyone.* He must see something because he pulls me into a bone-crushing hug.

"We can do this, Keres," he whispers in my ear. "I know we can." He pulls away to look at me again, arms still around

232

my waist. I can see the cherry tree branch I hold in my hand peeking around his neck. The delicate pink petals seem to mock his strong square jaw.

"Go with me?" he asks, pleads, begs, resting his forehead against mine, pulling his hands to my face.

"Anywhere," I whisper back.

Wex's lips touch mine, lightly at first. Then he devours me, hungry and desperate. We kiss each other, completely concealed by the dense boughs of pink cherry blossoms, drenched in light from the blood-red sunset.

Chapter Twenty-Two

I still feel the taste of Wex on me the next morning and it makes me lighter than air. How do people hide this feeling? The heavy rocks in my stomach have been completely eclipsed by a kissing-induced upsurge of joy. I will go anywhere with Wex.

When Abbot sends me to Marum and Statric in ink production, I literally skip through the Warren. Marum hands me a small, weathered notebook. "It's the next set of inks for you. Work your way through them. I have my own assignments today. Statric can explain any unfamiliar components to you. She's scavenged them all." He waves his hand to dismiss me from his work area.

I flip through the yellowing pages briefly to see a labyrinth of diagrams weave between lengthy handwritten paragraphs of explanations and instruction.

"The most appropriate place to start is the beginning, Keres," Statric says in her unnaturally glossy voice behind me.

"I will help you." Statric floats down the shelves of little glass jars and dusty boxes, picking up several and handing them to me, "Sactine flies are extremely difficult to trap due to their ability to analyze situational danger, so exercise caution with the wings in this casket. Also, be aware that the ginger root costs us a great deal at the markets. Be sure not to use more than what is called for." As she hands me jar and box upon envelope and phial, I place them next to the brewing bowls. When more than twenty different containers litter the surface of the table, Statric finally ceases to circle the room. She stands opposite to me and watches my hands with a keen eye while I begin following the directions for an ink titled, "Expiscor, Part A."

"This is a face tattoo," I say slowly. Face and head ink is extremely advanced magus. Anyone on the hall with one has built up over a decade of strength and control.

"Abbot believes you are ready," Statric replies calmly.

"What if I'm not?"

"That is for Abbot to determine. Please, continue."

My hands shake, clinking the glass lid against the rim of the jar holding dried strawberry leaves. I have never felt less ready in my life. Abbot's intense desire to cover me in ink is certainly blinding him to my abilities.

After an hour, Statric watching me as if her own life depended on the ink I'm brewing, I pour the bowl of sable-colored liquid into a phial and cork it. I hold the phial out between my thumb and forefinger and look at it with one eye closed. This plain glass tube contains something deadly. As I make up my mind to find Abbot so he can stamp me, Statric flips the page of the notebook, "Here is the next one, Keres. You will find the water caltrop in the dark red box on the bottom shelf."

I place the Expiscor, Part A ink in a rack and retrieve the bat-shaped pods as directed. I suppose Statric will have me brew under her until she is required elsewhere in the Warren. Over the last few days, the level of activity in the Warren has intensified. I have seen more Tutelas in the halls, hurrying in and out of the libraries and combat simulators in the last two days than I did my entire first three months. Everyone wears a haggard, drawn look, and none of them will meet my eye. I have started using the tree behind my left ear several times a day in order to concentrate on what is before me and not what I imagine is taking place behind the pensive expressions.

When Statric has watched me brew three more ink blends, she nods in approval at the rack of tubes. "Abbot will not be able to see you until this afternoon. He and Marmet are in council with the Doyens today. You are to meet with Zink in his den, and he will apply the inks for Civi, Ancile, and Integro groups. His placement is perfect and he is best suited to train you in their uses. The urban combat simulator is reserved for your use this afternoon, should you require practical application." She extends the ink rack to me, then turns her attention to inventorying which jars and boxes are nearing empty on the shelves.

I knock lightly on Zink's door and open it at the sound of his voice.

"Statric sent me," I say.

"Right, yes. I'm supposed to help you with the defensive magus."

I hold out the rack of ink to him and he hesitates before he takes it.

"Expiscor," he says in an undertone and shrugs his shoulders.

"Marum had me brew it first. Abbot says I'm ready."

Zink makes a circumspect noise through his teeth while he inserts the first tube of ink into his stamp. He walks over to me and kneels down so his eyes are level with my waist.

"We start with shields," he says, pressing the stamp to my left thigh with a click. "Speaking of shields," he says. The ink creeps around the circumference of my leg, forming small battle shields in different colors as it goes. "Mine's a line of hands," he says, watching intently.

He changes the ink tube out for the next and stamps my left ankle and my right thigh.

"That's a good start for now," he says, passing his fingers over the newly-formed image of the dapple gray horse I rode on the scavenge. He wears a look of complacence when he stands.

"What?" I ask him.

"It's like you think of me when you think of speed."

"I think of the horse."

"You think of what I did to the horse."

I roll my eyes. "Can you just teach me how to use these now?"

He holds out his hand in a "ladies first" gesture, bowing slightly. I stomp past him to the training area at the back of his den.

"The shields aren't going to do much for you with the single application of ink, but you will be able to throw something that can cover an area of maybe ten square feet. More if you end up being adept with the defensive magus. You'll have to keep reinforcing it until you start layering the

237

ink. Remember, though. Once you set up a shield, nothing on the outside can reach what's inside and anything from the inside that gets out will weaken it. Whatever or whoever is left inside won't be as protected as they were. So you won't be able to throw magus through the shield once it's set up. Try it, I'll chuck some stuff at you. See if I can break it."

I flick my fingers over the ring of shields and pull a bright golden dome over me. Zink lobs a wooden ball off of it, which shatters the dome on the second bounce. I pull another shield up, this time reinforcing it after every bounce of the ball. Zink switches to throwing a spinning star magus until he finally cracks through the golden light with a combination of his own shield tattoo and a blocking force with one sweep of his right hand.

"Loshee will be able to crack that with a toss of her braids. Hope you're ready," he says with a grin. "I'll let her beat you down. I'm no real threat. Give that horse a try, I'll throw the ball and you make it speed up." He tosses the wooden ball lightly in the air, I whisk a gush of wind towards it and it spins rapidly in the air before shooting forward. It smashes into a glass sculpture of a woman on Zink's desk.

"Oh! Zink, I'm so sorry!" I cry jumping forward to pick up the pieces of glass. "I should have aimed it, all I thought about was making it go faster." I place the delicate arm of the woman on the desk with a miserable gesture.

"Try healing it," he says quietly. "Use the stag and doe on your ankle and try."

I want to be very careful not to break it beyond even Zink's abilities, so I gently trace the ink with my thumb and hold my hand out over the glass pieces. Slowly, as if the sculpture is melting, it rejoins into its original form. The places that shattered show in ugly lesions of rough, raised glass. Pressure builds behind my eyes as I try again and again to smooth them out, but the scars remain. Zink rests his hand on mine to stay my inept attempts. He pulls from his own healing tattoo and the cracks dissolve seamlessly.

"You can't get so frantic. It causes mistakes. When you are healing or protecting, a calm mind and confidence is crucial," he says quietly, "Think of the healing magus like a bird. Soft, light and brittle. The slightest noise or movement will send it flying. A healing magus is easily fractured by any other thoughts in your mind. Like fear and doubt."

"I'll never be able to heal then. I'll just have to count on y-" I stop short on the word. I can't count on Zink. He won't be by my side forever. Zink fumbles with the papers on his desk and suggests we skip the simulator today and spend the afternoon in the Magus Library studying the theories behind restorative magusi.

#

Abbot never materializes for that afternoon's promised meeting, and the hours pass quietly. Zink and I lose ourselves in books until the lights blink and we mark our places, stacking the volumes neatly. We ride up the elevator together, wiping our minds simultaneously. We race down the street together until we reach the fork in the road, meeting Frehn who greets us with a whistle.

239

"Good day?" Frehn asks Zink.

"Won't complain," Zink answers with a grin.

Zink cuffs me on the ear and bolts towards the canteen. Frehn and I follow him slowly.

"Interesting development in the mines today," Frehn tells me, his hands shoved in his pockets.

"What's that?"

He shakes his head, "It'll have to wait for tonight. Wex will wanna hear this. Speaking of Wex..."

"What about him?" The strange hungry feeling aches inside me when I hear his name.

"You two were out kinda late last night. Anything you want to tell me?"

"Not a thing," I smile at him.

Frehn returns my grin and loops his arm around my neck, pulling me into a headlock, laughing at my attempts to break free.

PG3456 eats as calmly as possible and we meander back to our block, squelching our desire to make a mad dash to the relative safety of the common room. Once there, I check the painted hand, sound the all clear, and we dump our packs on the low table. The six of us take out our notebooks, by now filled with life saving information, and put our heads together waiting for Frehn's announcement.

"I've found the tunnel that leads out of the mines. I saw the light through it and everything. Explosives are on the same track, it won't take more than a drop to break through to the outside. And not much more to close it back up. I've already got a plan to move enough to the back wall."

Merit lets out a low whistle. "This is really happening." Harc opens the map she's been drawing of the city and places it over the one Merit and Wex have been collaborating on of things they have seen through the outer wall's bars.

"I've submerged two of the plastic crop preserve bags in the river by the concealed door in the outer wall," Wex says pointing at the place on map, "Merit and I will start moving the stash from the barn roof to those crop bags under the water. It will take a week or two to get it done without raising curiosity, but when we finish, Merit will send the twenty-four hour signal to Revvim. Then he, Revvim, will alert PG3453 to put their side of the plan into action. Poy and Sotter will disable the bullet train while Som, Flast and Drim set off the feint. When the diversion starts, we move. Poy, Revvim, and Sotter will meet with Keres, Doe, Frehn and me at the mouth of the mine. We will travel the mine in Frehn's cart to the place in the rock where the light shines through. We set the explosion to break out of the tunnel and set another one to close it off."

Merit takes over the plan now, pointing to places on the north side of the pastures. "At the same time, Harc and I meet the other half of PG3453- Flast, Drim and Som- here. I've only been able to train eight horses to run to the river at my signal but I may be able to get another one before it's time. Some of them are large so they can take two riders and still keep up with the smaller ones. Harc and I will retrieve the stash and we take the horses through the wall."

"And we meet two hours later here," Wex's finger taps a mountainside to the north of Chelon. "There's fresh water. The river that runs through the city comes from up there."

"What happens if one of us gets caught?" Doe asks quietly.

"We keep moving," Wex tells her solemnly. "No matter what happens, the rest of us have to keep moving."

No one makes a move, thinking about what this means. If we are separated, if one of us sprains an ankle running, if one of us falls off our horse, or the horse goes lame we leave them behind. With nothing to hold on to but the hope they will catch up. We know it's the only way that any of us will make it past The Mothers, who will chase us. It means absolute, excruciating, and prolonged death for whoever lags behind.

Doe's eyes go large, but she doesn't move to make an argument. We sit in silence, running the plan backwards and forwards in our minds looking for problems.

"What's the distraction?" I ask Wex.

"We don't know. I thought it was better if only PG3453 know that and only we know how we are getting out. In case someone finds out, the entire plan won't be compromised," Wex answers. "Once we are out of the mines and Merit's group makes it to this point," he indicates the base of the mountain, "we will send signals to let each other know we are safely out."

"Won't signals tell The Mothers where we are?" I ask.

"Not these signals," Harc says with relish. "I have shooting sparks from the factories. You can fire them from one place and they explode in a spark of color over another place. We trade them to other cities, they use them for celebrations. The only hole I see is PG3453. How do we know they aren't waiting for the crucial moment to turn us over to The Mothers mid-escape?"

Doe tucks her chin into her chest and Merit shifts his legs around on the floor. Frehn looks at Harc, a dangerous warning in his eyes, "I know."

"All we have is idle chatter on the Recreational Fields. We don't know anything about them. They could be spying on us for The Mothers, watching us like cats stalking barn mice just waiting for the right moment to pounce. You are the only one who has talked to any of them about the plan, talked to them about anything of real substance. How do you know they won't turn on us? What makes you so sure?"

"Do you think we have been the only ones tortured here? Do you think we are the only ones who suffer? Do you think the five in black were invented just for us? The Amendments Spire was only built for us?" Wex asks her harshly.

"No, I don't. But I think we are the only ones who will risk our lives to get out," Harc spits back. "Why do they want out so badly when the rest of the city simply accepts the persecution and The Mothers rule? We've got Keres, that's reason enough for us to run. What have they got?"

"Enough," Frehn says loudly. I blink back stinging tears. It feels like Harc has kicked me in the gut with her words.

"They feel the same way we do," Wex tells her. "They understand we have a better chance at life, a better chance for happiness on the other side of the wall. That's all the reason I need."

"Sotter will not let us down," Frehn says folding his arms across his chest and looking defiantly at Harc.

"Fine, but I won't help them."

"Oh, Harc," Doe says, reproach reflecting in every corner of her face. "Harc, you wouldn't let someone fall behind."

Harc doesn't answer. Her expression is hard and her body rigid. Merit stands and takes her by the hand, leaving the common room with her.

"She can't forget what Sotter did for her, for us." Wex says. "And from what Merit's told me, The Mothers remind her every chance they get that she is constantly punished because of Keres, stoking the flames to keep anger alive in her. Harc is struggling."

I stare at the map, not seeing anything before me. "She blames me," I say.

No one answers. Of course she blames me. I have been the reason for every punishment levied against us. My inability to keep still, my scarcity of obedience, my uncontrollable temper, The Mothers' anger against me, against my Unspoken status, maybe even against the knowledge that I am the Catalyst, has manifested in near endless unimaginable pain for PG3456 in their effort to control me. Harc has me to thank for her agony, for Merit's torment. And now she is indebted to Sotter and PG3453 for protecting her over the stolen scissors.

Wex carefully packs up the notebooks and maps. Frehn and Doe whisper together on the sofa. I stand in the center of the room, waves of compassion for Harc, alternating with resentment, crashing over me. My heart aches inside my chest, tears welling in my eyes. Wex stops folding the maps, noticing at my quivering lip. He open his arms to me, and I fall into them sobbing, utterly submerged in grief and regret. Frehn and

Doe stop whispering and move to the other side of the room. Wex holds my head in one hand, the other wrapped around me, and lets me cry.

Weak as water. That's what I've become. Weak, no longer the hot tears of anger, now I cry every time my feelings are hurt. I push off Wex in a quick movement and brush the back of my hand under my nose.

"I'm fine. Long day. I'm tired," I make excuses, walking towards my bedroom. We both know the truth is that I'm scared. Terrified of losing Harc, of PG3456 breaking, fracturing under the physical and psychological warfare The Mothers are waging against us, the strain of escape and surviving once we are on the outside. Without The Mothers to unite against, what do Harc and I have to hold us together?

I lay down on my round bed and pull the thought magus over my eyes to the back of my head. I picture the crystal box with pewter corners that holds the different colors of rope knotted together in five places sitting on the table. Next to it, is a gray dove in a wire cage. I open the cage door and the dove flies towards me in a fury. Its beating wings whip my face and its feet claw at my eyes before it circles the room as it climbs up the endless ceiling.

#

When I finally see Abbot again, it's late afternoon eleven days after PG3456's plan for escape is formed. Wex and Merit will be ready to send the twenty-four hour signal to PG3453 in less than two days. I am mentally exhausted from

245

the constant feeling of tense anticipation. Every movement or word from a Mother makes my heart jump into my throat, choking me momentarily.

The week's training sessions with Loshee and Zink are nothing but an unending stream of catastrophes. Speed is the only tattoo on my lower body I can use with any skill. Loshee even had me run simulations without Zink, thinking that his presence was allowing me to feel protected which would in turn distract my mind from sending the required signals to produce proper shields. No luck. I was killed in the combat simulator no less than nine times this morning alone. I don't even remember going to lunch.

"Looks like we finally hit the wall," Abbot says as he bangs open my den door. "Guess we will just have to hope you kill or contain everything before it has a chance to do any real damage."

"That's a cheerful outlook," I say from under a sofa cushion.

"Bluebird of happiness, that's me. Now get up," he yanks the cushion away and prods me with his boot. "You have more ink now than seventy percent of the people on the hall. Everyone has a specialty. They may have ink outside that specialty, but they can't throw anything of substance with it. So stop whining."

I wasn't aware I was whining. I wasn't aware I have the energy to put into whining. Abbot's boot connects with my back and I roll over on the sofa scowling up at him.

"You should get up when I ask you nicely."

"I'm sorry, I missed the nice part."

I slide off the sofa and walk to the free weights, assuming I'm in for a grueling training session. When I turn towards Abbot for instruction, I see him looking at the Expiscor ink, still untouched in the rack, on the edge of my desk. His face has gone dark, his eyes take on a dull, matte light. His hand hovers over the glass tube for a second, then he picks it up and walks towards me.

"You know what this is."

"Expiscor, Part A. It is stamped around the left eye." Abbot nods and he turns the tube upside down, sliding it into his stamp.

"And you know what it does."

"It discovers my enemies."

He nods again. "And what happens if you falter when pulling from it?"

"The ink could read my mistake as the act of someone who would do me harm. And it would work in conjunction with any additional ink used on the Expiscor nerve group, parts b through e for example, and act accordingly." That's verbatim from a book in the Magus Library. I spent hours pouring over it, fascinated by the abilities of the face tattoos.

"And that means what?"

"If a facial or cranial magus is pulled poorly, the thrower risks incredible pain and the veritable possibility of death.

"Yes. Stand still." He comes at me with the stamp raised. I'm held in perfect fear while he moves the stamp around my eye, looking for the precise spot. When he finds it, he inhales sharply and clicks the stamp. The piercing pain I've grown so accustomed to pricks through my body.

"It's not a matter of concentration, or a clear mind that's important for the Expiscor group," Abbot says pulling the stamp away and blinking at the new pattern of ink. "But I see you already have a good idea how to use it."

I turn my head slowly towards the wall of mirrors. Spilling from the corner of my eye is a stylized spider web, with two tiny stars sparkling on its delicate threads. While Abbot talks about the theory of enemy location and detection, I look fixedly at the triangle of web dripping down the side of my face until it begins to swirl out of shape. It morphs into two beautifully delicate comet trails spreading out from the two stars that were caught on the web.

"Don't pull from it unless it's life or death. Not even to practice. It's not wise to go looking for your enemies. Like thought clarification, this is an intangible magus and addictive."

I already use the tree tattoo too much- it's too difficult concentrating without it. Last night I used it to be able to sleep. I do not want to become obsessed with knowing who has it in for me, who wants me dead.

"Why stamp me if I'm not supposed to use it?" I ask Abbot petulantly.

"Because you will need it one day. The longer the ink stays in contact with the Expiscor nerve group, the more accurate it will be when you have to pull from it." Abbot leaves me gazing at my reflection. I stand in front of the mirrors until the lights signal dinner time. When Zink meets me at my den door, he starts at the sight of the Expiscor tattoo around my eye.

"At least it's got a soft pattern on you," he says. "Some are really harsh lines. I'm glad it doesn't look severe in the pattern form."

"Me too. I already have trouble with Frehn wanting to lick the one on my neck. I don't want to think about what he would want to do with this one."

"It's strange the different reactions people have. Delsum, my Banded parter, is terrified of them. She makes me turn off all the lights before I change. She doesn't want to see them. Lucky for her my specialty is on my legs and not my face," he punches the call button for the elevator. He has never talked about his PG before, though I have talked him deaf about mine.

"What's it like, being Banded?"

"Not so different from not being Banded. Ask Journer, she loves her partner. It's probably different for her."

"Oh."

The elevator lights quiver and the car vibrates slightly, I seize hold of Zink as he grasps at the side of the car. The door opens with the car a few feet lower than the floor of the Gratis Building. We have to climb out.

"What was that?" I ask, panic racing across my chest. Before Zink can answer, an explosion breaks the windows to our left. Zink flings his body against mine and we go flying across the smooth marble floor.

Keepers begin to run past us, their shoes grinding in the broken glass. Zink and I struggle to our feet, pushing out the

249

doors past the Keepers and run with all our might to the northeast of the city. As we top the hill, just as the mouth of the mine comes into sight, fire and rock explode from the entrance, spraying a wave of heat and shrapnel on us.

Chapter Twenty-Three

The ground shakes under my feet and I fall to all fours, panting. Zink covers me with his body, his arms flung over my head. From the mine entrance, smoke and fire pour past the bullet train parked at the platform. A tidal wave of miners who would have been walking leisurely towards the canteen for dinner surge out of the mouth of the mine in a vomitus mass of blood and flesh.

Healers are running in from the east, catching stumbling people and dousing them in water to quench the flames that rage through their clothes. Screams ring from every direction, Mothers swarming the scene making tutting noises and exaggerated moans in turns.

"Frehn!" I howl, "Frehn!" I struggle against Zink's weight to get up.

"We'll find him, Keres. Try and stay calm," Zink tells me, keeping tight hold on my arm, pulling me to my feet. "He's always one of the first ones out for the day because of the cart. He's never late, Keres.".

What if he chose today to move the explosives to our escape tunnel? What if that explosion was him?

"Zink, there's someth-"

"No, Keres," he cuts my words in half, "There's nothing. We will find him."

I can only whimper slightly and we move towards the mine, searching every face trying to see past the gore and flame and mud. I look for his green eyes in a sea of indistinguishable grime covered faces. People are running at random, Play Groups looking for their members. Zink and I hang on to each other tightly while we rip through the crowd. Everything feels like it's been slowed down. Soon bodies start appearing, slung over the edges of rail carts and across shoulders of friends. A boy stumbles past me with blood gushing from the side of his head. The entire left side of his face, from his ear to his chin, completely gone. His orange service uniform wet and clinging to his body with blood.

My stomach lurches at the sight of the butchered people surrounding me as we advance on the mine entrance. Zink and I lift our shirts over our noses and mouths to keep from choking on the smoke. I scream Frehn's name over and over, trying to make myself heard over the strange wailing that fills the air. Zink pulls me forward, deeper into the accumulation of bodies and blood. The Mothers hold their tunics close to their legs so as not to get them wet in the sticky red pools forming around the people on the ground, their eyes are triumphant with the pain.

"Zink, I have to find Doe before she sees this."

"There he is," Zink points over my shoulder. My head whips around and I see him. He is standing in his cart, the last in the line on the tracks, helping injured miners out of it and into the arms of their panic stricken Play Group members. I run towards him, yelling his name, blinded by tears.

"I'm alright, nothing Doe can't fix," he says to me, handing the last miner over to her Banded partner. "Just some scratches." He winces stepping over the side of the cart and I see both of the legs of his overalls are ripped to shreds. Zink and I get on either side of him and help him to the grass outside near the Healers' makeshift first aid station.

"Some of the explosives supply was being moved deeper, cart jumped the tracks, set off a chain reaction. No big cave-ins, but whoever was within five hundred feet of the cart didn't make it," Frehn says between gasps of pain. "I had just passed them going to pick up the last crew for the day. Force blew my cart off the track, had to reattach it before we could come up. We were miles deep."

"You can tell us later," I say to him. "Let's see how bad your legs are first."

Zink and I lower him to the grass and remove his pack so he can lay flat on the ground. I grab water bottles from a Healer's cart passing our position and gingerly try to wash the layers of clay and soot from his legs. He digs his fists into the ground, clutching at the grass, baring his teeth.

I turn to Zink, "Can you find PG3456?"

He nods and starts to move away, but Frehn grabs his arm, "And there's a girl in PG3453. Sotter, factories."

"I'll find them, don't worry."

I rip the legs off Frehn's uniform completely and continue to wash away the layers of earth and blood.

253

"When I saw the explosion, I thought- I thought it was you," I say, my voice catching.

"Plenty of time to confess your love for me when I'm all bandaged up."

The water removes the last wad of clay and I put the back of my hand over my mouth. Through layers of mutilated flesh, I can see the bright white of his shinbone. Where is Zink? I need his healing! Ointments and magus and something to take the gray look out of Frehn's face.

"Ok. Ok," I say casting franticly around my mind for what to do next. Blood has swirled back over the bone and is spilling over the edges of the wound. I wash it away again and take off my shirt to staunch the flow.

"Knew I would get you naked one day," he says winking up at me from the grass.

"Frehn! Shh!" I bend my head over the gaping hole in his leg to get better leverage in order to make the knot tight.

"Well, it's not exactly the way I imagined, but I'm not picky," he wipes the perspiration off his forehead and leaves his hand up to shade his eyes. "You are covered in ink."

Tell me something I don't know. I double-knot the shirt over his leg and will Zink to come back with PG3456. I need Doe to fix this. I need salves and real bandages. I cast a searching look over my shoulder for any sign of their return.

"I don't think there is anything so beautiful," Frehn says, reaching up and running his hand from my neck to my wrist.

"That's enough, Frehn. Be still. Doe will be here soon."

"Don't want anyone but you."

"You do not, just shut up and keep still."

"Frehn!" A tiny scream permeates the din around us.

"Doe! He needs-" I start but she has already flung her pack down beside him. She pulls out a small pouch of purple leaves and pops two in his mouth.

"Chew," she commands him.

Frehn catches my eye and smiles broadly, chewing on the leaves, "So much attention."

Doe unties my shirt and rinses the gash again with something that makes the broken tissue foam. She applies a paste from a jar in her pack and rolls gauzy white bandages tightly around his leg. Running her hands over Frehn's entire body, probing for more injuries she pauses while looking into his eyes. I feel like an intruder watching them exchange a wordless conversation. I stand and walk a few steps away to where Wex, Merit, Harc and Zink wait.

A minute later, Doe stands, "I have to do what I can for the others. Take him back to the common room. He won't be able to walk on his own for days, maybe weeks," she looks straight at Wex when she says this.

Wex shows he understands with a simple gesture of his hands. We will not be able to escape until Frehn heals completely. We are not able to get out through the mine anymore anyway so it makes little difference.

We advance on Frehn, and Zink bends low to help prepare him to stand. I hear Zink whisper something about Sotter. Wex is handing me his own shirt to put on, "You can't walk across Chelon with next to nothing on. Even in crisis. I'll get your shirt."

"Ah, let her go without it," mewls Frehn.

"Not even for you," Wex replies, helping Zink get Frehn to his feet. It's slow progress across the city to the Quad. Everyone we pass has tear-stained faces, long wet streaks slice through the dirt on their cheeks, people mourning their dead or crying for joy their PG members were hurt but not killed. Merit, Harc and I push through the crowd, making room for the others who are carrying Frehn now with their arms formed like a chair. Frehn's face is drawn, tight and has slipped from gray to green, as if the color of his eyes has faded down his skin with the river of sweat.

When we have Frehn stretched long on the sofa, Wex turns to Zink. "That's the second time you have carried one of us back to our block. Thank you," he shakes Zink's hand firmly in both of his.

"If we don't help each other, no one will," Zink says to him as he returns the firm grip.

I move to the window and watch the scene below. People running across the Quad, carrying miners through the doors of residence compounds, the near dead to the Healers' Building. Lavender robes swirl behind Mothers as they float through the crowd, holding their absurd rags out to dab at open wounds four times the size of the cloth. The Healers ricochet from one bloody trauma to the next while Keepers and Architects haul boards to repair the broken windows of the buildings near the blast. From my vantage point, I see Abbot and Journer walking calmly together across the courtyard. They are like two stoic crickets surrounded by a sea of agitated ants.

256

A howl of grief from outside the common room door makes me jump. Someone must have broken the news of a death to a woman somewhere on the residence hall. We all fall silent, listening to her scream out her loss. Harc covers her ears and rocks slightly.

"Is there nothing we can do, Zink?" I ask him desperately. "All this pain..."

"Nothing. Some things have to be left to nature," he says. His eyes are glassy with tears and his shoulders sag with the weight of helplessness.

The television blinks on, flooding the room with a bright blue light. A Mother appears on screen, an expression of sorrow pinned to her face like a mask, "Children, there has been an accident in Mineral Recovery. Your Mothers are tending to the wounded now." A snorting noise escapes Wex at those words. "Your Mothers are preparing boxed rations for your dinners in the canteen. Please send one representative from your Play Group to retrieve them. Tonight you may eat in your blocks, won't that be an exciting amusement for you? Only those kept in the Healers' Building will be excused from Service tomorrow. Be not afraid, your Mothers will protect you." The television goes dark with a small pop.

We stand watching the black screen, waiting for more. "I'll go get my PG's rations," Zink says, "Keres, come with me?"

I do not want to leave the common room. I do not want to go among the scene of grief and pain. But I move towards the door with him.

"Check your room first," he says quietly to me.

When I walk through my bedroom door, I don't have to look up. All five fingers of the hand over my door are pulsing an amber light.

Terror seizes my spine and I cannot move. Zink, seeing the light reflected around the room, pulls gently at the back of my shirt. I can feel my eyes pop, bulging from my head, my nostrils flare with fear. An ice-cold feeling plummets down my head and back. And I know, as certainly as if I had personally witnessed them plot, I know The Mothers discovered our plan to escape through the mines and they staged the explosion. They killed hundreds of people, destroyed thousands of lives to keep me inside Chelon's walls.

Zink pulls at me again and I sway into him. A rushing sound fills my ears and pulses through my head to my stomach.

"She will be back with dinners soon, rest up Frehn," Zink tells the others. He looks hard into Wex's face. Wex's eye twitches almost imperceptibly in response. Zink shunts me from the block and down the corridors. Before we reach the elevators, he quickly looks around and shoves me sideways into a Keeper's closet shutting us in complete darkness.

I can feel myself starting to hyperventilate. Zink's arms fold around me, "It's alright. It's going to be alright," he repeats over and over. "We are going to get through this."

"They know, Zink. They know. They will kill them," I start gagging, the visions of mangled people and bodies spilling from the mouth of the mine mixing with images of Wex being hacked into pieces by an axe-wielding Mother.

"If The Mothers wanted them dead, Frehn would have been killed in the explosion. They don't make mistakes."

258

"Does that mean we are going to be tortured with relentless, never-ending fear? Every morning I see them leave for Service might be my last? They will create catastrophes over and over until I break? What do they want from me?"

"The same thing they want from everyone else. Complete obedience. But they will not be able to get that from you. It's impossible." He holds me in the dark until I can breathe normally. "Listen to me, The Mothers will be overstimulated with the pain of today. They will not need to pursue PG3456 until things calm down. That gives you time to figure out how you are going to go forward. Because forward is the only direction you can go."

We leave the closet to retrieve the boxed rations, sidestepping the people returning from the canteen laden with white paper boxes. Three hours ago, the world was on fire. Now, the smoke is clearing and the people walk over the ashes as if nothing happened. When morning comes, the dead will already have been cremated in the pit and buried. The children of Chelon will continue as they did before, empty shells of human waste.

Zink and I stand in the line for our PGs' rations. When we return to the Quad, Zink leaves me for his residence compound. He has not seen his Play Group since lunch. It might as well have been a hundred years ago. I move in slow motion back to the block, forcing myself to move my feet at a natural pace. When I open the common room door, I see Doe has returned and is rewrapping Frehn's leg. We say nothing to each other that does not have a direct connection to the food

259

I've brought. We can all still see the light pulsing from the painted hand through my open door. We eat mechanically.

There are moments when the heavy feeling threatens to overcome me. Its long black smoke fingers sinking into my chest pushing me further away from those I love. Everything we have been building towards- the escape, life on the other side, relationships, love, freedom- detonated before our eyes, taking the lives of innocent people with it to the grave. The Heavy covers each of us as we wrestle with what the explosion means.

The warning bell sounds, signaling power down is approaching. The six of us remain in our places around the sofa. We reach out to each other, holding onto hands and arms. And we wait. I look into Wex's eyes and we agree in that instant that death is our only way out of Chelon, our only reprieve from The Mothers' cold-blooded tortures.

The one-minute warning sounds, and PG3456 remains positioned in a last display of unified defiance in the common room. I can feel Doe's pounding heartbeat through her hand. The only light comes from the pulsing hand over my bedroom door and the fire, still smoldering in the grate. No one comes to lock us in our rooms. The five in black do not make an appearance. One by one, we succumb to exhaustion and drift asleep around Frehn stretched out on the sofa.

My eyes have only just closed when I feel someone shaking me awake. I scuttle backwards at the sight of a small group of people in black crowded around the room, looking down at us.

"Keres," Abbot says urgently, "Wake up. You have to leave. They are coming."

Chapter Twenty-Four

"Who? Who's coming?" I splutter at Abbot. The tense
lines in his face reawaken all the fear in my body.

"Not here, we don't have time," he says pulling me off
the floor.

"I'm not leaving without PG3456," I say.

"Now is not the time to show your ignorance, Keres.
Look around you."

I turn my head to see Loshee and Statric waking up
Harc and Doe, coaxing them into their rooms. Holden and Zink
are carrying Frehn to his room while Wex and Merit follow at
Journer's signal. "Move," he orders me in a desperate voice,
dragging me to my room. He flings open my closet, throwing
clothes in my pack at random. I yank open drawers and add
anything I can lay my hands on to the bag.

Loshee appears at my door almost instantly, "They're
ready. There's no more time."

Abbot snatches the pack up with one hand and grabs
my arm with the other, pulling me back into the common room.
Frehn is standing on his own, but leaning against Zink, his face
drained of all color. Abbot gazes over their rigid faces as if
taking inventory. He gives Statric a pained look and barrels out
of the common room door into the hall, my arm still in his

death grip. We all run quickly and without making a noise out of the residence compound and through the Quad, sticking close to the trees and sides of buildings. At a sound up the street, Abbot flings me around a corner. We all hold our breath. Crouching against a building, the Tulelas' covering our bodies with their own, their black clothes make us disappear in the dark. I can hear footsteps on the gravel street and I shut my eyes against the terror of being caught by the night patrol of Mothers. The sound passes and we creep through the trees, low to the ground all the way to the Gratis Building.

Inside, Loshee jumps over the Keeper's desk and buzzes the doors of the elevator. Everyone but Statric and Holden cram in the car, as the two of them nod to Abbot and dash out of the building, back into the night. I open my mouth to thank them but am silenced by the doors closing. Silence reigns, save for our heavy breathing and Loshee's clicking beads, until our shoes connect with the floor of the hall. We pass right through to the Warren, running down the long hall.

"Abbot!" Marum shouts, making all of us jump. He is running towards us from the cross section of hall. Panting, he thrusts something towards Abbot, "Here, it's ready."

Abbot snatches a thin wooden box from him and shoves it in my pack. He drags me further down, almost to the end of the hall, and looks behind us for the first time, "Everyone here?" he asks Marum.

"They went down a minute before you arrived. Half of the others are already installed in the Burrow. Serees came, the others declined."

Abbot's jaw clenches and he slams his fist into the wall in front of him. Doe lets a strangled cry escape before covering her mouth with her hands. When he pulls his fist away from the wall, the floor begins to drop from underneath our feet. Harc looks wildly around for something to grab, Frehn loops his free arm around Doe's trembling body. The floor moves like an elevator, quickly but smoothly, deeper into the earth than the Warren itself. When we finally come to a stop, my stomach feels like it was left behind on our residence block.

"Get them to the horses. We will follow you," Abbot says, pulling me off the section of Warren floor. I watch as PG3456 is gently but urgently guided by Zink, Loshee and Journer through the immense space and towards a large rolling door. Abbot drops the pack and turns to me, looking savage. He clasps my shoulders with his hands and tries to steady his breath.

"You have to leave Chelon."

"Wh-"

"The Audauxx are hunting, they are coming here. They can't find you."

"What are Audauxx?"

"Not what, who. Tutelas who have forgotten their purpose," his eyes jump around my face, "They want the Catalyst."

"Me? What for?"

"You are one half of the ultimate weapon, Keres. Born in the seventh minute, of the seventh hour, on the seventh day, of the seventh month, of the seventh year of the seventy-seventh century. You are the most powerful Tutelas ever to be

264

born. You are the Catalyst. And we can't protect you here. You have to reach the safe city. You have to get to Credo Cantus. Tell them the Audauxx are moving. They will know who you are and what to do. We will hold them off for as long as it takes, but you have to reach Credo Cantus. The whole world will be hunting you once they know the Audauxx have discovered your existence. If you get caught, if you are killed, everything we have been protecting for thousands of years will be gone."

"Gone?"

"Humanity will be erased."

"You're coming with me? You and Zink?"

The corners of his eyes twitch and an expression of heartbreak covers his gruff features. "No. We have to stay here and protect what's left."

"I can't go alone, Abbot. I'll be dead in minutes!"

"You will not be alone. PG3456 is being apprised of the situation now. Well, to the best of our ability."

"We have no defenses, no food. We'll be hunted down and murdered! Abbot! They will die! And I'll die trying to protect them! The guard ink will make sure of that!" My heart feels like it will burst with horror. Real panic like I have never felt before traps me.

Abbot yanks at my shirt, exposing the black smoke finger tattoo on my upper sternum. "This will hurt," he says, thrusting something sharp into my chest. I fall backwards and hit the floor flat on my back, unable to breathe. I put my hand to the place where I'm certain I will feel a knife. For a split second I think he has stabbed me in the heart. My fingers come away wet with black ink and blood. The front of my shirt is quickly turning a dark, dirty red color. I look up at Abbot, trying to make sense of what has happened. In his right hand he holds a wide, flat silver blade. My blood is dripping off the serrated edge of tiny scoop-shaped razors to the floor.

"You have no guard now," he says as he flings the tool across the floor. I struggle and roll around the floor, gasping for air.

"Listen to me," Abbot kneels down in front of me, putting both his hands on my shoulders and looking hard into my breathless face. "You will always have a choice. Being marked as the Catalyst has no effect on who you are. It makes no difference. You are in control of you, what you do and what is done to you. There is no question the Catalyst will be compelled to wield the weapon, but when you do, no matter who is forcing you, you will have a choice. A choice to destroy all human life or to save it. Remember that."

I stare at his wild eyes, looking from one to the other. His whole face is fierce with the earnestness of his words. When I reach out to touch him, my hand is warm and wet with the blood and ink from my chest.

"We are out of time." Abbot wrenches me up suddenly before I can reassure him. He drags me across the room towards the rolling door PG3456 went through. I lift my hand to the place my guard tattoo once was, trying to feel what has happened to my body. My skin is already rough with scabbing and congealed blood, my shirt still wet with ink and blood. When we pass through the doors, I stop short. Spread before me is an expanse of rolling pasture, nine horses in harness wait by a hitching post. Sotter is among the seven or so already mounted, talking quickly to Frehn, who still leans against Zink.

"PG3453," I say.

"We knew Sotter wouldn't leave without them. Frehn wouldn't leave without her and you wouldn't leave without Frehn. They had to come. Complicates everything nicely. It will be a miracle if any of you make it out alive."

"What about you? What will happen to you and the Warren?"

"The Tutelas have gone underground as of tonight. We took as many people as would come with us. Some refused. They have been left on the surface and to The Mothers. There's nothing we can do for them now." Abbot begins to jog forward to the horses, and I follow. His Play Group chose to stay above ground, only his Banded partner, Serees, trusting him enough to follow him.

Journer is talking to the group. "Saddlebags are loaded with supplies. Don't follow the river, that's where they will look for you first. Two days' travel from here, there is another river due northwest. Get to it. You each have enough water," she pats a cluster of large flasks tied to one of the saddles.

"And Harc, everyone has one of your shooting sparks in case you are forced to separate." Harc forces a hard little smile to her lips in answer.

Abbot stops me beside the same dapple-gray horse I rode on the scavenge. "That tunnel leads to the north side of the city," Abbot says pointing. "When you get to the end of the tunnel, you will only be a few hundred feet from the outer wall. Don't slow down and don't turn back for anything." He clasps my head in both his hands. "You're going to be fine. I had some supplies to help you continue your training packed in your saddlebags. When I see you again, I expect you to have at least tripled your abilities." He kisses me hard on the forehead and throws me up into the saddle.

Loshee hands me the dragon wing wristbows and attaches the quivers of bolts to the front of the saddle. She moves to each member of PG3456 and 3453 handing them weapons, swords and spears, telling them quickly how to use them. Then Zink helps Frehn climb up behind me. "He's not strong enough to ride alone yet. It will be at least two days before he is back to normal."

I look around at my friends, faces firm and brave, ready for the coming war. They watch me to make the first move. I look back down at Zink and Abbot, who stand close to my legs. Zink reaches up and grabs my outstretched hand. "Be careful, and I'll see you soon," he tells me.

I try to smile at him and pull my chin high as I look at Abbot. I nudge my heels into my horse's sides and we move towards the tunnel leading above ground. I turn in my saddle to look at Abbot, Zink, Loshee and Journer one more time. They stand together, solid and un-moveable, like warriors facing certain death. Abbot wipes his left thumb across his lips and slowly holds out his palm. A warm sensation covers my body like a blanket.

Frehn's arm around my waist tightens in a hug. We enter the tunnel and walk the horses slowly up the inclining earth floor. Round doors slide mechanically as we pass through different sections of the tunnel. It's several tense minutes before we see the moonlight reflecting water, signaling our approach to exit. I pull back on the reins and turn to face everyone. Eleven pairs of anxious eyes look back at me waiting for a plan to deliver them to safety. Wex and Doe are riding together on the same horse as are Flast and Drim.

"Get out your maps," I tell them. "We will run together towards the rocky place here," pointing to a series of boulders marked on the map three miles northwest of Chelon. "If pursued, split up into threes. Flast and Drim, with Som and Harc. Poy and Revvim with Wex and Doe. Sotter and Merit will follow me and Frehn. If that happens, we regroup in the woods here." I point to a place about halfway up the slope of a mountain to the northeast of Chelon. "They will see us heading for the northwest and assume we will be trying for the river. Don't stop for anything. Don't turn back. We will wait until the morning to leave from the regroup spot. If you haven't been able to get there before we leave, keep moving north, northeast until you come to this river. Follow the river upstream. Does everyone understand?" They each nod and refold the maps, safely putting them in pockets or pouches.

"Alright. On my signal." I hold up my hand, watching the night outside the tunnel. When I'm sure there's nothing lurking on the other side, I swing my arm down, digging my heels into the dapple gray. My horse rears slightly and we shoot out from the tunnel, hooves pounding. Seconds later I hear the horn. We've been seen already. The Mothers must have discovered empty beds in the residence blocks and have been on the watch.

We tear through the forest at breakneck pace, Frehn gripping me and the saddle tightly. "Can you see anyone?" I call to him. He turns in the saddle and I hear him stifle a cry. Straining my neck, I look behind us. Five masked figures in black mounted on mammoth horses are charging towards us, their robes flying revealing inner linings as red as hawthorn berries.

I shoot a web of light from my wristbow, attaching it to trees hoping to impede their path. The five in black avoid it easily. "Go!" I shout and two groups split from my left and right sides.

One of the black figures gives chase to Wex's group and one gains quickly on Harc's leaving three thundering after mine. "Take the reins," I yell to Frehn. He holds them tightly while I turn my body around in the saddle, facing Frehn.

"What are you doing?!" Frehn yells over the sound of six sets of hooves hammering the ground beneath us.

"Starting offensive maneuvers," I say calmly back. Leaning around him, I shoot a series of green light darts from my wristbow, while sending trees crashing to the ground from a flick of my wings tattoo. The darts connect with one of the figures in black, knocking it from its horse. The figure in the lead methodically peels back its black robe, revealing a long red stick. By the curve of the hip now exposed, I can tell the figure in black is a woman. She pulls the stick from its sheath and tucks it into her shoulder, looking down it at us. I hurl a wall of red light to protect our flank as a spark emits from the stick and something tiny and gold shoots through the air at us. It splits the light wall in two and drops out of sight.

"They have long guns!" Sotter yells to me.

I glance up at Frehn's face, his skin ghostly white. We can't keep going at this pace. It will kill him. Lunging to the side again, I fire off a bolt of lightning and follow it quickly with a net. The lightning just misses the woman and explodes against the large tree she swerves around, but the net wraps around her arms as she raises them for a second shot. Frehn lurches in the saddle, slumping over me. "Frehn! Oh fie!" I scream, "Fie!"

Savagery boils over inside. I fire my wristbows, and a flash of white light floods the forest, blinding me. Smoke curls around the trees, obscuring the scene. The woman in black bellows in pain as the red long gun comes flying from the smoke, spinning end over end, connecting with a sickening thud against the back of Merit's head. His eyes flutter, and his body goes limp as if his spine is being pulled out of him. He tips off the saddle and we are out of sight before his body hits the ground.

All sound rushes from me. The forest that closes around the scene takes on an artificial quality as we gallop away from Merit. An emptiness floods through my body as I stare behind us, waiting for Merit to reappear. To gallop forward from the smoke and woods, whole and alive. I envision Harc before me in a silent scream of agony, her face and hands shaking with the incomprehensible truth. Merit is gone.

Frehn's head lolls to the side at a sickening angle, his eyes rolled into the back of his head. As if I am knocked forward, sounds bursts around me once more, thrusting me back into consciousness. I feel desperately around his back,

271

looking for the bullet entry, but I don't have time to locate it before the third figure in black has caught up with us again. The figure's robe flying open behind it like a cape, the deep red lining creating a chilling image of streaming blood. Feminine curves are silhouetted against it. Eyes blaze behind the mask as she inches closer, horse hooves and snorts blotting out every other sound. I wrap the reins around Frehn's partially limp body to tie him to me. "Hold on to me, Frehn, hold on," I tell him. I glance to my right where Sotter urges her horse to keep pace with us, her face bloodless, wet with tears but her expression resolute.

The woman in black reaches for something on the back of her saddle and I send a wave of ice at her chest. I make contact with her, and I can see the ice form a shell around her torso but it doesn't slow her movements. A green band of smoke issues from my wristbows, wrapping around the woman, crushing her. It shatters the ice shell and squeezes the woman tightly, trying to crush the life out of her. And she still reaches for her weapon, pulling it forward, firing wildly as I pull a force push off my shoulder with my finger tips and hurl it at her. It connects with the bullet that has just left her red gun, reversing its direction, smashing it into her chest. A piercing screech fills the forest, then deafening silence.

We push the horses faster for what feels like hours, until we reach the base of the mountain and locate a small pond. Letting the horses drink, Sotter and I pull Frehn from the saddle and search for the bullet hole.

"There," Sotter's finger points to a tiny red mark under his scapula.

"Is that all?" relief spreads through me. No blood, it can't be that bad.

"It's a biting bullet." Sotter starts ransacking the saddlebags. "We have to dig it out before it chews its way through his heart."

I stare at her. "Chews its way?"

"They bore into the skin and make their way to the nearest vital organ. They are slow though. I was assigned to the factory that makes them for the last few months."

"Slow," I repeat looking at the mark.

Sotter kneels down next to Frehn. She opens a medical supply box and hands me a knife. "Cut him, hold one side open with the knife. I need to be able to see it." My mouth hangs open, staring at her. She must be crazy. "Do it!" she roars. I plunge the knife into the back of his shoulder and cut towards the center of his back, pressing the blade against one side of the gash.

"Hold still," Sotter inserts a long pair of metal tweezers deep into the open cut. I turn my head and wish I could stop my ears to the sound of metal pushing against Frehn's muscle tissue. "Ok, you can let go," she finally says. I pull the knife away and she presses a bandage to the cut.

"Did you get it?" I ask tentatively.

"Yeah. But it wasn't clean. We need Doe."

We plaster his back with strips from the medical box that we dunk in the pond water and wave ammonia under his nose. He convulses and opens his eyes.

"Back on the horse, Frehn." I tell him. I pull a movement magus from my arm and use it to place him in the saddle, then I climb up in front of him. Sotter mounts her horse and we turn up the mountainside. Frehn's head lolls against my shoulder as we climb. Half an hour or so later he starts muttering about tattoos and magic and we stop to force some water into his mouth. Sotter walks her horse close to mine so she can keep close watch on Frehn's face.

"You can do magic," she says to me after a while.

I wait for the black smoke fingers to press into my chest before I remember they have been scraped off my body. I look down at my shirt, still stained with my blood, and then back at her.

"Yes."

"Can the other Unspoken?"

"Yes."

A distant whistling sounds through the trees, followed by a rolling boom. Sotter and I sit straight up, looking around us. My wristbows are raised. But the sound is miles away. We nudge our horses into a canter, anxious to put as much distance between us and the rumbling as possible. When we reach an outcropping on the mountainside, we cautiously edge our way to the cliff. Chelon is deep in the valley below us. The Amendments Spire protrudes above the trees and buildings like a broken bone. Seeing the two walls enclosing our former home makes us reach for each others' hands. Our eyes are pulled beyond the city where an unending mass undulates through the small mountain pass like a snake. Twenty catapults stand in a line a few miles ahead of the massive army, sending green gaseous balls of fire whistling through the air at the walls of Chelon. From our cliff, we see the impact before we hear the explosion. The horses strain against their bits nervously.

"We can't help them now," Sotter says quietly.

"No," I whisper. "We can't help them now."

I pull the reins and turn my dapple gray around. "I think I'll call you Odin," I whisper to him, patting his neck. "You have just delivered me from Hell." I pull Frehn's arms tighter around me, trying to dispel the solitude, the rage and the image of Merit's frail, broken body on the forest floor miles away.

I can end this. The torture, the war, I can end it all. I have the choice to obliterate the pain, to decimate The Mothers and The Audauxx, to ensure that the suffering ends. Abbot said I will have to use the weapon, it's my destiny as the Catalyst, but that it is up to me how I choose to use it. The humanity I have known has ached for centuries, fear and torture suffocating its every move. I have the power to empty the earth, to let the world breathe without choking on the agony of life.

Everything I learned in the Warren, the grueling hours with Zink and Loshee in the combat simulators, Abbot struggling against my own anger to teach me self-control, was leading up to this. Abbot knew I would be hunted. He knew I would not be able to stay inside the walls of Chelon. He and Zink both tried to tell me The Mothers were not my true enemy. They were only a horrifying obstacle, but not a threat to my, or PG3456's, life. The Audauxx and their desire to use me in their lust for control has always been the reason for my training. They were a part of what I was not yet ready to know, things Abbot said would destroy me. Everything Abbot worked so tirelessly to ingrain into me floods my mind- never throw magus in anger, always have a clear idea of the ultimate desired result when pulling from my ink, push forward through pain, fulfill my own destiny as the Catalyst, the ability to choose rebirth or destruction, developing the physical strength to escape the double walls, the command over intusmagus to evade The Mothers, to reach the safe city, to rise above the hunger for power.

Frehn moves his head, pushing his face into my neck. His warm breath against my ear drives everything else from my thoughts and the full force of love burns up through my chest.

In that moment, I make my choice. I failed to save Merit, I failed to preserve love for Harc. But there is still a chance that I can save Statric and Holden, Abbot and Serees. And Wex. I will reach the safe city. I will fight the Audauxx. I will save love. This is my true destiny.

As Sotter and I start silently back up the mountain in search of the regroup location, blue and gold sparks create a glimmering trail over the tree tops. Someone is safe. Someone fired the signal.

We can't help anyone in Chelon now, but we can help those who are willing to fight. We have to reach Credo Cantus.

End of Book One.